ONE

The clack-clack sound of the young woman's heels on the pavement cut sharply back into the night as the last wail of the warning siren died away, restoring an uneasy quiet. Early evening cloud had dangled a hint of a promise of respite from bombings and she had been craving a four-inch bath followed by a dance-blistered feet-up, but plainly the blasted, sodding enemy had other ideas, so now she was hurrying up Haverstock Hill in the hateful impenetrable darkness of blackout, the air still stinking from the last raid, her next-to-useless tissue-covered torch pointed down at her feet, her eyes trying to stay fixed on the white-painted line that marked the pavement's edge, hoping like bloody billy-o to reach home before the raid began.

Not that home was safe these days, but she couldn't bear the shelters, had thought she was going to suffocate the one time she'd tried squeezing in on a platform at Kings Cross. She was a sociable type, Lord knew, but it had been no party down there; it had smelled disgusting and sounded even worse, full of snores and farting and babies crying, and worse, there'd been insects, even mosquitoes – in *London* – and she'd been bitten to shreds and not slept a single wink, and she'd determined that it was simply not a place fit for dying. So tonight, as soon as she got home, she was going to duck under her very own and *private* kitchen table and just take her chances of being a sitting duck if a bomb did have her name on it and, frankly, anything seemed better right now than being out all alone in this bloody awful pitch-darkness.

She loathed the blackout, had needed a night light as a little kid in Dungeness and had never really grown out of it. So the brightness of city life had been one of the many things she'd loved about moving to London – until this ghastly war had come along and snuffed all the lights out.

A new sound startled her.

Sounds, more like, from somewhere behind her.

Weird, grating, creaking, rasping sounds, a bit like teeth grinding,

PREY

Also by Hilary Norman

The Detective Sam Becket thrillers

MIND GAMES
LAST RUN
SHIMMER *
CAGED *
HELL *
ECLIPSE *
FEAR AND LOATHING *

Novels

IN LOVE AND FRIENDSHIP
CHATEAU ELLA
SHATTERED STARS
FASCINATION
SPELLBOUND
LAURA
IF I SHOULD DIE
SUSANNA
THE KEY TO SUSANNA
THE PACT
TOO CLOSE
BLIND FEAR
DEADLY GAMES
TWISTED MINDS
NO ESCAPE
GUILT
COMPULSION
RALPH'S CHILDREN
WHIRLWIND*

* *available from Severn House*

PREY

Hilary Norman

SEVERN
HOUSE

First world edition published in Great Britain and the USA in 2024
by Severn House, an imprint of Canongate Books Ltd,
14 High Street, Edinburgh EH1 1TE.

Trade paperback edition first published in Great Britain and the USA in 2025
by Severn House, an imprint of Canongate Books Ltd.

severnhouse.com

British Library Cataloguing-in-Publication Data
A CIP catalogue record for this title is available from the British Library.

ISBN-13: 978-1-4483-1349-5 (cased)
ISBN-13: 978-1-4483-1664-9 (trade paper)
ISBN-13: 978-1-4483-1350-1 (e-book)

Typeset by Palimpsest Book Production Ltd.,
Falkirk, Stirlingshire, Scotland.
Printed and bound in Great Britain by
CPI Group (UK) Ltd, Croydon CR0 4YY

The manufacturer's authorised representative in the EU for product
safety is Authorised Rep Compliance Ltd, 71 Lower Baggot
Street, Dublin D02 P593 Ireland (arccompliance.com)

Praise for Hilary Norman

"An outstanding psychological thriller with bizarre twists and unexpected turns"
Booklist Starred Review of *Whirlwind*

"Well-crafted . . . Norman skillfully examines such themes as hypocrisy, cruelty, forgiveness, and redemption in this unsettling novel"
Publishers Weekly on *Whirlwind*

"The stunning conclusion will have readers reeling. Norman's latest features her trademark suspense, intriguing characters, and an intense plot. This fine series just keeps getting better"
Booklist on *Fear and Loathing*

"Tight prose combined with well-drawn characters and skillfully evoked locales ensures a satisfying, high-pressure ride"
Publishers Weekly on *Fear and Loathing*

"Two thumbs up for this shivery, keep-'em-guessing mystery"
Booklist on *Eclipse*

"Norman weaves multiple strands with ease, building tension to a climax that doesn't disappoint"
Kirkus Reviews on *Eclipse*

"Grabs readers from the first page and doesn't let go . . . this dark psychological thriller is packed with plenty of action and enough twists to keep even dedicated fans guessing. Highly recommended"
Library Journal on *Eclipse*

About the author

Hilary Norman's first novel, *In Love and Friendship*, was a *New York Times* best-seller, and her work has been published in many languages. She has travelled extensively throughout Europe and lived for a time in the US. She now lives in London. *Prey* is her twenty-sixth novel.

www.hilarynorman.co.uk
www.hilary-norman.com

For my husband
JONATHAN KERN
Simply the best.
With all my love, forever.
1949 – 2022

Acknowledgments

My gratitude to the following:

Guy Slater, for endless patience, generosity and wisdom

Severn House and Canongate, my publishers, with special thanks to Tina Pietron, my marvellous editor, Rachel Slatter and Anna Harrisson

Euan Thorneycroft and Jessica Lee at A.M. Heath, my agents for almost four decades

My parents, Henry and Herta Norman, for their reminiscences of life in wartime Hampstead, their stories never forgotten

My family – David, Foksy, Neal, Gabriella and Aleksandra – for helping to keep me (almost) sane through dark times

Susan Sheldon, my dearest friend, for doing the same

Marilyn and Brian Hart for all their loving support

Lee Birch, for decades of kindness

John Levite for Belsize Park knowledge

Misty, sweet, constant canine companion, who must get a mention!

And above all: Jonathan Kern. My beloved husband, partner, best friend, and always astute (and forbearing) first reader. I will cherish memories of our final, pleasurable researches and plentiful cups of coffee around Hampstead and Belsize Park – and all the many shared research adventures that came before.

Author's Note

Calla House is fictitious, as are all characters.

'Fear is sharp-sighted'

Miguel de Cervantes, 'Don Quixote'

PART ONE

April 1941

but magnified. Rhythmic, too, and really creepy. *Grate, creak, squeal.* Over and over.

She stopped for a second, turned, saw nothing but blackness. Started walking again, even more quickly now, the sounds still trailing her.

Pursuing her, she felt.

She told herself not to be an idiot, but kept hurrying, risked casting another look back over her shoulder, saw a shape now, coming closer – someone pushing something, she thought – saw what it was, something ordinary enough that ought not to have scared her at all. But it did, it really did, made the hairs on the back of her neck and even her nipples stand right out, chilled her deep inside, and an involuntary moan of fear escaped her and she stopped hurrying and began to run.

Oh dear God, help me, she prayed silently, her breath coming in gasps as her heels clattered on the pavement, and she still didn't comprehend why she felt so terrified because this was not a bomb or a mine or gas or even a *Nazi*, but she knew, she just *knew* that this was something even worse, coming closer . . .

Her right shoe collided with a broken bit of stone and she stumbled, fought to stay upright, lost and fell down hard.

The grating, creaking, squealing thing stopped. Right behind her.

'Oh dear,' a voice said. 'Oh dearie dear.'

She scrambled to get up, heart hammering, the icy sensation of terror filling her whole body now.

Her left heel caught on the hem of her coat.

'Let me help you,' the voice said.

'I'm all right,' she said shakily.

'Course you are,' the voice said.

The raid began, some distance away, ack-ack first from the battery up on Primrose Hill, shells bursting in the sky, searchlights seeking the bombers, criss-crossing, then the first strike, the first *explosion*, defence and attack combining, deafening, shaking the earth.

Obliterating those other, much smaller sounds of terror and violent assault on another Hampstead hill, but bringing enough spasmodic flashes of light to illuminate the spectre of the young woman being dragged over the pavement and into a side road by her slim ankles.

Blood ran in a dark rivulet through her red hair and over her forehead, rolled down one cheek and over her pretty, youthful jawline, her attacker grunting with effort; and another bomb exploded, closer this time, and on the horizon fires glowed from earth to sky.

For a moment there was only the ack-ack, and then . . .

Grate, creak, squeal.

And the hideous orchestra of the air raid started up again.

TWO

He had been on an errand in Bloomsbury, had been walking back to Goodge Street Station, passing the jagged, hideous, blackened cavities and bombsites of Tottenham Court Road, when he'd caught his first glimpse of her.

A young woman in a particularly eye-catching coat – quite a decent garment for these times, oversized checks of black and red wool sewn together almost like patchwork, the coat cut for some other female, too big for this one but with a pleasing swing to it as she moved, jauntily and entirely oblivious of him.

It was her hair, of course, that had marked her out. Like red tulips bathed in sunlight even on a cloudy early evening.

He had held back, waiting to see where she went, had tried to fix his eyes on the top of her crimson head as a small crowd threatened to swallow her up, had spied one of the bold checks instead, had hastened then so as not to lose her.

She had walked into the station and his heart rate had sped up, adrenaline surging, though he knew she might yet be travelling south, had restrained himself again as she'd approached the lift, had let a layer of passengers step in ahead of him before entering, and they had shifted for him considerately, waiting for the gates to close, and then, as they had begun their noisy descent, he had maintained a downward gaze, not permitting himself a better view of his new target.

His *quarry*, he now felt certain, his pulses racing.

After that, there had been more waiting on the platform, and then boarding. But the delay had not mattered to him by then, for she had been going north.

His prey.

Going his way.

The hair was duller now – now that he had her – brought to life again by the patchy moonlight and searing flashes of explosion, and then, in the pinkish glow of distant fires, there were ripples of Rita Hayworth. All extinguished again by darkness as the two of them went on their way.

Grate, creak, squeal.

The blackout his dear friend, he often thought, folding him into itself, devouring him, rendering him invisible.

Life felt excellent in rare moments such as these. It had not always been so, had been worse than hard. Worse than most people could begin to imagine.

He was owed so much.

Taking his due now, finally, and Christ knew he'd earned it.

A cloud covered the moon, then shifted west, beams stroking the hair.

His, soon.

'Be there soon, dearie dear,' he said softly.

THREE

Alfred Ashcroft had been born in 1902 while his father, Ronald, a serving British army corporal fighting in the second Boer War, lay wounded in a hospital far from home. By the time the soldier returned to their somewhat shabby flat near Camden Town, he was, like many others, a physically and psychologically damaged man with intense anger issues.

It had been just mother and son till then. Lilian Ashcroft had been a beautiful woman with glorious, long, flame-coloured hair, and as a young child Alfred had loved stroking it, adored it especially when she bent over him and let the silken strands caress his cheeks. As he grew a little older, she allowed him to stand on a stool beside her dressing table and brush it, but once Ronald was home everything changed. Father resented his son's close relationship with his mother, mocked when he saw Alfred brushing or plaiting Lilian's hair, denigrated him, shouted at his wife for permitting it, called her perverted, called the boy a freak. He beat Lilian regularly and viciously and made her life – and their son's – a misery.

In 1912, when Alfred was ten, Lilian hanged herself and Ronald shot himself through the mouth. The boy found them, experienced pure gladness that their tormentor was dead; felt terrible numbness as he stood on a chair, carving through the washing line that had gouged deep into Lilian's lovely neck. He was not aware at the time of truly *thinking* about how this tragedy had come to pass. He only felt the weight of her still warm body as he lowered her, almost dropping her, to the floor. He did not even glance back at his father, had seen enough of that ghastly, hideous destruction to stay with him forever. He cradled his beloved mother for a long time, then took a pillow from the bed she had shared with the monster, rested her head on it and went in search of two things: the wedding photograph that stood on a shelf in the sitting room and a pair of scissors from the kitchen. He removed the photograph from its frame and carefully cut his father out of the picture, realizing for the first time as the blades sliced through the paper what his mind had been too deadened to consider before: that his mother had *not* done that to herself, would never have done that to *him*, would not have left the son she so loved; that the brute must have done it to her and then shot himself.

'Bastard!' Alfred had sobbed, had closed the blades of the scissors and turned them into a dagger, stabbing his father's image over and over, cutting his own fingers, heedless of pain or his own blood. 'You dirty, evil *bastard*.'

He heard knocking then, at their front door, froze, waiting until it stopped and the sound of footsteps faded.

He looked down at the photograph, at his mother, severed at last from the devil who had destroyed her, had wrecked their lives, hers and his, twice over, once when he'd come back from war, and again now. She'd looked dignified in her simple wedding dress, but the black-and-white photograph didn't do her justice, and there was nothing now left of her true physical beauty except that glorious hair. So he went back to the bedroom, knelt beside her and, very carefully and tenderly, he cut off her thick, still shining plait, carried it to his room and hid it, knowing that someone would come soon, and if anyone found out, they would ridicule him or call him wicked as *he* had often done.

'He did it,' he told one of the policemen who came because a neighbour had heard the shot and gone to call them.

'My father,' he said, saw the busybody neighbour hovering behind them, goggle-eyed. He was icily clear about what he was saying, because whether his mother had put that washing line around her own neck or whether his father had done it to her, either way he was a murderer.

The ambulance was a new motor vehicle, for they had been horse-drawn till recently, but Alfred wished that his mother could have been taken away by beautiful horses – though his father could go straight to hell in a dustbin so far as he was concerned.

'He did it,' he told the policeman again.

'We know,' the man said kindly.

'I mean he did that to my mother,' Alfred insisted.

He went on telling everyone who would listen, or pretend to listen, over the next days and weeks, but no one paid any attention. They told him there was no doubt that Lilian had committed suicide, that sadly both his parents had died by their own hand, that the husband had plainly shot himself out of grief. Alfred did his best to explain what Ronald had been like, said that they must have seen the bruises on his mother's face and arms, but then he gave up arguing because she had been buried by then – beside *him*, which seemed the wickedest thing of all – but whatever they said, he still knew without a shred of doubt that even if his mother had hanged herself – which he still doubted, would *always* doubt – she would only have done it to escape the cruelty. His father had been the beast who had driven her to it, and though Alfred was glad that the army pistol had blown the corporal's face to bloody mincemeat, he also believed with all his heart that instant death was far better than he deserved.

From then on, yearning despairingly to see his mother again, he became obsessed whenever he saw a red-haired woman, though it was never the *right* shade of red, never the colour of flame. He wanted, needed to touch Lilian's hair again, to stroke his own face with it, close his eyes, make-believe that she was with him again. When he knew he was alone and it was safe, he took out the plaited hair and held it close to his face, breathed in the remnants of her scent, kissed it reverently and felt just a little comforted.

He was sent to live with foster parents in Palmers Green: a chemist and his teacher wife, who were both very busy but kind to him, and Alfred did well at school, found that he liked escaping into learning and seldom got into trouble, until he befriended a red-headed boy whose mother had hair of *almost* the right shade. He wangled an invitation to the other boy's home, but the mother quickly became unsettled because Alfred kept staring at her, and then, after tea, when he asked to visit the bathroom, the curious lady followed him, caught him removing strands of her hair from a brush and told him to leave, reported his behaviour to the school and to his foster parents. Denounced for unacceptable conduct and humiliated, Alfred cut himself off emotionally, focused only on work, but in 1914, with the school leaving age being twelve and his foster father leaving to fight for their country, his education was cut off.

His foster father wrote to him, asked him to take good care of his wife and to always remember to be useful to her. So young Alfred helped around the house, dug the beds in their garden and planted vegetables as his war effort task and pleaded with his foster mother – who was volunteering at the local hospital and knitting for the troops – to teach him in her spare time. She was glad to oblige, observed with satisfaction his growing adeptness with mathematics and his hunger for delving into her husband's old textbooks, and a closeness grew between them. Until, while she was visiting a primary school in Poplar in June of 1917, she was killed in a daylight air raid. Alfred Ashcroft would have been entirely alone then but for a friend of his foster mother's, another teacher who promised him a home until his foster father returned from the war, encouraging him to continue with his studies, moved by the boy's earnest wish to follow in his footsteps as a chemist.

His foster father did come home, but succumbed to Spanish flu soon after, despite young Alfred's efforts to nurse him back to health. Aged sixteen, with the backing of his unofficial adoptive mother, he went back to school, buried himself in his till-then fragmented education, excelled at chemistry and physics, moved on to train as a pharmacy dispenser, passed the examinations – and finally, a young man without friends or any wish for a social life, he opened his own pharmacy in Kentish Town.

His mother, he thought, would have been proud of him.

FOUR

For Harriet Yorke, it began in the spring of 1941, seven months after the start of the London Blitz, during one of her nightly walks with George, her small Cairn terrier, the outings frowned upon by Louisa, Felix and Jack, her tenants and dear friends, who all worried about her venturing out after blackout but were also almost resigned to her blithely ignoring them.

'George's bladder doesn't care about rules,' she had told them more than once. 'And you know he won't go in the garden.'

George had been stung once, by a bee, and held the lilies responsible, whether in bloom or not, which reassured Harriet since she knew that not only were calla lilies – for which their house was named – not actual lilies at all, but they were also highly toxic. And walking was good for her, too, she told her friends.

'Not in a raid,' Felix had said darkly, in his heavily-accented English.

More complaints during her Thursday night walk – just after the All Clear had sounded – from Mr Bilton, the local Air Raid Precautions warden who had loomed out of the darkness and sighed pointedly as he saw that Harriet had left her gas mask at home *again*, then looked sternly down at George.

'I know, Mr Bilton, he's still not evacuated,' Harriet had said. 'And I'm awfully sorry about the mask, and I absolutely promise to remember it next time.'

'You're WVS, Miss Yorke, so you know better than most how bad it's been. We could get another packet any time.'

The warden was right, of course, she knew that, and he was doubly correct, considering that she did volunteer for the Women's Voluntary Service and was therefore involved in all sorts relating to the often nightly raids. This evening she had been off-duty and had spent the raid in the basement of Calla House, but she was certain it must have been nothing short of nightmarish for thousands of Londoners who'd been far less lucky, and coming upstairs after the All Clear, they had all rather shakily counted their blessings.

She had apologized again to Mr Bilton, then walked on more

briskly, her masked torch pointed downward, along the pitch-black, white-kerbed avenue, until a strange and rather ugly sound halted her and the dog in their tracks.

Something like a vixen's scream, but more muffled.

She listened for another moment, then walked on, stopping at regular intervals for George's tree inspections before turning back.

'Just one more stop,' she told the dog, 'then home.'

He had been about to oblige her near Glenilla Road when they heard another sound, an odd rasping or rather screeching, something like old lift gates in need of oil, quieter but repeating, on and on.

Harriet peered into the dark and saw the silhouette of a man in a hat and coat walking towards her from the side road, pushing a wheelchair which was clearly the source of the sounds.

George growled.

There was a person in the wheelchair, Harriet saw as the man came closer, slumped beneath a blanket – a woman, she thought from the shape, though the face was obscured by a shawl.

A front wheel of the chair struck a broken paving stone and it veered a little off-course, the man cursing under his breath.

'Need some help?' Harriet offered.

'No, thank you.' He pushed harder at the chair, but the wheel was caught, and instinctively Harriet moved forward to assist.

'We're fine.' The man sounded brusque, then added, more politely, 'She enjoys her little outings.'

Harriet smiled towards the chair's invisible occupant.

The man gave a more energetic shove and the chair surmounted the jagged paving stone and, as he passed Harriet, the moon sailed out from behind a cloud and she noticed a female hand resting on the blanket, dark-varnished nails visible, a small mole on the knuckle of the index finger.

A whiff of something unpleasant wafted upward on the breeze, made Harriet wrinkle her nose.

'Good night,' the man said and turned into the avenue, walking away from them, melting slowly into the night.

Harriet stood still for several seconds, oddly unnerved, waiting for the wheelchair's sounds to disappear entirely.

And George growled again.

FIVE

Alfred had married. He had met the young woman who would become his fiancée at the end of a dispiriting Sunday afternoon in 1928 when he had been hanging around the Palm Court in the Waldorf Hotel on the pretext of meeting a fellow pharmacist for tea, when he was actually hoping for a glimpse of the actress Clara Bow, who had been rumoured to be staying there during her London visit. Miss Bow was, in fact, neither at the hotel nor in London, but Alfred had seen a colour poster publicizing The It Girl's new film titled *Red Hair*, and had been galvanized by her wonderful flame-coloured curls into an instant fandom that he had all too soon realized had been wholly absurd. In fact, *he* had made himself ridiculous, humiliatingly so, had gone clothes shopping in readiness, was dressed in a three-piece suit with an elegant waistcoat and trousers with creases, had even been talked into adding a bow tie and a trilby.

Emily Williams had emerged from the Palm Court after taking afternoon tea with her mother, Jane, and was on her way to the ladies' cloakroom when she had tripped and almost fallen – if Alfred had not caught her.

She had liked what she had seen, her good mood augmented by the glass of champagne that her mother had encouraged, being her birthday and with her stockbroker husband meeting them later for dinner. The young man who had saved her from embarrassment was quite nice-looking, well-groomed and very much a gentleman.

'You must have a drink with us,' Emily Williams had told Alfred. 'My mother will want to thank you.'

'That's very kind,' Alfred had responded, a little flustered but encouraged by the upturn in fortune, 'but really unnecessary. I just happened to be standing here.'

'But you caught me so elegantly,' Emily had said, and giggled, then blushed a little. 'I'm sorry – are you waiting for someone?'

'Not any more,' Alfred had told her, charmed by her pink cheeks.

Years later, he wasn't sure if she had ever charmed him again. Neither could he recall ever hearing her repeat that giggle.

Nor was he sure if he ought not to curse Miss Clara Bow for the change of destiny that she'd unwittingly set in motion that afternoon.

Emily was not a redhead. Alfred had decided long ago that he could never marry a woman with hair the colour of his mother's, that it would feel terribly wrong, as if he had chosen some kind of under-study. Emily had brown, ordinary hair, a good-looking, dignified young woman who took pride in her appearance and who was – and Alfred had considered himself a lucky man at the time – attracted to the quite pleasant-looking and intelligent young pharmacist. He had subsequently courted her and they had got along well, but he was still aware, in 1930, that he was wedding Emily Williams for convention's sake, rather than for love.

Her stockbroker father, Hugo Williams, had mistrusted his son-in-law from their first encounter, regularly referred to him, sneeringly, as a *chemist*, never a pharmacist, but, encouraged by wife Jane, he had nonetheless bought the couple a house in West Hampstead that Alfred could not have dreamed of affording. The young man felt that he would rather have bought a modest flat and been his own man, but Emily had sharply told him to be grateful, and so he was, because he had no appetite for conflict.

He had never loved any woman apart from his mother, had felt only moderately interested in the 'mechanics' of intercourse, suffi-ciently to oblige his wife in the early days and then, after a rather long wait – providing his father-in-law with more grounds for disparagement – to produce a son and daughter. Frederick, known from birth in 1935 as Freddy, had slightly reddish hair – not at all like Lilian's, more of a russet-brown – but Alfred adored the boy, lavished cuddles on him, bought a Kodak camera, took countless photographs of him and loved stroking his hair. Emily appreciated his fondness for the boy at the outset, but then she tired of it – as, she realized, she was in general tiring of the husband who she should never have married; who was, as Hugo had repeatedly told her, beneath her.

'Leave Freddy's hair alone,' Emily told him. 'All that fussing with it isn't normal.'

Jarringly and upsettingly reminded of his father's resentment of his mother's closeness to him, Alfred withdrew from Emily, concen-trated all his attentions on his work and on Freddy, scarcely bothering with Amelia, his daughter, born in 1937, who had her mother's dull

hair and seemed altogether too much like Emily to greatly interest
him.

Redheads, however, continued to attract his focus, and when he
did so in his wife's presence, she objected strenuously to him eyeing
other women.

'It's very odd, in any case, for you to be drawn to ginger heads
when most aesthetically-minded people are repelled by them.'

'And it's very odd of you to use such an offensive term' – Alfred
took exception – 'though perhaps you've forgotten that my poor
late mother had beautiful red hair.'

Emily knew about his childhood tragedy but had no empathy,
regarded the sorry tale as sordid and scandalous and therefore not
to be spoken of; and after that exchange, Alfred knew better than
to mention either red hair or his mother to his wife, but in his ever-
increasing desire to find – or at least touch – hair with some
semblance of his mother's beauty, he secretly visited Clarkson's in
Wardour Street and chose an expensive wig of almost the right
shade, which he then hid at the back of a desk drawer in his office
behind the shop. A personal possession for his eyes only – and
surely a husband was entitled to at least a measure of privacy.

Until one early-closing Wednesday afternoon, Emily arrived unexpectedly and, seating herself behind the desk while Alfred worked at
his dispensing table, she idly opened drawers and came upon the wig.

'What *is* this fixation with red hair?' she demanded. 'And what
on earth do you *want* with such a hideous thing?'

'I've been considering stocking wigs for women with alopecia,'
Alfred dissembled, but the flush on his cheeks and the way he
snatched it from Emily betrayed him.

'Please get rid of it,' she said.

'Why should I?'

'Because frankly you're lucky to have found anyone to marry
you with your unsavoury past and your constant ogling other women,
and I wonder all the time why I didn't listen to my father when he
told me not to trust you.'

'And I wish to Christ that you had.'

'You're just an *embarrassment*,' she hissed, grabbing the wig
back and tossing it into the wastepaper basket.

That had been a pivotal moment in their marriage, for Alfred
found afterwards that he hated her almost as much as he had loathed
his father. He wondered what she would say if she knew that he

kept his mother's plaited hair wrapped in tissue paper at the back of his safe in the shop; he pictured in his mind a horrific scene where Emily took it out, maliciously unplaited it and threw it in a dustbin, decided that he might kill her if that came to pass.

Feeling somewhat guilty about that dark fantasy, he banished such ideas, worked harder than ever, remained an excellent pharmacist, was visited frequently by customers who preferred to entrust their symptoms to a discreet gentleman rather than to a doctor who might look down on them. The business thrived, but although Alfred found it impossible to halt his 'private' thoughts, he managed to keep them safely concealed from his wife. He felt, in many ways, emotionally numbed, found excuses to stay overnight in the vacant flat over the shop, told himself that such small bolts for freedom made him more able to tolerate family life with better grace.

As troubles swirled around Europe and another war appeared to be looming, Alfred began to consider volunteering, remembering his foster father telling him that chemists and pharmacists would be needed during conflicts and feeling that perhaps enlisting might really be the making of him. And more appealingly, that it would remove him honourably from Emily, whose chief pleasure in life seemed, increasingly, to be berating and belittling him.

Still wanting to appear a good husband and father, he suggested, one weekend in the spring of 1939, a Sunday outing to London Zoo. Walking around, propelling Amelia's pushchair (while wishing that he were the one strolling with Freddy), Alfred's eye was captured by a young woman with particularly shiny red hair.

Emily noticed and became instantly furious.

'This fixation has to stop, Alfred,' she told him. 'The woman looks like one of those hideous orangutangs, for heaven's sake – or maybe that's what your precious mother looked like.'

Alfred let go of the pushchair and slapped her.

Emily gasped, Amelia screamed, Freddy cried, and strangers all around stared in shock and open condemnation.

'That was the absolute last straw,' Emily said, her hand shaking as she held it to her burning cheek. 'You will never have the chance to do anything like that again.'

Back home, she told him to leave, reminded him that he had assaulted her before numerous witnesses, and Alfred, his hatred burgeoning, but ashamed to have lost control in front of his beloved son, complied and moved into the flat over the shop.

When Emily told her father, Hugo, outraged, announced that he would go immediately to Kentish Town and give Alfred the thrashing he deserved.

'And under no circumstances are you to take him back,' he told Emily.

Jane Williams, however, opposed any suggestion of violence, especially, she said, as it might rebound on them, and vehemently advised against the scandal of divorce.

'And you need to consider very carefully, my darling,' she counselled her daughter. 'Separation is one thing – probably best for a while in the circumstances – but let's not make any drastic decisions.'

'Your mother's probably right,' Hugo admitted reluctantly. 'But if your so-called husband ever lays so much as a *finger* on you again, or causes you even a glimmer of humiliation, I promise he will be properly dealt with.'

Missing Freddy, but otherwise relieved to be a free man, Alfred concentrated on taking solicitous and meticulous care of Kentish Town's residents. He listened to and read the news, still debating volunteering but anxious now that if he did so, he might never see his son again.

Suppressed anxiety and isolation heightened his obsession, and one afternoon, passing a hairdressing salon just as a woman with fiery-coloured hair was entering, Alfred hung around outside for a few minutes, then realized that another woman was observing him and quickly moved away – but not before he had seen the red hair being cut and then swept up.

Back in his cramped flat over the pharmacy, he could not get the tresses out of his mind. Intensely excited, unable to focus on anything else, he waited until all the shops in that row had closed, then returned with a torch, walked around to the back alley and saw two dustbins outside the salon. His heart pounding, conscious that his actions were irrational, even bizarre, but entirely unable to stop himself, he took the lid off one bin and shone his torch into its depths. Ignoring the pungent smell of bleach, accustomed as a pharmacist to chemical odours, he found a small pile of hair cuttings, plucked them out, replaced the lid and made his way back to the flat.

In his tiny bathroom he washed the hair and left it to dry, then tenderly combed the short lengths through. He went downstairs, unlocked the back entrance to the shop, shut himself in securely, opened the safe and took out his old treasure. Placing his mother's plait on a clean, pressed piece of linen, he shone light on it, then placed the hair retrieved from the salon's dustbin close to, but not touching, the plait.

It was not the same. It did not come close.

Disgusted, with it and with himself, he threw out the impostor hair, returned to his office and sank down. Gently, reverently, he stroked Lilian Ashcroft's hair as he had done many times over almost three decades, held it to his nostrils, breathed in a scent that he was aware had long since been imaginary, then kissed it, tears in his eyes, wrapped it up again and returned it to the safe.

With war now looming closer, he visited his wife, told her of his wish to volunteer before conscription, to do his bit for their country, and Emily shrugged, but Alfred felt that she was not quite as dismissive as usual, so he took the opportunity to say that he would like to take Freddy out for an afternoon. At first she refused, but the boy had overheard and begged his mother to permit it.

The happy father took his son to Lyon's Corner House, and they had a fine tea, all going splendidly until, out of the corner of his eye, Alfred noticed that one of the 'nippies' – as the waitresses there were known – had shiny red curls beneath her cap.

He stood up. 'Excuse me, Freddy.'

'Daddy, where are you going?' the boy asked.

'To wash my hands.'

'Can I come?'

Alfred didn't answer, just walked away. He felt powerless, as if there were a magnetic field between those curls and his right hand.

The squeal was loud enough to make heads turn.

'He pulled my *hair*!' the waitress accused.

'It was my cufflink,' Alfred said, scarlet with mortification, explaining to the manager who had hurried over. 'I coughed and raised my hand to cover my mouth, and the dratted thing caught on the young lady's hair and I am dreadfully sorry.'

The manager accepted with good grace and the waitress was made to apologize to Alfred for making such a fuss, but Freddy was giggling as his father returned to the table, his cheeks still hot.

Back in West Hampstead, Emily invited him in, saying that she needed him to change a light bulb.

'Since you're here,' she said.

'Gladly,' he said, returned to good humour, grateful to have been allowed time with Freddy.

He was halfway up the stepladder when disaster struck.

'You should have heard her, Mummy,' Freddy said joyously. 'It was so funny. Daddy went to wash his hands, but then this waitress *screamed* because she said that my daddy pulled her hair, but then she had to say sorry because it wasn't Daddy's fault.'

Emily's eyes turned icy. 'What colour was her hair, Freddy? The waitress's. Do you remember?'

'It was red,' he said. 'Like a tomato. But pretty.'

Emily waited until Alfred had put away the stepladder, then told Freddy to take Amelia and wait in the kitchen while she saw their father out.

Alfred kissed them both as they passed, ruffled Freddy's hair, then followed his wife into the hall.

Waited for sentence to be passed.

'You might just as well sign up right away,' she told him at the front door, 'because you will not be seeing our children again for a very long time.'

And then she closed the door and went to telephone her father.

Back in his tiny flat, Alfred took his white handkerchief from his pocket and saw immediately that the red curl he had tugged out of the waitress's scalp was obviously dyed.

Uncertain, yet again, what disgusted him more, the cheap and nasty imitation hair or the foolhardy, possibly insane and utterly *pointless* act that had risked his future as Freddy's father.

Depressed, he threw the curl away.

Five days later, just after dusk, on his way back from buying sixpence worth of fish and chips from a shop in Chalk Farm, Alfred was set upon by three thugs who tossed his plaice and chips into the gutter and dragged him into the back of a van. After a long, brutal beating and kicking, accompanied by torrents of vicious verbal abuse and threats of what more would happen to him if he survived and tried to lay blame, Alfred, senseless, beyond pain but severely injured, was dumped near the Pancras Gasworks.

Discarded again.

SIX

'George never growls,' Harriet had said to Jack very late that April night in 1941, following the curiously disturbing encounter with the stranger and the wheelchair a little earlier. 'He barks, but I don't think I've ever heard him growl.'

She had been working at the easel in her top-floor flat, painting the monochrome journal she had begun in the early days of the 'phoney' war – when all kinds of government restrictions had come into effect but no bombs had been dropped and heightened tensions had given way to anti-climax and a degree of relaxation – when Jack, who had been on a late shift at the club, had knocked softly, as he often did these nights when neither of them could sleep, and now they were sitting on her sofa, drinking tea and smoking, George snuggled between them, an old recording of 'Mack the Knife' playing softly on the gramophone.

'*Und der Haifisch, der hat Zähne . . .*'

'And the shark, he has teeth . . .'

Harriet's father, Peter Yorke, had been a British army lieutenant when he was badly wounded in 1917 during the Battle of Arras and invalided out and – soon after the signing of the Armistice – finally brought home to his French-born wife Eugénie, their one-year-old daughter Harriet and Calla House, the home in London's Belsize Park bequeathed to him by his parents.

Harriet had been conceived during a weekend leave in 1915, Peter unable to meet her till now. Despite the physical and psychological pain that still plagued him and, for a long time, prevented him from returning either to service or to his work as an architect, his enchantment with their red-haired little girl cured his initial depression and inspired him to sketch Harriet countless times, easing the path back to full-time work at the Bloomsbury firm.

In 1921, Eugénie died in childbirth, their premature son Louis dying soon after, but again it was five-year-old Harriet who saved Peter from drowning in grief. Bereft and confused as she was by the loss of both her *maman* and the promised brother or sister who now existed for her only in a few of her father's rough sketches, she clung to Peter and to Ginny Wilkins, the cleaner who had, until Eugénie's death, come in twice a week but who had now given up her own flat and other jobs to come and live full-time in Calla House as housekeeper and unofficial nanny. Ginny had been a blessing, a kind, reassuring female presence, a jolly person despite her own war widowhood.

Harriet loved every minute spent with her father, most especially when he brought work home at the weekends. She never felt ignored as he worked, was intrigued by the altered energy that overcame her daddy when he drew, though even at that early age the mostly linear lines of architecture were not for her. Whatever kind of building Peter Yorke was creating, Harriet gazed through every window and doorway into the space within and felt an urge to fill it with people or dogs and cats and activity.

Which she did – just once – when her father left plans for a detached cottage on the drawing board in his top-floor home office. Harriet was seven now, and the results of her efforts were reasonably accomplished but almost cost Peter his job. Ginny Wilkins purchased and fitted a lock on the office door and bought a supply of used paper and crayons and, as Harriet showed ever more signs of artistic ability, Ginny took her to art galleries and museums, and bought her, one Christmas, a 'grown-up' sketch pad and some pastels and, for her next birthday, her first set of watercolour paints. By her eleventh birthday Harriet was a happy all-rounder, doing well at her school near Hampstead Heath, excelling at languages and making friends easily. Eugénie had been tri-lingual, and her daughter appeared to have inherited her knack, and within a few years Peter was urged to encourage her to up her game and aim for Oxford to study modern languages – except that he knew that Harriet's heart was leading her towards a different goal: first The Slade School of Fine Art and then, perhaps, a year in Paris.

And then life had intervened.

In the spring of 1932, when Harriet was almost seventeen, after a period of restlessness and dissatisfaction with the direction of his career, Peter gave in to a long-buried impulse and bought Lowena (a Cornish word for 'joy'), a cottage near Carbis Bay in Cornwall. It was a dream he had shared with Eugénie, put on hold by the Great War, then crushed by her death; but now, driven by an edginess that reminded him of his post-war depression, and after lengthy consultations with Harriet, he finally made the move, setting up a one-man architectural practice and quite swiftly building up a small local clientele. In an enviable position to afford his new home, he made over Calla House to Harriet, advised her to rent out two floors and to keep the whole top floor for herself, primarily because it had the best light for painting.

'But you'll be alone,' Harriet said, fearing for him and alarmed by his generous, but daunting, decision. 'And whatever Ginny says about wanting to retire to Wales, it's shocking to even think of ripping away her home with us.'

Ginny, however, was adamant that life with her sister in Swansea was what she wanted, and Peter was immovable, so Harriet insisted that half the top floor would always remain his.

'And you will have a room in Lowena whenever you need a break,' Peter countered. And surely no budding artist in her right mind, he added, would turn down a second home so close to St Ives, where the clarity of light said to be unique had been drawing in talent since the end of the last century, and was in fact home to a prestigious Society of Artists . . .

Peter was blithely confident in her ability to organize the house *and* to study at The Slade. Harriet was not remotely sure but forced herself to be supportive, and finally, in the summer of 1933, the move to Cornwall was complete.

Just a few months later, however, Peter fell seriously ill, a wartime wound coming back to haunt him, necessitating surgery, followed by a post-operative infection, his recovery hampered by a recurrence of depression. Harriet abandoned London and Calla House – still undivided – to go to Cornwall, where she stayed in the cottage near Carbis Bay for more than a year, seeing him through the worst and finding for him a young secretary-cum-housekeeper named Penny Tippet, before returning to Belsize Park in early 1935 to find Calla House in urgent need of repairs after a major burst pipe and consequent flood, even the calla lilies in the garden (which Eugénie had adored) close to extinction.

It was time, Harriet accepted, for pragmatic action on all fronts. She might still have fought to get her place at The Slade, but instead she applied for a job at the BBC, which was said to take a progressive approach to women on its staff. Having no shorthand skills but finding typing easy to master, she worked as a clerk for the Empire Service at Broadcasting House, took regular short breaks in

Cornwall, organized the conversion of the house into three flats, keeping, as planned, the top floor for herself and her father, found tenants and painted in what little spare time she had.

With unfortunate hiccups in the plumbing and electrics, the tenants gave notice and Harriet's confidence plummeted, but far greater unease was darkening the whole country's mood with the worrying news from Europe, so when a new job came Harriet's way because of her language skills, she grabbed it and got back on track.

Several wishes were granted in swift succession, restoring her confidence: hot running water; light switches functioning; and then, in 1938, wonderful tenants for the ground-floor flat. Louisa and Felix Brandt were Jewish refugees from Berlin, a charming couple in their late fifties. They were reticent about their experiences, both outwardly calm, grateful for their freedom and for having been saved from possible internment by a generous acquaintance who had paid the required sum of fifty pounds for each of them to guarantee that neither Felix – a history professor banned from teaching in Germany – nor Louisa – a violinist with a chamber ensemble in Berlin who had managed to smuggle out her cherished instrument – would become a financial burden to the British government.

To help make ends meet, the Brandts had sold both Louisa's and her late mother's engagement rings and two brooches, an antique watch of her father's and a little silver, and though Felix's poor English and painful arthritis prevented him from working, Louisa – after several pleasant afternoons chatting to fellow refugees over *Kaffee und Kuchen* in the Cosmo on Finchley Road (increasingly a home from home for many who had fled Nazism) – was soon giving private music lessons in the living room as well as selling the delicious apple cakes and loaves she baked.

The couple frequently showed their gratitude for the warmth of Harriet's welcome, inviting her for modest suppers, but as their friendship developed, Harriet saw that even the smallest pleasures they experienced seemed instantly tainted by guilt and fears for their son, still in Germany because his wife had not felt able to part from her parents.

More good luck arrived with a tenant for the first-floor flat: Jack Jerome, a young music student, tall, dark, attractive, able to pay the rent and, best of all, fun to be around. He asked Harriet's permission to haul his upright piano up the staircase with a friend, and she was pleased to grant it, even if it might mean listening to hours of repetitive practice. Once Jack discovered, however, that not only was Louisa an accomplished violinist, but that she was also content to abandon classics and improvise with him, Harriet was soon opening her door to enjoy the marvellous bursts of jazz filtering up to her floor.

'Are we not disturbing you?' Louisa regularly asked.

'On the contrary,' Harriet told her.

And after that, there was no stopping the music.

Until Jack joined the RAF and, for a time, Calla House seemed to fall almost silent.

SEVEN

Flying was in Jack's blood, his father having served in the Royal Flying Corps in the last war, flying photo-reconnaissance missions over France, posted missing in June of 1917. Jack's mother Iris had kept Lieutenant Jeremy 'Jerry' Jerome's memory proudly alive for their son, conceived on a leave not long before his death, but when, on his eighteenth birthday, Jack had announced his intention to join the RAF Volunteer Reserve, Iris had been aghast. She'd been well aware of his love of gliding, had supported his membership of the Surrey Gliding Club, had known of his desire to join the Brooklands Flying Club, and his passion for aircraft was evident in his bedroom at home, his walls covered with his own certificates and photographs of heroic fighter pilots of the Great War – Jerry Jerome in pride of place. Iris's only son's declaration that he planned to join up, however, had been more than she could bear.

Realizing the depth of her distress Jack had given way and gone with his other love, of music, being a passable pianist with a taste for jazz and, more recently, swing; but he was just keen enough to study classically and fortunate enough to be accepted at the Royal College of Music in London – and face it, there was nothing else he would rather have done, except, of course, flying. Still, he was doing his best to knuckle down to college discipline, and he had found himself an excellent base in Belsize Park, a first-floor flat in a charming house owned by a very attractive redhead, an artist with a day job at the BBC.

Iris Jerome could breathe again, but not for long, because early in 1939, with shadows of another war threatening to spread over Europe, Jack broke the news that he now felt duty-bound to put his music career on hold and to join the Volunteer Reserve. No discussion this time, no permission needed, he was twenty-two years old and determined to be in place if, and when, the time came.

Jack had begun training at Hatfield's Elementary Flying Training School as a pilot. Posted in due course to Brize Norton, and then, training completed, he joined his squadron at an RAF base in Suffolk. Happy as Larry and raring to go and Hitler be damned.

Harriet had left the BBC at around the same time and volunteered for duty in the ATS – the Auxiliary Territorial Service – her father proud and dismayed in equal measure.

'Cornwall's filling up with artists,' Peter said, reminding her that she had a base ready and waiting. 'And wouldn't you rather paint and keep your old dad company instead of having to do whatever humdrum kitchen or office job they allocate you?'

'For one thing,' Harriet said, 'you have Penny for company, and actually what I'm hoping for is driving duty – far from humdrum. I have a licence, I'm a terrible cook, I detest filing, and though I'm now really quite a nifty typist, I'm trying to keep that under wraps.'

With no basic training yet established, however, she had started out peeling potatoes at a barracks in Aldershot until fortune had smiled on her in the shape of the work she had hoped for, and in the space of just three months she was driving army lorries and a rather handsome Humber, in which she chauffeured several colonels and a major. But then in the spring, a call came from Penny to say that Peter had suffered a relapse of his depression and Penny believed that he really would benefit from seeing her.

Duly discharged, Harriet headed southwest and, working with the calm, steadfast Penny and a sensible St Ives doctor, she helped her father through several bleak, but slowly improving weeks – before Louisa Brandt telephoned at the end of July to tell her that Jack had been badly injured in a crash during a test flight.

'His life is not in danger,' Louisa reassured her, 'which is why he is back here with us, but he has lost the sight of his left eye, and his other injuries will take time to recover from.'

'So no more flying,' Harriet said. 'Shouldn't he go home?'

'He's refusing to go to his mother. I think he's right,' Louisa said. 'I feel he needs company of his own age. Your company, I would say.'

That news seemed to prod Peter Yorke back to life. He was furious with himself for the weakness that meant he was never likely to return to service, and angry with himself too for having disrupted his daughter's life yet again. So now he was insistent that Harriet return to London.

'It's clear that your friend – a young man and, by all accounts, a decent type – needs you more than I do, as do those poor refugees, and I dare say that Calla House could use your care again too. Though what you really ought to be doing, wherever you are, is concentrate on your art, and maybe you could still get into The Slade.'

'I doubt that,' Harriet said.

'And I realize that I'm rather illogically pushing you back to the capital at a time when there's talk of evacuations, but I simply will not have you wasting your life on me a moment longer.'

Back home, she found she had swapped one angry middle-aged man for an angry young one, scarred on the left side of his face, wearing an eye patch yet no less attractive for that, but equally furious with himself because his accident in a Hawker Hurricane had been his own blasted fault.

'So I'm damned lucky to be more or less in one piece,' Jack told her on her first evening back, 'and I'm not at all sure that you should have come back from a relatively safe place—'

'Cornwall's probably a bit of a target too,' Harriet said.

'All the more reason to admit that I'm bloody glad to see you,' he said, 'even if it is only with one decent eye.'

Days later, war was declared. Harriet went back to the BBC to a job in European Services, nabbing the job partly because of her fluent French and adequate German and Italian – and between that and volunteering part-time for the WVS, keeping tabs on Jack and the house with Louisa's help, grabbing the odd day or two to visit her father, life was hectic and, despite the pervading air of alarm, she had seldom felt more energized.

On Saturday June 29th, 1940 – eleven days after she had listened in Lowena's snug sitting room with Peter and Penny to Mr Churchill preparing the nation for the Battle of Britain about to begin – news came of two high explosive bombs dropped on Merrifield, Torpoint, some fifty or so miles as the crow flew from Peter's cottage. Penny sent a telegram assuring Harriet that they were fine, that her dad's mood was spry, that he was relieved in the circumstances that Harriet was in London, and sending orders that she was to stay there even if – especially if – the Luftwaffe targeted St Ives.

'Both of you should come to Calla House,' Harriet responded. 'We have a decent basement, remember, perfect for use as a shelter.'

'Peter and Penny staying put,' her father telegraphed back.

Six days later three more bombs fell on Charlestown, a mile or so outside St Austell and even closer. Lowena was unscathed, but later the same day, Peter suffered a massive heart attack and died in Penny's arms.

Following the funeral, grief-stricken and still reeling, Harriet discovered that her father's will had been made long ago, leaving everything to her with no reference to Penny, who had not yet come into his life. Deeply concerned, Harriet contacted Peter's solicitor to see if she could change this in Penny's favour or, at the very least, state legally that Lowena would be her home for life. Penny would not hear of the idea, said that she had loved her years with Peter.

'I will mourn his loss forever, darling Harriet, but I'm all right financially, I intend to train as a nurse to try and be of some use, and I do not want to stay in Cornwall, and most certainly not in Lowena.'

Life and the war moved forward. Harriet continued to work for the BBC and the WVS, to take care of Calla House as best she could, to support Louisa and Felix – whose sporadic communications with their son and daughter-in-law via letters and then by plainly censored postcards had now entirely ceased – and to bully Jack into doing his physiotherapy exercises. And in what little spare time she had, she worked on her black-and-white painted journal.

As the Battle of Britain raged on, Jack, who had been kindness itself to Harriet after her father's death, became agitated and depressed, frustrated by the office job he had been allocated at the War Ministry, beset by guilt because but for his own carelessness he would be in the air and not 'flying a desk' or in the 'chair force' as the *real* flyers called the safe jobs men like Jack were condemned to. Harriet encouraged him out of his dark moods and, as his injured arm became strong enough to allow him to play jazz piano three evenings a week at April's, a Soho bar, and to fill in part-time at the Windmill Theatre, he entered a far happier state.

On September 7th, 1940, Luftwaffe bombers rained devastation on the docks of the East End, and the terror of *Blitzkrieg* was underway. In December, a delayed-action high explosive bomb caused deaths and considerable damage to Broadcasting House, and European Services moved to a disused skating rink in Maida Vale before being relocated to Bush House. They were now broadcasting in thirty-four languages, Harriet translating into and from her three, and typing day in, day out, and it was good to feel somewhere close to the heart of the organization through which the Prime Minister exhorted the nation to show defiance of the Nazis.

Jack often came upstairs after work at the War Ministry, or often even later after his stints at April's. The music and friends he made there and at the Windmill were helping to keep him buoyant, but he sorely missed what he had never quite had: the camaraderie and – insanely, he admitted – the dangers of what he ought to have been doing. Most of all, the loss of a chance to really play his part, to make a bit of a difference.

Harriet's relationship with Jack was platonic, though if she were totally honest with herself, there had been moments that had felt – at least to her – like something more than mere neighbourliness between them. Perhaps a *lot* more, she had mused once, recently, walking up the stairs after a couple of late drinks in his living room – but then she'd shaken herself out of it, remembered that she was his landlady and that it would be foolish to risk rocking that boat for something that would very likely, in these uncertain times, come to grief.

Not that Jack Jerome had once given the slightest indication of being attracted to her. They were just becoming friends, and good friends at that.

The bombings, terrifying as they too often were, had brought all the residents of Calla House closer. Whole nights sometimes spent in the basement, Felix in charge of the tea thermos and biscuits, Louisa bringing her violin, Jack often limping back and forth, furious with himself again for his uselessness. And Harriet, when she was not undertaking WVS duties, calming herself by consoling George, who hated being shut in anywhere.

'It's extraordinary, really,' she said one night when they were all sheltering together, 'the things you can get used to.'

The raid had been underway for a while, but nothing nearby yet.

And then, as if to pour scorn on Harriet's words, a big one landed much too close for comfort, powerful enough to shake Calla House, to send their teacups crashing to the floor and to push Louisa, still clutching her violin and bow, into Felix's arms.

'I spoke too soon,' Harriet said after a shaky silence.

Jack had moved closer to her too, put an arm around her shoulders.

'I should be working,' she said. 'I should be out there.'

'You can't leave now,' Louisa said agitatedly.

'I know,' Harriet said. 'Don't worry.'

'Plenty of help needed tomorrow,' Jack said.

'Bloody close, wasn't it?' she said.

She felt his arm tighten around her, was intensely glad of it.

'Louisa, do you think you could play some more?' Jack asked.

Louisa nodded, raised the instrument, and Harriet, with great regret, eased away from Jack and started to pick up the broken teacups.

'More glue needed,' she said.

EIGHT

Alfred, having been left for dead after the beating, had not been found till morning and taken to St Pancras Hospital where strenuous efforts had been made to save him. His disappearance had been unnoticed until an agitated customer, who had brought an urgent prescription into the pharmacy the previous morning, had gone to the local police station to complain.

When Emily was eventually located and informed that a man believed to be her husband was critically ill and that she was needed to confirm his identity, she telephoned her father – now a lieutenant colonel in the army – to ask him to take on the task.

'He's not expected to survive,' she told him.

'Cheaper than divorce,' Hugo Williams said.

Alfred did survive, but his injuries were so serious that his recovery took several months. During the time he languished in hospital, war was declared, the Kentish Town pharmacy lost to him and, finally, he was ruled medically unfit for service and then divorced by Emily on grounds of desertion, a letter to him from Williams pointing out that he could count himself damned lucky that she had not cited cruelty or incurable insanity as grounds.

Physically barely strong enough to visit his old shop to ask for his property, Alfred was told that everything had been handed over to Lieutenant Colonel Williams, his father-in-law.

Still limping heavily and walking with a stick, Alfred took a bus to West Hampstead. The house that had never really felt like his home looked only a little less daunting than his wife as she answered the doorbell.

Emily was alone, the children in the countryside with her mother, where she would shortly be re-joining them.

'You look dreadful,' she said, with no hint of sympathy.

She had allowed him in as far as the entrance hall.

'And those glasses . . .'

Alfred fingered his spectacles. 'My injuries affected my vision.' He paused. 'If you had come to visit me in hospital just once, you would realize now how greatly improved I am.'

'That's good,' Emily said, 'though of no interest to me. I would not be seeing you today if my father were not serving with his battalion.'

Her coldness leaving no room for hope, he asked for their evacuation address, but Emily refused to give it.

'I'm entitled to see my children.'

She laughed. 'You're entitled to nothing except that.' She pointed to a single suitcase in a corner of the hall. 'Your belongings.'

'My wallet was missing when I was found.' Alfred's mouth was dry. 'There were photographs. Precious to me. Of the children. One of my mother.'

'I know nothing about that,' Emily said.

He bit down hard on his hate.

'Will you at least give me a photograph of Freddy and Amelia?'

'If I find a spare one, I will have it sent to you.'

Alfred turned towards the suitcase, then back to her. 'What did your father do with my belongings from Kentish Town?'

'Nothing to do with me,' she said. 'Though if you're wondering about that disgusting *thing* you kept locked in your safe, that's gone for good. My father burned it –' she nodded towards the living room – 'in the fireplace.' She took a step closer to him. 'Even the ashes stank, if you want to know, vile degenerate that you are.'

She watched his expression, malice in her eyes.

'Would you like to hit me again?' she asked. 'Then you could take up residence in prison and lose your certification as a pharmacist, and that really would be the end of you, and good riddance.'

Over time, Alfred salvaged what he could of his dignity, his bitterness strengthening him, pushing him forward. He took a job as manager and dispensing pharmacist in Belsize Park with a one-room flat over the shop, and began again. He was tougher than the Williamses thought, he reminded himself. They probably could not have imagined how much he had endured as a boy – more than most could imagine – and he had overcome it all; and his foster parents had been decent, he allowed that he had been fortunate there, but of course they had been snatched away too, as everyone and everything precious had been stolen from him. And then the terror and savage humiliation of the beating and the subsequent months of agony, and the knowledge – of that he had no doubt – that Lieutenant Colonel Hugo Williams and his ice-cold bitch of a daughter had been behind it all – would never help him, because they knew full well that he would not dare to make an accusation, and that even if he did, he could never prove it.

But he had come through without a single soul to help him.

He remembered that his foster father, the chemist, had written to him when he'd had to leave school, advising him to always help himself. Alfred did so now. Determined to grow stronger, he began to exercise, lifted weights at night, teaching himself to overcome his residual physical weaknesses, though nothing, he had been told by a doctor in hospital, was likely to rid him of two of the impairments that his assailants had left him with: impotence and sterility. Alfred told himself that neither of those was of great consequence to him. He had two children he was not allowed to see (and his beloved Freddy was almost certainly being poisoned against him); and sex had never been important to him.

Back pain, digestive problems, headaches, eyes that tired easily. All were manageable through mind over matter assisted by his pharmaceutical expertise and his unrelenting physical training.

Not so his inner rage and loathing.

He blamed *her* more than him. It was perhaps possible to understand a father's vengeance against a useless and – in Hugo Williams's eyes – perverted son-in-law. But for a woman – a wife and mother – to be so devoid of soft-heartedness, to be so utterly cruel . . . Emily stood alongside his own monstrous father in his personal canon of evildoers. Never to be forgiven.

Nevertheless he did well, was a fine manager, trusted by the proprietor who was serving overseas and grateful for Alfred, who worked diligently and presented a calm exterior to customers.

He still longed for his mother, that pain greater than ever when he allowed it to disturb his focus. He yearned for Lilian, dreamed of her gentleness and of her glorious hair, and in his dreams he brushed it, stroked it, breathed in her scent, plaited it for her – but then he would wake and have nothing.

He discovered through painstaking research that his parents' wedding photograph had been published in the *Gazette*. By dint of earnest persuasion and a fee, he was granted a copy, which he framed behind glass and kissed each night. Not that it brought her back in any kind of satisfactory manner, for the demurely veiled, grave-faced bride standing beside the man who would ultimately end her life, had nothing in common with the warm, loving mother he had worshipped as a boy.

He turned to fantasy.

With no wife to criticize or mock, so long as he maintained his façade in working hours, Alfred granted himself permission to indulge his imagination. If he were, after all this time, to find another woman with exactly the right shade of hair, he fancied that he would woo her – and now that most of his visible wounds had healed he wasn't too bad to look at – he never had been film star material – and with time he would become even stronger. And maybe this fantasy woman would like him well enough to stay with him; though maybe he might not like *her*, but if the hair was true flame, like Lilian's, then he would find a way to keep her.

His impotence made the make-believe even better, for hadn't he married Emily Williams because she did not remind him of his mother? Because even the notion of making love to some kind of 'substitute' was unconscionable. But making her his, *keeping* her, that was different.

And anyway, it was just fantasy.

Or maybe not.

Maybe one day, that was what would happen.

He would make it so.

It became his great preoccupation. During working hours, he was still able to concentrate, to maintain his composure and profession-alism, but in his free hours and at night, he devised scenarios and plans. He was clever enough, after all, had proved that in his younger days, with his studiousness and determination to achieve, and he would succeed one day with this too. It was just a matter of time and patience. He was not yet forty, and he was doing well again, had money set aside, and he would find a way to have what he wanted, and he had *earned* it, and unless an enemy bomb put him out of his half-submerged pain, he had time on his side, and with a war on, no one was going to notice him much unless he chose to let them.

On September 7th, 1940, the first bombing raid exploded on London, and soon night-time raids became an all too regular horror for the population. But for Alfred, his fantasizing and planning seemed suddenly to come tantalizingly close to fruition. Now he *knew* exactly what he would do if and when he found *her*. He had assembled all that he might need in whatever circumstances might come to pass.

He was ready.

It was just a matter of time.

It came so swiftly, so unexpectedly, the decisions he made so breathtakingly quick-fire that afterwards he could scarcely believe that it was Alfred Ashcroft, once innocent victim, who had been at the centre of the action.

Prowling the West End, as he had grown accustomed to doing sometimes, before blackout, he saw the woman – and perhaps it was a trick of the dying sunlight, but the hair was *right*, he was certain of it, he had found *her*, and his heart pounded so loudly when he stared at her that he felt sure she would hear it, but she just smiled at him and he removed his hat as a gentleman ought, and she seemed amused by that.

'It'll be a quid,' she said.

That altered everything.

He realized what she was and what a fool *he* was – though he had, of course, seen prostitutes before and she hadn't looked that sort, but that was what she was – and it was *she* who had made a fool out of him, and that made him angry; but infinitely worse, he saw now that her hair was dyed, of *course* it was, which made her doubly fraudulent, and in a great flash of revelation he found that he hated her as much as he had ever hated anyone.

Suddenly she embodied his father and Emily and Hugo Williams and the thugs who had tried to destroy him – somehow they were all rolled into this one deceitful whore. And on one level he realized that he could simply walk away, perhaps hand over her 'quid' to avoid nastiness, could just go home, but his anger was burning so vividly: a very different kind of flame than that of his mother's glorious hair, this was a white raging heat, and through it he saw clearly, decisively, that it made good sense to do this *now*, today, this very evening, because it was a perfect opportunity for a rehearsal, to see how all his planning really worked out.

So Alfred Ashcroft – a changed man, no longer victim but avenger – smiled at the dyed-red prostitute and gave her ten shillings, told her she would get the rest when they reached their destination.

'If it's too far,' she said, 'it'll have to be another quid on top when we get there, because time is money.'

'All right,' Ashcroft said. 'Because I like you.'

And that clinched their business arrangement, and she went with him.

And when they came to his special place, everything was ready. Just as he had planned it.

NINE

'**A**nd George didn't *just* growl at that man, you know,' Harriet told Jack in her sitting room-cum-studio, unable to push the strange wheelchair couple from her mind. 'He really bared his teeth.'

'If you'd only waited for me to get home, I could have come along.'

'George doesn't do waiting, you know that.' She thought back. 'Don't you think it's a strange time to choose for a stroll with someone in a wheelchair?'

'Maybe they were late getting back from somewhere.'

'He said that she enjoyed her "little outings".'

'There you are then,' Jack said.

'She never said a word.'

'Maybe she can't speak.'

Harriet absorbed that possibility. 'I did hear that odd scream a few moments earlier. I thought it was probably a fox or an owl, but . . .'

'Bet it was a fox,' Jack said. 'Or even a cat. Everything sounds spooky in the blackout, Harry.'

'Mm,' she said.

Not far away, in a cold, dark basement, an old wheelchair stood in the middle of an almost bare concrete floor.

There was no electric light switched on in the room, but a crack in a window frame to the left of the blackout blind was allowing in just enough moonlight to illuminate part of the chair and the area around it.

Scattered cuttings, long strands of hair, gleamed almost vermilion on the concrete.

A woman's hand rested on the right arm of the chair, nails varnished dark red, a small mole on the knuckle of the index finger.

Congealed streaks of blood were visible on the woman's head, where patches of her scalp had been exposed, her hair having been brutally cropped, and her face – the skin now tinged a bluish-purple, another dried trickle of blood below her nose – was distorted by terror, and by murder.

She wore a man's shirt, buttoned neatly to the hollow above her clavicle.

Her underwear was intact, but she wore no shoes or stockings.

Those stockings – made of precious nylon, so hard to come by, nylon being needed to make parachutes amongst other wartime necessities – had been used to bind her to the wheelchair.

She had only been dead for a few hours.

TEN

Very early on Friday morning, while Hampstead still licked its latest grievous wounds of destruction, its air bitter with the ugly fumes that bore no relation to wood or bonfire smoke, Harriet was taking care of Calla House business before changing to go to work. For now, she was wearing stained dungarees, a scarf turban covering most of her auburn hair, and she was balanced near the top of an old, unsteady ladder attending to a blocked gutter on the east side of the house while Jack, down below, gripped the ladder tightly, frustrated by her refusal to let him do the job for her.

Someone was watching them.

Through a window on the opposite side of the avenue.

Just watching.

For now.

The bombers returned that night, raining terror closer to Calla House than ever, though Harriet, on WVS duty, spent the raid away from home in a public shelter, caring for a child whose mother was very unwell.

She was still on duty early on Saturday morning as ARP Services toiled on a row of houses that had been destroyed by a parachute mine on Thursday night in Fellows Road, part of the estate owned by Eton College. An all too familiar, terrible and grisly scene these days, though Heavy Rescue had already departed, badly-wounded and shocked survivors taken away and many bodies removed, but men in tin hats still dug for remains in the devastation, after which the site would be fenced up and made as safe as possible.

Harriet, in her WVS beret and overalls, bringing tea and sandwiches on a tray strung around her neck to two plainly weary men, was in turn directed by them to another man digging alone some distance away. She picked her way carefully over hillocks of debris, broken concrete slabs, shattered glass and general wreckage to offer him refreshments, but the man kept on doggedly working, his tin hat, face, hair and clothes coated in grime and soot, only his spectacles glinting in the sun.

'Nothing for me, thank you, dear,' he said.

There was something vaguely familiar about his voice.

'Have we met?' she asked.

'I don't believe so,' he said, still digging.

'Won't you take some tea, at least?' she encouraged.

'Nothing for me,' he said again. 'Thank you.'

And went on digging.

Harriet looked around for a thirstier volunteer, but then something caught her attention in the debris over to her right and she began to make her way towards it, but was halted halfway by the sorry sight of a child's doll, partially buried, its grime-coated eyes open and one arm, smashed to eggshell, exposed. Her thoughts flew in anguish to the doll's likely owner, then swiftly, urgently, pushed her on to what she had first spotted.

A human hand, part protruding from a pile of rubble.

'It's all right.' The man's voice came from behind. 'I've seen her.'

Harriet took another step closer, stooped, saw that it was indeed female.

'Leave her,' the man said. 'Nothing you can do.'

'She might be alive.' Harriet's stomach clenched.

'No pulse,' he said, 'and cold. She's long gone. Like most of the other poor devils under this lot. They'll come for her soon, don't worry.'

Harriet stared at the hand for another second.

A voice, from a distance, called out, 'You coming or what?'

'Coming!' the man shouted back, laid down his shovel and looked at Harriet. 'All right, dear?' he asked.

She felt dismissed, looked back at the hand, disconcerted.

Because, the tragedy aside, it had also triggered a memory. Of that other hand, the one she had seen two nights ago, fingers tipped with varnish, a small mole on one knuckle.

She looked back at the grime-coated man, saw that his spectacles were still focused on her.

'All right?' he asked again.

'Fine,' Harriet said, and moved quickly on.

At the Windmill Theatre, after playing for the lunchtime show and still in the heightened spirits that the place always lent him, Jack was passing the dancers' dressing room when the door opened and Dora, a gorgeous brunette, stuck her head out.

'You seen Babs, ducky?'

Jack thought. A pretty girl, as he recalled, though they were all so bloody marvellous, on- and off-stage, doing their damnedest to lift the morale of their audiences with their routines and famous nude tableaux . . .

'Only no one's seen her since she left here on Thursday,' Dora went on. 'And I think she's got digs near you. You're up in Hampstead, aren't you, with all the nobs?'

Jack grinned. 'Belsize Park. And she might not have gone home. Chap in her life? Someone special?'

'Not as special as her job,' Dora said. 'Babs Woodruff would never miss a single show, let alone a day and a half.'

That evening, downstairs in Felix's and Louisa's flat, over a supper of goulash soup – redolent with garlic and the paprika that Jack had found in Soho and handed over – he mentioned the missing dancer.

'The scream you thought you heard,' he said to Harriet. 'That was on Thursday evening, wasn't it?'

'Scream?' Louisa was instantly anxious.

'It was nothing,' Harriet reassured her. 'Just a fox.'

'It put the wind up you,' Jack said.

'If only you would stop walking alone at night, *Liebling*,' Felix said.

'I'm not alone,' Harriet said. 'I have George.'

'Hah,' Louisa dismissed.

Preferring not to cause more upset, Harriet held back until she and Jack were on their way upstairs.

'I haven't had a chance to tell you,' she said. 'About the hand.'

'Hand?'

They paused while she quietly told her grisly tale, then continued up, bypassing Jack's flat, going up to Harriet's.

'I know it's a bit mad, but I'm as sure as I can be that it was the same one,' she finished.

In her sitting room Jack wandered across to her latest painting, depicting Friday night's shelter, the anxious child and her sick mother.

'This is very good,' he said, then turned away from the easel. 'But your couple with the wheelchair?' He pulled a sceptical face. 'Bit far-fetched, surely.'

'I realize that.'

He shrugged. 'I suppose they could have gone on to Fellows Road and been damnably unlucky.'

'I suppose they could,' Harriet said.

After a moment, Jack said, 'You didn't actually describe the woman.'

'I couldn't. She was too bundled-up.'

'Only Babs – the missing dancer I mentioned who lives nearby – is rather pretty with very long legs.'

Harriet stared. 'You're surely not suggesting the woman in the wheelchair was Babs?'

'Of course not,' Jack said. 'That's even madder.'

Harriet's brow wrinkled as she thought back. 'I really can't remember anything else. It was much too dark.'

'Doesn't matter anyway,' Jack dismissed. 'Far too much of a coincidence.'

'More than enough of a coincidence seeing the same hand again – *maybe* the same one – half buried.' Harriet shuddered. 'That could happen to any of us, of course, any night.'

Jack took another moment. 'Was it young or old, would you say? The hand.'

Harriet thought again. 'In the street, it was too dark to tell – I think I may have assumed it was old because she was so bundled-up and in that ancient wheelchair.'

'And on the bombsite?'

'I didn't see wrinkles or age spots, just the mole and varnish – but then I wasn't looking in a forensic kind of way. I was too transfixed by the awfulness.'

'But it could have been a young hand,' Jack said.

Harriet shrugged. 'I suppose it could.'

Coincidences notwithstanding and with a few free hours to spare the next day, they arranged to meet at the Windmill and found Dora in the canteen with her friend, Milly, who had a photograph of Babs – still missing – for Harriet to look at.

'Told you I wouldn't recognize her,' Harriet said to Jack.

'Talk about getting carried away,' Dora said. 'Blimey, Jack.'

'Do you know,' Harriet asked the dancers, 'if Babs has a mole on her hand?'

Dora and Milly both shook their heads.

'Can't say I ever looked that closely,' Milly said.

Harriet sniffed the air. 'Do you mind if I ask what scent you're wearing, Milly?'

'Not wearing any,' she said.

'Just Eau de Milly.' Jack grinned.

Sleep had annoyingly been eluding Harriet – such a dratted *waste* with no raid and a whole night off – when it struck her. She pulled on her dressing gown, careful not to disturb George, snoring on her eiderdown, padded down to the first floor and knocked quietly on Jack's front door.

'It's open, Harry,' he called.

Always a night owl, Jack was in his kitchen, smoking a Senior Service cigarette and reading a Father Brown mystery.

'What's up?' He put down the book and pulled out a chair for her.

'What's the name of the make-up they use in the theatre?'

'Greasepaint?' Jack queried.

She shook her head. 'The make.'

'Max Factor?' Jack said. 'Leichner?'

'That's the one,' Harriet said. 'I remember it from a play I acted in at school – and I think that's what I sniffed on Milly today. And *that* was what I smelled on Thursday night on the woman in the wheelchair. Except there was another smell, too, that distracted me – sweeter, quite sickly.'

They sat in silence for a few moments.

'Not exactly proof of anything, is it?' said Jack.

'I suppose not. Though there was the scream.'

'Not a fox or cat then,' Jack said.

'I don't know – maybe. But the woman was slumped over very unnaturally.'

'First time you've mentioned that. Sure you're not embellishing?'

'Not entirely,' Harriet admitted.

'Still something, though,' Jack mused.

'Maybe,' Harriet said again.

ELEVEN

They called in at Hampstead Police Station next day, were received politely enough, they both agreed afterwards, but both felt equally certain that no one was going to act on Harriet's virtual non-information.

'Not really much they can do in the circumstances, is there?' Jack said. 'Not nearly enough to go on for them to go digging – and hopefully they're right and Babs is just off somewhere living it up with a beau.'

'Bet she isn't,' Harriet said, with foreboding.

She was in Jack's living room, arranging things for the small party they were throwing that evening for Louisa's and Felix's wedding anniversary, when Jack came in with a prescription for Felix's tablets. Louisa had intended to fetch them herself from Smith's, the chemist's near the tube station, he told Harriet, but it was raining and Louisa had had a hairdo, so Jack had offered to go for her, but then he'd remembered the Don't-You-Know-There's-A-War-On-Bouillabaisse he was cooking for the party.

'I'll go,' Harriet said. 'I need some cold cream anyway.'

She popped George into the handlebar basket of the man's bicycle she shared with Jack – though he seldom used it, his blind eye making it hard to ride in a straight line – pedalled up the avenue to Haverstock Hill, crossed the road and parked it at the kerb, glanced up at the sign to check – G. Smith & Son Dispensing Chemist – and went inside.

The man behind the counter at the back of the shop looked so different in his immaculate white coat that it took several moments for her to be certain.

'Hello again,' she said warmly.

The man looked enquiringly at her. 'Yes, madam?'

She smiled. 'I wasn't quite sure, without your tin hat and all that terrible grime.' She saw that he was mystified. 'You were clearing up the other morning after the raid,' she explained. 'I was the nuisance trying to foist one of my dreadful sandwiches on you.'

'Ah. The WVS lady.' Now he returned her smile. 'What can I do for you, madam?'

Harriet fished for the prescription in her jacket pocket and passed it over, told him she was collecting it for Mr Felix Brandt, that she'd been given to understand they kept the tablets for him.

'Indeed we do.' The chemist reached for a book and pen. 'May I have your name and address, since you're not the patient?'

'Of course,' Harriet said. 'Same address. The Brandts live in Flat One, I'm in Flat Three.'

He wrote her details in the book, then moved behind a partition to the dispensing area.

'Did they get that poor woman out, Mr Smith?' Harriet asked.

The chemist looked up, frowning, and the light from the lamp above his dispensing table reflected on his spectacles. 'Of course.'

'It was just . . .' Harriet felt a little thrown. 'Seeing her hand like that. So terribly sad.'

'Yes, indeed.'

'Was she identified?'

'Not while I was on duty.'

He began to dispense Felix's tablets and Harriet found her Pond's cold cream and browsed until the chemist had tipped the pills into an envelope and sealed it.

'How is Mr Brandt?' he asked.

'Celebrating his wedding anniversary today,' Harriet said.

'Nice day for it –' he looked down at his book – 'Miss Yorke.'

She nodded. 'Did I get your name right? Mr Smith?'

He made out a bill, tidily straightening the carbon paper behind it, then handed the top copy to her, and as Harriet got the money from her purse, she felt that he was watching oddly intently.

'Ashcroft,' he said. 'Dispensing pharmacist and manager. Mr Smith is the proprietor, serving overseas.'

'Thank you, Mr Ashcroft,' Harriet said, and turned to go.

Feeling curiously, and rather uncomfortably certain, too, that the pharmacist was still watching her as she left the shop, got back on the bicycle and pedalled away.

'I'm not sure,' she told Jack later as they worked in the Brandts' kitchen, transferring food on to serving dishes as guests began to arrive, 'how I managed to stay calm once I realized.'

Louisa came in with a swish of black silk and long pearls, two more relics of the past she'd managed to salvage when she and Felix had fled Berlin. 'The bouillabaisse smells wonderful, Jack – so kind of you both. Much more than we deserve.'

'It's absolutely what you deserve,' Harriet said.

'You just go back to your guests,' Jack told her.

'But I must help you.'

'No, you must *not*,' Harriet insisted. She waited until Louisa was out of the room. 'I thought there was something wrong about the man, even on the bombsite. But today, in the shop, I called him Mr Smith because that's the name we use, isn't it – Smith's – and it's on the sign outside, and he didn't correct me, which is nothing, I know.'

'But you said you asked if you'd got that right, and—'

'And he said his name was Ashcroft. "Ashcroft. Dispensing pharmacist". I know it sounds silly, but that felt a bit peculiar too – the way he said it, the pharmacist bit – sort of self-importantly.'

'He's probably proud of it,' Jack said, reasonably.

'And why not, and I wouldn't mention it, but . . .' She trailed off for a moment. 'But then, as I was leaving, it suddenly all came together. His face, his voice, the way he looked at me – most of all *that*. He gave me the creeps, Jack.' She hesitated. 'And he wasn't really looking at my face – I think he was looking at my *hair*, which seemed even stranger.'

'It's very nice hair.'

'Thank you.'

'Still not exactly evidence of anything, is it, Harry?' Jack said.

'Except we might – possibly – be talking about . . .' Harriet hesitated. 'There's something I haven't mentioned – I didn't really register it at the time. Everything and everyone on these bombsites is always covered in soot and dirt. Mr Ashcroft was too, same as all the rescue workers.'

'But?'

'But that hand looked . . .' She paused. 'Not exactly clean, obviously. But not as grimy as everything else.'

'One of those things, maybe,' Jack tried to dismiss.

Harriet shook her head. 'I'm beginning to wonder if that poor woman was buried by a Nazi bomb at all. And how come Heavy Rescue didn't spot her?'

'I expect a lot gets shifted while they're working – the hand might not have been visible before. Except then—'

'It would not have been almost clean.' She took a breath. 'And one more thing.'

Jack smiled. 'Yes, Sherlock.'

'I know Milly and Dora didn't remember, but you need to see if anyone else at the Windmill knows if Babs had – has – a mole on her hand.'

Watching again, from the grimy window on the opposite side of the road.

Blackout partially raised.

Eyes fixed on Calla House.

A party was in progress on the ground floor. Moving shadows just visible beyond heavy blackout curtains – the visitors he'd spied arriving earlier.

All right for some.

Later that night, long after most of the guests had departed, after Jack and one of Louisa's music students had carried the piano downstairs so that Jack and the night owl could play jazz piano with Louisa accompanying on violin; after the student had finally left and the washing up had been done and everyone had retired to bed, George, up in Harriet's bedroom, began to whine.

Harriet groaned, looked at her alarm clock.

'George, it's after two. Go back to sleep.'

The dog went on whining with mounting determination until his mistress, done in as she was, gave in, pulled on a jumper and slacks and the ancient grubby white plimsolls she used for dog walking, and took him quietly downstairs.

'Short version,' she told him outside. 'No arguments.'

It was quite lovely. Cold, but starry and mercifully peaceful.

Until George halted abruptly, ears pricking.

'What is it, boy?' Harriet asked.

The dog growled.

Inside Calla House, Jack, till then sound asleep, woke up and, feeling unaccountably disturbed, sat bolt upright.

At the corner of Glenilla Road, the dog was sniffing at yet another tree and Harriet's patience was dissipating.

'Come on, George.'

She heard it then.

The sound from that other night.

Something grating, creaking.

She turned, peered uneasily into the blackness, saw nothing.

The sounds grew louder, coming closer, then stopped.

And now she saw it. The wheelchair, stationary.

Empty this time.

No one pushing it.

Like something out of a ghost story.

George growled again, more loudly this time, and Harriet, unnerved, felt goosebumps along her spine.

'Come on.' She tugged hard at the dog's lead, began to turn . . .

He was on her instantly, pinioning her arms and pressing a pad of something wet, sickly-smelling – *revolting* – over her nose and mouth.

Harriet choked, struggled madly, knew it was hopeless, felt herself begin to go under.

Down into the dark.

TWELVE

She woke, feeling sick and dizzy and terrified.

In the depths of a hellish nightmare.

She tried to move, but her arms were trapped behind her, her wrists bound together with something. She looked down, saw that some kind of thin, knotted black cord was tethering her by the waist to a chair.

She remembered.

The wheelchair. First seen on the walk with George. The woman slumped in it. The man in the hat and coat. The hand. Her and Jack's fears for the missing dancer.

Her mind zigzagged weakly back and forth in an effort to make sense of *this*.

The man. At the bombsite and then at the chemist's. The light over his dispensing table glinting on his spectacles. The same pair that she'd seen catching the sunlight that early morning.

Smith.

No – Ashcroft.

Her heart began to pound.

It was the *wheelchair* she was tied to, in a large, cold, damp-smelling room with a stone floor.

She turned her head to the right, realized that someone was standing in the shadows, motionless.

The figure moved. Walking slowly, calmly, towards her.

Harriet blinked hard, trying to focus more clearly, but she already knew that it was him. No hat or coat now, but the spectacles were the same.

He was wearing a crisp white coat, the same kind that he had worn in the chemist's.

Ashcroft, the ARP rescuer. Felix's pharmacist.

Respectable member of society.

She noticed his hands.

He was wearing gloves. White, too.

Fear made her heart hammer in her chest, and suddenly George flew back into her mind and she turned her head left and right, craning to look around.

'Where's George?' Her voice was hoarse. 'What have you done with my dog?!'

THIRTEEN

'Where the hell are they?'

It was almost four in the morning, and Jack – returned minutes ago after a fruitless search for Harriet and George – was smoking agitatedly and pacing back and forth in Louisa's and Felix's kitchen, the elderly couple looking on anxiously, untouched teacups on the table.

'Perhaps George is just wanting one of his long walks,' Louisa said.

She had been trying, unsuccessfully, to bolster both men's spirits, though Felix's stress was less obvious than Jack's, her husband's reactions subdued by the pain tablets he had swallowed at bedtime. Earlier, as Louisa had answered Jack's urgent knocking on their front door, Felix had imagined he must have slept through an air-raid warning, muttering curses against Hitler as he'd stumbled out of bed.

No bombs this time. A different kind of threat, quite preposterous sounding, they had both thought at first as Jack had shared his fears about the missing dancer – those fears mounting now with Harriet and the dog being nowhere to be found.

'This is no ordinary walk,' Jack said now, still pacing, his limp growing more evident. '*Why* didn't I go up to check on her sooner?'

'Why would you?' Felix paused. 'Why did you check at all?'

Louisa threw him a look that told him it was none of their business.

'Because I knew something was up,' Jack said. 'I woke up and just *knew* something was very wrong, but then I talked myself out of it and dozed off, and by the time . . .' He looked at his wristwatch. 'Christ knows when she actually left.'

'It could still be something simple,' Louisa said, her creased forehead belying her words. 'Harriet says that George sometimes runs after a fox. She might just be chasing after him—'

'Not a fox,' Jack said grimly. 'More like a rat.' He slumped down on to a chair. 'I've been too slow – once she'd gone for your tablets, Felix, and told the chemist this address . . .' He stubbed his cigarette out violently. 'Stupid, *stupid* girl to go out alone in the middle of the night.'

'So what can we do?' Felix asked.

Jack lit another cigarette, stood, picked up his old leather jacket from where he'd slung it over the back of a chair. 'I'm going back out and I'm not giving up till I've found them.' He put on the jacket. 'Felix, you phone the police, tell them everything Harriet said – from the beginning, if you have to – about the woman in the wheelchair and the hand—'

'But you already told them at the police station,' Felix said.

'Not about the mole on the hand.' Jack's face was grim. 'And Harriet hadn't made the connection with Ashcroft when we went to the station, and she hadn't seen the bastard staring after her when she left the shop – the sign says G. Smith, but he told her his name was Ashcroft.'

'I know him,' Felix said.

'So do I.' Louisa looked confounded. 'He's a good chemist.'

'Pharmacist.' Jack stressed the word darkly. 'He'll probably be registered. Felix, please call the police. We shouldn't waste any more time.'

'And what can I do?' Louisa asked.

'Make sure Felix doesn't leave anything out. Make sure they know they need to take immediate action. Tell them we're very likely talking about murder.'

FOURTEEN

A shcroft stood in front of Harriet.

'You're frightened,' he said.

She didn't answer. Her mouth was dry and she still felt sick.

'I'm sorry for that.'

'Then please stop this. I don't know why I'm here, but if you untie me, let me go—'

'You won't tell anyone what's happened,' he said.

'That's right. You've made some kind of mistake.'

'No.' He shook his head. 'No mistake.'

'Please.' Harriet licked her lips. 'Please tell me what you've done to my dog.'

'Nothing.' He was dismissive. 'It ran off.'

Harriet thought about George, remembered him barking, growling, hoped to heaven it was true, that he had run away, and she prayed, against the odds, that the dog had found his way back to Calla House.

She felt her teeth begin to chatter.

'You're feeling unwell, Miss Yorke,' the chemist said. 'It's the effects of the chloroform. Not very nice, I know, but it will pass.'

She stared at him, taking in his face. It was ordinary, the eyes hard to see behind the rather strong-looking glasses. His hair was brown and neatly combed, his lips thin, chin average – everything average. Respectable – she thought for the second time.

She tore her eyes from him, took in the rest of the room again.

There was not much to take in. A hanging rail of clothes – women's garments, so far as she could see, nothing that caught the eye except for a red-and-black checked coat. Two pairs of grey curtains covering something on a wall, she thought, rather than a window, since she could see the window opposite her, its blackout securely down.

Women's clothes on the rail, almost certainly.

Babs Woodruff – or her image of her as described by Jack – sprang into her mind. And then the hand.

Her teeth began to chatter again.

'Don't worry about the clothes,' Ashcroft said, quite gently. 'I hang them appropriately out of respect. Though I will, in due course, have to incinerate them.'

Harriet's mind ran ahead to horrifying possibilities of what 'in due course' might mean, and she cut them out, forced herself *not* to think about them.

She looked down at herself, as if to check.

She was wearing the same jumper and slacks and plimsolls that she'd pulled on for her walk with George earlier.

When had that been? She had lost all sense of time, though it had been late night when she had been dragged off the pavement, and judging by the blackout at the window, it was still night – or maybe it was the *next* night, though she didn't think so, she didn't feel as she thought she might if she had been unconscious for so long . . .

'What's the time?' she asked.

'Time doesn't matter,' the chemist replied.

She looked down again, focusing on the chair to which she was tethered at the waist.

'Why am I tied to this thing?'

'Practicality. Convenience.' Ashcroft paused. 'A small element of theatricality, perhaps, I admit. Continuity.'

The last word chilled her most.

And the way that he was staring at her.

Not at her face.

At her hair. Again.

In the kitchen at Calla House, Felix was on the telephone, Louisa hovering over him impatiently.

'Of course we appreciate your problems, sergeant,' he said.

Louisa seized the receiver. 'That's not true, sergeant,' she said, emotion making her accent stronger than usual. 'We do *not* appreciate your problems. Two young women are now missing, both from Belsize Park – one almost certainly murdered and the other in mortal danger – and my husband has already told you who to look for. Ashcroft, the chemist.'

'But the name on the shop—' Felix added.

'Smith,' Louisa said. 'G. Smith is the name on the . . .' She wavered. '*Ladenschild.*' She glared at her husband. 'What's the word?'

'Sign,' Felix supplied.

'The sign on the shop is G. Smith & Son, but the man you must find told Miss Yorke his name is Ashcroft. And we know this man, he is the . . .' She sought the right word again, anxiety provoking confusion. '*Apotheker.*' She looked at Felix again, then found the word herself. 'Pharmacist.'

They heard barking. Louisa slammed down the receiver and rushed ahead of Felix out through the hall to the front door, tore it open.

The terrier trotted into the house, his lead trailing, claws clattering across the linoleum.

'George!' Louisa plucked him up, delight swiftly giving way to fresh alarm. 'But where's Harriet?'

'George!' Jack's voice called out of the dark, and then he loomed into view, his gait more uneven than before. He saw Louisa at the open door, stopped.

'I heard George and ran after him. Is she back?'

Harriet's arms and shoulders were painful, she was discovering as the effects of the chloroform continued to wear off, and she realized now that the tether tight around her waist was not made of rope but of stretched, twisted nylon stockings, probably a pair tied together.

Nylons too, around her wrists behind her – and who had they belonged to, she dreaded to wonder? – and she had started trying to see if she could unfasten those wrist knots, was so far getting absolutely nowhere, though at least the chemist had not yet noticed.

'I have something to show you,' Ashcroft said.

He moved swiftly to the back of the chair and she stilled her fingers before he took off the handbrake and wheeled her to the left, towards one of the two pairs of curtains.

He reached for a cord to the right, drew it open and revealed a meticulously set-out display of photographs attached with drawing pins to a board on the wall.

Black-and-white images of women with two things in common.

There were five photos, all of different women, all tied to a wheelchair. The same one, Harriet was as certain as she could be, as the one in which she was seated.

Not seated. *Trapped.*

They all looked terrified.

Something was clipped to each photograph.

Hair. Locks of hair tied together with black ribbon.

The third thing, perhaps, that the women had in common, though she couldn't tell from the photographs.

Red hair. Different shades, but all red.

And now Harriet knew why he had been staring at her hair.

'This is bloody insanity,' Jack snapped, slammed the phone down, missed the hook, left the receiver dangling. 'Coincidence, my backside.'

Louisa gently replaced the phone.

'I'm sorry, Louisa, but what more do they *need*, for the love of God?'

He pulled on his jacket again.

'Jack, what are you doing now?' Felix asked.

'What I said I was going to do. Find Harriet. Now that we know she hasn't even got her dog. For a start, I'm going to do what the police ought to be doing. Going to that blasted chemist's.'

'What are you thinking, Miss Yorke?' Ashcroft asked.

Harriet said nothing, feeling suddenly that it was vital she not say the wrong thing to this man. Her abductor. A possible murderer.

'Presumably that I'm mad,' he said.

He pushed the wheelchair and Harriet back to the centre of the room.

'Cat got your tongue?' he said.

Her mouth felt very dry again.

'Not that it really matters to me what you think,' he said. 'I stopped caring about what other people thought of me some time ago.' The eyes behind the spectacles were cold. 'Normal people. Isn't that how you would regard yourself? As "normal"?'

He walked to the garment rail, pulled off a pale silk stocking.

She forced herself to speak. 'I don't think I've ever thought about being normal or otherwise.'

'Ordinary then.' Ashcroft fondled the stocking. 'Is that a better word to describe you, Harriet?'

'Why not?' Her eyes were on the stocking.

He ran the silk between his fingers, watching her face.

Then pulled the stocking taut.

FIFTEEN

Outside the chemist's in Haverstock Hill Jack pounded on the door, but getting no answer he banged on the residential door to the right of the shop.

'Oy!' The blackout over the window above the next shop snapped up, the window opened and a man in a vest leaned out. 'What's the bleeding racket?'

'I'm looking for Ashcroft.' Jack stood back. 'The chemist.'

'It's the middle of the effing night,' the man said.

'It's very urgent,' Jack said. 'Matter of life and death.'

'So's my sleep,' the man said. 'One flaming night without a fucking raid and I get effing Long John Silver banging on the bloody door. Now sod off.'

The window slammed and the blind came down.

Jack stood still for a moment, considering, then turned around, spotted a loose lump of concrete near the kerb, picked it up and, without another moment's hesitation, lobbed it through the shop window.

At Calla House, a police officer was taking details from Louisa and Felix.

'Do you have a photograph of Miss Yorke?'

'I don't think so,' Louisa said. 'Jack – Mr Jerome – probably—'

'*Weihnachten*.' Felix went to the dresser, opened a drawer. 'At Christmas, we had . . .' He found an envelope, pulled out several snaps. 'Here. She has red hair.' He gave one to the policeman. 'But what you really need is a photograph of Mr Ashcroft, officer.'

'Find him,' Louisa said, 'and we think you'll find Miss Yorke.'

'And Mr Jerome?' the officer said. 'Where exactly has he gone?'

'He's looking for Harriet,' Felix said. 'As we told you.'

'Or Mr Ashcroft?' The man's voice was heavy with disapproval.

'Someone had to do something,' Louisa said.

Ashcroft, still holding the silk stocking, had seen Harriet flinch.

'Are you afraid I'm going to strangle you, Miss Yorke?'

'Are you?' She felt very ill again.

'There's no danger of that,' he said. 'I apologize for causing you that kind of fear.' He looked downwards, towards Harriet's plimsolls. 'Socks with those shoes – if you call them shoes. No silk stockings for you.'

She shook her head, wordless again.

'Usually in trousers, Miss Yorke. Except on the bombsite in your uniform, of course. You looked very smart. Worthy of respect. Although . . .'

Harriet stared at him. 'Although?'

'The beret was covering your hair.' He looked suddenly sad. 'And last week, in your overalls – dungarees, I think they're called – that turban thing. To have that hair and to conceal it, not to seem to bother with it at all . . .'

'You've been watching me.'

A new chill had clamped over her heart, and behind the chair her fingers found a knot and began to work at it.

The chemist didn't answer.

'Since when?' she asked. 'Why?'

Her eyes flicked nervously to the photographs on the board.

Knew what she had, till now, tried to suppress.

She was in the hands of a madman.

'You know what they say about curiosity, Miss Yorke,' Ashcroft said.

Jack was inside the chemist's shop behind the counter, rifling through paperwork, hunting for Ashcroft's home address, when the man from next door appeared in pyjamas and slippers, brandishing a rounder's bat.

'All I'm after is Ashcroft's damned address.' Jack ignored the threat, went on searching, swept useless papers and files aside, a box of prescriptions scattering on the floor.

'He lives over the sodding shop, pillock,' the man said.

Jack stopped ransacking. 'Where's the door?'

'He's not there,' the man said.

Jack gritted his teeth. 'Do you know where he is, sir?'

'Nope.'

In frustration, Jack punched the typewriter on the desk and it teetered on the edge, then crashed to the floor.

'That'll cost you, pillock,' the neighbour said, apparently enjoying the spectacle. 'I've called the coppers.'

'Good,' Jack said.

And went on hunting.

'I knew that you'd recognized me,' Ashcroft told Harriet. 'You weren't entirely sure at the bombsite, but—'

'I'd seen her hand on Thursday night,' Harriet said. 'There was a mole. I remembered it.'

'Bad luck for you,' Ashcroft said.

'I've told people about it. About you.'

'I daresay.' Ashcroft turned away. 'I can't see the arthritic Mr Brandt doing much more than lifting a phone, though maybe your friend – the young man who held the ladder for you on Friday morning – bit of a limp, I noticed, is that why—'

'What did you *do* to her?' Anger rushed suddenly through Harriet, almost blotting out the fear. 'And why? Why her? And why have you been watching us?'

'Not "us". You. Too many questions. Why Miss Woodruff?' Ashcroft moved behind the rail to a table partly in view, came back holding a small cardboard box. 'I didn't know her name until I saw her identity card. I didn't know any of their names before I took them.'

He held out the box for her to see.

Several cards inside. Five, Harriet thought, considering the photographs, and her heart thumped hard, dread squeezing her stomach.

'Barbara Woodruff.' Ashcroft fingered one of the cards.

Babs. From the Windmill. All doubt gone now.

'A common sort,' Ashcroft said, 'but with a certain sense of style.' He nodded towards the checked coat on the clothes rail. 'And a very nice coat, I noticed.'

'You killed her for her coat?' Harriet's horror mixed with incredulity.

'Not her coat,' Ashcroft said. 'But I had no alternative anyway once I'd found her. I could hardly let her go, any more than I had the others.'

She hardly dared speak it.

'Her hair then.'

'I saw her first from a distance in poor light.' He shrugged. 'I misjudged the colour. I took it for perfection. I was mistaken, as I have been each time. And each time I feel guilt, and shame – at which I'm well practiced, having been made to feel shameful by too many people in my life – and that makes me feel angry.' He made a gesture with his hands, of resignation. 'After I saw you that Thursday night, I brought her back here. Did what I had to do.' He looked at her expression, went on. 'Then I waited for the next raid on Friday night. Less chance of seeing other people. I took her to the bombsite where you and I met for the second time – and buried her. It wasn't easy, but I'd done it before, so I knew what I was doing. When I was finished, I left and came back after Heavy Rescue were done.' He paused. 'The hand being exposed – probably by their labours – was unlucky. Especially for you.'

'My God,' Harriet said.

'You're disgusted,' Ashcroft said. 'Outraged.'

'Yes,' she said, fervently. '*Yes.*'

'Naturally,' the chemist said. 'You're not the first, as I said.'

He moved abruptly, stepped behind the rail, emerged with something else in his hand. Scissors.

Harriet gasped.

'I saw you first some weeks ago, riding a bicycle that was too big for you. Your hair was flying in the breeze. Just for a moment it reminded me of her so strongly that I could hardly breathe.' He came back, stood close beside her, stroked a few strands of her hair with his left hand, made her flinch. 'It's not perfect, of course, not long enough and too wayward and auburn, rather than the colour of flame, and it's not as fine, but I realized a long time ago that it never could be perfect.' He caressed her head with his palm. 'And at least it's natural auburn, you're not a fake, like so many.'

Harriet's eyes were fixed on the scissors' sharp blades.

'I would very much like to keep you,' he said. 'Knowing that I could come here and perhaps talk to you sometimes. You're intelligent, for one thing, and there's no artifice about you. But mostly I'd want to keep you so that I could do this whenever I felt the need.' He touched her hair again, and she cringed. 'Your hair would grow longer, and I could close my eyes and pretend, as I used to when I still had her beautiful plait.'

What in God's name did that mean? When he had her *plait*? Whose plait? Panic grew inside her head, feeling like a pounding heartbeat out of control in her brain, and she thought she was going to faint.

He wanted to *keep* her. Like a pet, to be stroked at will. Here, perhaps, wherever *here* was, tied to this wheelchair. Or perhaps he had a cage prepared for her.

'Don't worry,' he said, a smile in his voice. 'I can't keep you now. Not when others may try to find you.'

'They will,' she said quickly, trying to slow the drumbeat in her head. 'I'm sure they already are. So you should let me go while you still can.'

'Anyway . . .' He stooped and brushed the top of her head with his lips. 'It isn't perfect, and however hard I tried to fantasize, I would know the truth and have to accept it.'

He stepped away again, back behind the rail, and the thrum of her heart was back in her chest, where it belonged, her head was clearer, and perhaps he had put away the scissors. But after a moment he reappeared with something else in his right hand – a framed photograph – but the scissors were still in his left, and the pounding rose again, up into her throat.

'This is all I have of her.' He stood gazing at the image. 'They left me with nothing, but I managed to locate this. It is her, yet it isn't, not really. It's false, because she's standing beside *him*, bride and devil, and she isn't the person I knew so completely, not the woman who loved me, who adored me, who was the kindest, softest, most beautiful person I've ever known.'

He came to her side and held out the photograph for her to see.

'You can't see her hair because of the veil, and of course it's monochrome, but still, it's something . . .'

'Your . . .' Harriet licked her dry lips, fought to keep her tone level. 'Your mother?'

'Lilian Ashcroft,' he said.

She heard reverence in his voice.

He turned, took away the photograph, a restlessness in his movements now, as if he were suddenly hurrying, and this time, he returned without the scissors but with a camera and flashgun.

Harriet looked at the photographs on the board, and froze.

'Look at me,' he said.

It was an order.

'What for?' she said.

The flash blinded her.

'Before,' the chemist said.

He attended to the camera for a few moments, then set it down carefully on the floor. Disappeared again behind the board, then came back with the scissors.

Now she knew what they were for.

'Please,' Harriet said. 'Don't.'

She jerked her head away, but Ashcroft took a small handful of hair and snipped at it.

'What a fuss,' he said, crossly, looked at the curls in his hand, and nodded. 'To go with your "before" photograph,' he said.

The word hung in the air.

Another word in her mind.

After.

SIXTEEN

'I don't give a damn if you lock me up and throw away the bloody key, so long as you find Harriet first.'

Jack was in an interview room at Hampstead Police Station with a detective inspector named Greenaway. A middle-aged, stout man with keen and interested brown eyes.

'I'd strongly recommend that you try to calm down, Mr Jerome,' Greenaway told him.

'If the blasted fool who dragged me here had taken one moment to listen to me instead of wasting valuable—'

'Mr Jerome.'

'Harriet Yorke has been abducted by a man who—'

'Jerome.' Greenaway's voice was louder, more commanding. 'You were arrested for breaking and entering and—'

'But I told—'

'Enough,' Greenaway said.

'For God's—'

'*Enough*!' said the detective inspector.

SEVENTEEN

'You kill innocent women for their *hair*,' Harriet said.

'Innocent people are dying every day,' Ashcroft said.

'That's war,' she said. 'You're not fighting a war.'

'Think I didn't want to fight, Miss Yorke?' he said. 'I can assure you I did – I was all set to volunteer, told my wife I was going to sign up before conscription. Private Ashcroft doing his bit for king and country, trying to make his wife and children proud.'

He saw her expression.

'Surprise you, does it? Me married with children?'

'I don't know,' Harriet said. 'I don't know anything about you.'

'True. Lots of thing you don't know.'

She kept quiet.

'I can't remember a time when I wasn't drawn to red hair – except, of course, before I lost her. If I saw a red-haired woman, I would sometimes follow her, would wish that I could touch it but know that I couldn't.' Ashcroft paused. 'I tried to control it. It was very innocent back then. I never hurt anyone. I had no desire to hurt anyone then.'

'What changed?' Harriet was curious despite herself.

'Initially, my wife's lack of understanding. She knew how my mother had died, she knew how dreadful it had been for me, and she was my *wife*, so I made the mistake of trying to explain the attraction to her. Her disapproval, her coldness turned something harmless into a compulsion that sometimes took me over, made me do foolish things. But still, I never hurt a living soul.'

He moved away again, and Harriet continued her battle with her wrist knots, but fearing what might be about to happen, and finding herself horribly fascinated by the fragments of the chemist's past, she asked, 'What happened to your mother?'

'My father killed her,' Ashcroft answered.

He was by the rail of clothes again, but his face seemed different, his expression less cold, less detached than it had been.

'She was hanging when I found her. And he was dead, too, he'd shot himself through the mouth. I was ten.'

A wave of compassion for the ten-year-old boy startled her.

'I'm so sorry,' she said.

'Yes,' he said. 'Thank you.'

Harriet wanted him to go on, wanted to distract him for as long as possible, still had no idea what time it was, how long had passed since she'd been taken, but she thought that either Jack or the Brandts must have realized by now that she was missing – and she prayed that George had found his way home, and—

'My life changed forever.' Ashcroft cut into her thoughts. 'And not for the better. If something good came my way, it was soon destroyed. A dark pattern, if you like. I focused on my talents, meagre as they were, worked hard, picked a wife I hoped would be good for me, but I was soon disappointed.' He paused, was silent for a few seconds. 'My reactions to red hair became more intense, more compulsive – still trying to recreate my mother, which was pitiful, obviously . . .'

'Understandable,' Harriet said.

'Please don't pretend you understand,' Ashcroft said.

The softening was gone. Harriet's struggle with the knots became fiercer.

'There were incidents – several. My wife threw me out, backed as she always was by her father, who had despised me from the instant he'd heard about me, before he'd even met me. I wasn't sorry to leave, except for the loss of my son, who I loved with all my heart. I concentrated on my work, on the pharmacy – I had a shop in Kentish Town then, I was respected. But then I slipped up again, my wife learned about it, told her father, and lo and behold, a few days later I was attacked, most brutally, with the direst of threats, and left for dead.'

He moved abruptly to the back of the wheelchair and, without commenting on what she'd been doing, checked and tightened the knots in the nylons, cutting deeper into Harriet's wrists and plunging her into fresh, silent despair.

'It was too much.' He continued as if he had not paused, standing beside her again. 'They crossed a line.' He shuddered, took a breath. 'In here.' He laid a hand over his heart. 'And in here.' He moved the hand to his head. 'So once I recovered, many months later, I began to cross my own line – like crossing a border, I suppose, from being a quite benign person with an innocuous occasional craving for *this*— '

Harriet's curl of hair was still in his hand.

'There was no harm in it, really, before. An idiosyncrasy, no more. But the line I'd crossed after they did that to me – that, and worse – changed me, drove me downward. Turned me into a man who decided to take what I wanted, and to punish them for what they'd done to me.'

Harriet's compassion drained away. This man was sharing with her what he clearly saw as justifiable motivation for *murder*, his account both plausible and horrifying, but he had drugged and abducted her because he knew she had recognized him and because she had seen Babs Woodruff's hand sticking out from beneath the rubble on the bombsite and because he had been following her because her hair was *red*. And she had seen photographs of five women, and he had shown her the box of identity cards, said he hadn't known any of their names before he'd taken them.

Them.

And whatever had been done to him, this man was unquestionably mad, terrifyingly composed but deranged, and she was in the most grievous, imminent danger, and she needed to be more careful than she had ever been in her whole life . . .

'But you aren't punishing the people who did those things to you.' Her voice was almost steady, reasonable, as if that might enable her to get through to him. 'You're murdering random strangers, women who've done you no harm at all.'

Except me. That thought jarred her. She was the one woman who would most certainly report him, given the chance.

'Only because I see no other way, once I've begun – once I've taken these "random" women.' Ashcroft gave a small smile. 'I must tell you, Miss Yorke, that I've never explained myself to anyone before. It's a compliment to you, really. But it was a woman who ruined me. My wife. She set my father-in-law and his thugs on me and stole my son. It was *her* wish, her doing.'

He stepped away, then paused, looked at Harriet's face.

'It's become an addiction – I recognize that – as strong as morphine or any other kind.'

He moved behind the rail, back to the partially visible table, reappeared swiftly, the scissors in his hand again, and was on her before she could even gasp. And this time, though she jerked her head away, he took a handful of hair and snipped, then grabbed more, his strength seeming to grow, along with his anger – she *felt* it – or rather rage, or perhaps it was a different kind of intense emotion, because he, too, was gasping as he cut, and though she had closed her eyes in defence, she thought he might be sobbing. He grabbed more, almost viciously now, and hacked at it, cutting close to her scalp, and she cried out in pain and terror, her own rage filling her, at him and at herself too for her helplessness, for her idiocy in having gone out alone at night despite her friends' warnings.

He paused, and she opened her eyes, saw him lift some of the severed hair to his nostrils, smell it and nod. 'Good. Amami, I suppose. I sell so much of it these days. Not much else to choose from.'

It was more than bizarre, the switch from tortured savagery to purveyor of shampoo.

'Now keep still,' he said. 'Don't want you bleeding.'

He went on cutting, going more carefully now, in control of himself, Harriet thought, taking her hair in long strands while tears ran down her cheeks until, finally finished, he moved away from the wheelchair again and collected from somewhere behind the rail an empty paper bag.

He tucked most of the fallen hair into it, folded the top of the bag neatly, as if he were wrapping a purchase from his shop, then walked to the far right corner of the room and placed the bag on the floor there.

She had not noticed that corner before, had not had reason to look.

But now she saw that her hair had joined a small heap of similar bags.

Ashcroft gave a sigh, returned to the unseen place behind the rail and came back with the camera and flashgun.

'What now?' she asked.

The flash blinded her again.

And of course, she knew.

This was the *after*.

'Why did you do that?' she made herself ask, though her voice quivered a little. 'Why take my picture?' Her fingers were busy again behind her back, and achieving something, she thought, a tiny hole made by one of her nails, but not enough, nowhere *near* enough.

'A memento,' Ashcroft answered. 'To go with the others.'

He set down the camera and flashgun, came to the back of the chair, and instantly Harriet stilled her hands, prayed he wouldn't spot the hole she'd made, but he said nothing, took off the brake and moved her again, wheeled the chair over to the second curtained section of wall.

He pulled another cord.

It was another display of photographs. Of the same women as on the first board, she thought, but could not be certain. All were slumped now in the wheelchair. All with ragged, almost bald scalps. The clothes they had worn in the first set of photos now gone, each woman dressed in a man's shirt. Their faces horribly contorted.

Any faint lingering doubt or hope obliterated.

'I'm sorry to frighten you,' Ashcroft said.

Harriet's eyes veered from the pictures to his face, saw that he was looking at them, not at her. Behind the chair, her fingernail located the hole in the nylon again, tore at it while her mind worked frantically.

'If you're sorry,' she said, 'untie me.'

'I can't do that.' Ashcroft sounded quite gentle, as he had earlier. 'You'll try to bolt and I'll have to stop you, maybe hurt you.' He saw her eyes return to the photos, saw the intensity of her fear. 'I can't let you go now, Harriet. You must realize that.'

She made herself look away from the poor dead women, back at him.

'I could help you,' she said.

'Of course you could.' Ashcroft's smile was sad. 'All the way to the gallows.'

EIGHTEEN

Having been escorted to Greenaway's office at the police station and trusted to be left alone while the detective inspector made enquiries, Jack paced between filing cabinets and the desk, smoking and quietly cursing, his anxiety and impatience growing by the second, not knowing how much longer he'd be able to contain his frustration.

At last, DI Greenaway entered, holding a piece of paper.

'Harriet?' Jack said before the door was closed.

'I'm taking a gamble on you, Mr Jerome,' Greenaway said, 'so don't let me down, there's a good chap.'

'You've found Ashcroft.'

'Not yet,' Greenaway said. 'But we do have an address.'

Ashcroft checked his wristwatch.

'Time to move on.'

'Where to?' Harriet asked, alarmed. 'Why?'

'Since, as you say, you told people about me, I daresay they'll have told the police by now.' He saw panic in her eyes. 'You needn't worry. I shan't be doing to you what I did to those other ladies.' His tone was soft, almost kind. 'And just to reassure you, I only removed their clothing in order to make identification more difficult. There was nothing sexual in it, Miss Yorke, nor in anything I have done. I took their clothes purely for practical reasons, as with their stockings. I had dragged them by their ankles – I'd had to, you see, there was no other way – so it was a matter of removing fingerprints. And afterwards, I burned the stockings, as I will the clothing.'

Harriet forced herself to look again at the photographs of the poor dead women, then back at him. 'What did you do then?' Her voice was almost a whisper.

'I smothered them,' Ashcroft answered. 'I had to do that so that no one would doubt that they had been suffocated in the bombing.' He saw that she was aghast. 'They knew nothing about it, Miss Yorke, they were unconscious. Though I can't claim that I was being merciful, because the hatred – not really of them, but of my wife and her father – was – is – still in me. Before that though, when I cut the hair, it does seem to become a kind of frenzy – rage against them for not being what I need them to be, for being *pretenders*, though that rage doesn't last long. And I think perhaps I was a little rough with you, Harriet, when I took your lovely hair – lovely, but not quite *right* – and I apologize for that too.'

He paused, waiting, perhaps, for a response, getting none.

'But when I finish them,' he went on, 'which I truly abhor doing, I do hate them again too, for *making* me do it because I know I can't trust them enough to let them survive. I can't trust anyone any more.'

The words seemed to echo in the cold, damp air.

'Why do you photograph them?' She asked the question because she knew she was running out of time, and because she found that she wanted to know.

'That's a very personal question, Harriet.'

'I think I have a right to ask it.'

He nodded. 'It's a tribute. To my mother. I talk to her sometimes, to that little photograph, in case she's watching. And I imagine she's horrified, because she was so kind, so soft and womanly. But it's my way of showing her that there has never been, never will be, anyone to compare. That this is a kind of homage to her.'

Harriet said nothing, felt beyond words.

'I know I've failed her utterly,' he went on. 'That it was always going to be impossible. That there was only one. I must have known I was acting irrationally – I'm an intelligent man – and yes, bad things were done to me, evil things, but still . . . The first time, that rage overwhelmed me, took over, made it almost easy. And I had planned it all out before that – I'd enjoyed that so much, the strategizing, because it had helped me to forget.' He sighed. 'But after the first I found that I couldn't stop, partly because that would have meant acknowledging what I had become. Mad. Wicked. Useless. As my father said. And the others long after him. And I am sorry.'

A tear slid down from behind the spectacles.

'You could stop it now.' Harriet fought to suppress her revulsion. 'It's not too late.'

'Of course it is, and you know that. You're not a stupid woman.' He took off his glasses and wiped his eyes, and Harriet noticed that one of his light brown eyes was oddly flecked. 'I wish you'd seen her. Or at least the plait. I cut it off, you see, after I'd taken her down when I found her hanging – I apologize if I've already told you that.'

He put his glasses back on.

'No,' Harriet said. 'You haven't.'

'It was so very beautiful, and I kept it safe for years – it was my treasure, and no harm to anyone – but they stole it and burned it – my wife took pleasure in telling me that – and I will never forgive them. Never.'

'I can understand that,' she said.

'I know,' he said, 'that I am mad. And I would like to stop. But I don't think I can. I expect, ultimately, that I will *be* stopped. Time will tell.'

Harriet shuddered.

'You really don't need to be so frightened,' he said. 'I told you I'm not going to do to you what I did to them.' He smiled. 'Something a little more special for you, Harriet.'

He left her side again, returned to the table, stooped, his back to her.

'What are you doing now?' Fear surged higher because the talking, his introspection, was clearly over. The little hole in the nylon had grown, but it was useless, she knew that now.

'Don't fret,' Ashcroft said. 'Not much longer.'

He straightened up, came around the rail, carrying a small glass bottle in one hand, a cotton pad in the other, and Harriet's panic blossomed into full-blown terror, and she tried to rock the chair into movement, tears springing to her eyes. She thought about Jack, about her father, about her—

Her nose caught the smell of the bottle's contents, remembered it from earlier.

'No!' she cried out. 'Please, not again.'

Ashcroft was already tilting the bottle over the pad. 'It'll help you, Harriet.'

'No! I'll be quiet.'

'Of course you won't be.' He was harder again now.

She went into a fresh semi-frenzy of panic, desperately trying to free herself.

'Calm down, please, or I shall have to hurt you.'

He set the bottle down on the floor and came at her with the pad in his right hand, tried to tilt back her head with his left, but Harriet cried out, turned her face away.

'Keep still,' he said harshly, and grasped at what was left of her hair, yanked it hard, making her cry out again in pain and terror as he forced the pad over her nose and mouth.

She fought it with all she had, before the awful sensation flooded over her, through her.

And was gone.

NINETEEN

J ack and DI Greenaway waited outside the police station on Rosslyn Hill for their car to be brought round, Jack in an agony of impatience, badgering to know the address they had discovered, the policeman giving nothing away.

Less than a mile away, in a side road in the near pitch-darkness of blackout, the sounds made by the wheelchair seemed unnaturally loud to Ashcroft as, his pharmacy white coat removed and returned to his outdoor attire of hat and coat, he pushed Harriet along the pavement.

Grating, creaking, screeching.

A scarf wrapped around Harriet's shorn head and face, a blanket covering the rest of her.

Dead to the world.

A constable named Miller was driving the Wolseley, Greenaway in the front passenger seat, Jack in the back of the police car as it turned off Haverstock Hill and he realized, peering through the dark, where they were.

'You're not dumping me,' he said flatly.

'No,' Greenaway said placidly, 'we're not.'

'But this is where I live,' Jack said.

'Correct,' the inspector said.

'He's in our road?' Jack burst, beside himself.

'Not far now,' Ashcroft said to Harriet's huddled, inert form.

No traffic. No signs of human life anywhere.

From somewhere, the sound of an owl hooting.

'Such peace still to be found at times, even in this war,' he said. 'Don't you think, Miss Yorke?'

He paused for a moment, patted the scarf.

'Nearly there,' he said.

And began pushing again.

* * *

'There, sir,' said PC Miller.

'Pull over,' Greenaway said.

Jack stared through his window, silently cursing his useless eye, unbearably tense.

'You will stay in the car, Mr Jerome, till you're told otherwise.'

Jack didn't answer, trying to make out the building almost directly opposite Calla House, knowing he'd seen it a thousand times in daylight, oblivious of the slightest danger.

'That's an order,' Greenaway said.

'Yes, sir,' Jack said.

He waited as the two policemen got out and walked to the front door, waited as Greenaway knocked, and then, very quietly, he opened his door and got out of the Wolseley, his own focus on something he had just spotted.

A tiny chink of light from the basement.

The constable saw him heading for the steps, nudged the inspector.

'What the *hell* d'you think you're playing at, man?' Greenaway hissed.

Jack lifted a finger to his lips, pointed to the light, and the DI nodded, tapped Miller on the arm, gestured for him to go ahead down to the basement.

The younger man knocked on the basement door.

'For God's sake,' Jack said.

Miller knocked again, and Jack went down the steps, elbowed the constable out of the way and tried the doorknob.

'You can't do that, sir,' PC Miller said.

'A bloody murderer's hardly going to answer, is he?'

Jack took a couple of steps back, launched himself at the door, failed to budge it. The constable moved as if to grab him . . .

'Let him get on with it, Miller,' Greenaway said grimly.

Jack shouldered the door, felt it give a little.

'Better his bones than yours, constable,' Greenaway said.

Jack stepped back again, went for it one more time.

With a crack and groan, the door flew open.

Ashcroft and Harriet were approaching the Fellows Road bombsite. Several family houses within the devastated area, the whole now boarded up for safety.

Ashcroft knew what he was looking for, but darkness made

precision difficult. He took his masked torch from a pocket, searching for the gap between boards that he had made on his last visit.

He found it, put on the gloves he used in his ARP work, expanded the space with an effort and put away the torch.

'Right,' he said, forced the wheelchair through, then turned, did his best to bring the boards roughly together again.

'Not far now, dearie dear,' he said.

It was a phrase he always employed at some stage of his missions, and he recognized that he spoke it in a manner quite different from his usual way of speaking. And he didn't know exactly why he did it, except that he had thought, the first time, of one of the fairy tales his mother had read to him, of the wolf in the fairy tale disguising his voice to Little Red Riding Hood, and somehow it had stuck, had become part of it.

He had not always been mad, he thought, and found that he was close to weeping again.

'Oh dear God,' Jack said. 'I think that's Babs.'

He and Greenaway stared, with escalating horror, at the two boards of photographs on the walls, while Miller stood guard outside on the steps.

'Babs Woodruff, the dancer we told you about.' Jack's voice was choked with rage and fresh fear for Harriet. 'Christ almighty.'

'Yes.' Greenaway's anger was quiet but unmistakable. 'I'm very sorry.' Jack was still staring at the photographs and the detective gave him another moment. 'Would you recognize Miss Yorke's clothes, Mr Jerome?' He looked at the hanging rail. 'With that lot?'

Jack's dread intensified, but he stepped closer to the collection of women's clothes.

'No touching, sir,' Greenaway cautioned. 'Fingerprints.'

'It's hard, without moving them.' Jack scanned the garments, thought about Harriet's usual late-night dog-walking attire, always slacks and pullovers in winter, sometimes a blouse in summer. 'There's nothing I recognize,' he said, drank in that small relief.

And then the hair on the floor caught his eye and his throat constricted. A few cuttings, the kind one might see on a barber's floor that had escaped a broom.

Red. Auburn. Not unique, but distinctive – and Jack knew it well, had admired it from the first day he had met her.

He crouched down. 'That's Harriet's,' he said to Greenaway, feeling sick. 'I'm pretty sure.'

The policeman nodded, looked back at the clothes rail, saw there was a table behind it, a camera with flashgun, moved closer, then looked around and noticed the small heap of paper bags on the floor in a corner, squatted down, took a pencil from his inside pocket and pushed his way into several of the bags.

'Quite a collection.' He took a sharp intake of breath, tightened his lips, saw that Jack had seen it too. 'All red.' He raised a hand. 'Please, Mr Jerome, don't touch this either. This is important evidence.'

Jack's jaw was almost too tightly clenched to let him speak.

'If he's—'

Barking, sharp and fierce and familiar in the silence, stopped him.

Followed immediately by the air-raid warning.

'Fuck,' Jack said. 'Not now.'

Miller stuck his head around the door. 'Bit of a commotion out here, sir. Old couple saying they're Mr Jerome's friends.'

George, trailing his lead again, shot down the steps and into the basement before the PC could stop him, tail wagging furiously as he saw Jack – but an instant later, his hackles rose and he began to growl.

'Get shot of it, Miller,' Greenaway snapped.

'This is Harriet's dog.' Jack scooped George up, held him close, felt him trembling.

'I don't care whose dog he is,' Greenaway said. 'This is a crime scene.'

'But George was with Harriet when she first saw Ashcroft with the wheelchair. She said he growled like that then too. Something he never usually does.'

'A witness then,' Greenaway gave in, turned to Miller. 'Do not let anyone else in.'

'What about the warning, sir?' Miller enquired.

Greenaway looked at all the photographs and at the hair on the ground and the paper bags, then at Jack's desperate expression, and shook his head regretfully.

'We'll have to get you and your friends to shelter,' he said.

'I'm not going to a shelter while Harriet's missing,' Jack said.

'You'll do as you're damn well told, Mr Jerome,' Greenaway said.

The siren's wail was loud and clear over Fellows Road too, as Ashcroft, panting and sweating profusely, accepted that, strong as he thought he had become, he could propel the cumbersome old wheelchair no further. He pushed away the blanket covering Harriet and, swearing violently under his breath, began untying the nylon knots still securing her to the chair.

Jack brought George up the steps from the chemist's basement, closely followed by Greenaway.

'Is Harriet here?' Louisa hurried over.

'I want everyone in shelters right now,' Greenaway ordered.

'Jack, what's happening?' Felix, arthritis-hampered, his voice strained, called from the darkness.

'You'll have to go home,' Jack said.

'But what about Harriet?' Louisa protested.

Felix came into view. 'Is she down there?'

'No, Felix,' Jack said. 'But she was here.'

'So close to us,' Louisa said. '*Lieber Gott!*'

'That goes for you too, Mr Jerome.' Greenaway turned to Felix. 'You have a shelter, sir?'

'We have a basement,' Felix said. 'Across the road, in Miss Yorke's house.'

'Good,' Greenaway said. 'Get down there now, quick as you can.'

'You could join us, sir,' Louisa said.

'Thank you, madam,' Greenaway said, 'but we'll get ourselves back to the station.'

Jack glared at him. 'But Harriet—'

'Will have to wait till this lot's finished.' Greenaway looked back down at the basement. 'Get that door secured, PC Miller.'

'But you are with me now on this?' Jack said to Greenaway. 'You know this is life or death?'

'No doubt about that,' the inspector said.

'Come along, Jack,' Felix called.

Jack gripped the policeman's arm. 'Remember what Harriet told your colleagues about the Fellows Road bombsite.' He spoke rapidly.

'If that's where Ashcroft buried Babs, it might be where he's taken Harriet too.'

Greenaway nodded. 'I'll be speaking to the rescue people before first light.' He glanced upwards. 'Though I daresay they'll have plenty more on their hands by morning.'

'They'll need to search the whole site,' Jack said.

'It will be done,' Greenaway said. 'With or without Heavy Rescue.' He looked down at Jack's hand still clamped on his arm. 'The instant this lot's over. You have my word. All right?'

Jack removed his hand.

The sirens had just ceased, the sound still ringing in Ashcroft's ears as, gripping Harriet under her arms, he dragged her across the rubble towards one of the bombed houses. The chemist groaning now with every step.

He hadn't had quite this much trouble moving the others, but he seemed to have wrenched his back.

His victim a dead weight now.

Still silent, which was something.

In Calla House, Felix and Louisa went to their flat to fill the thermos flask with hot tea and to collect Louisa's violin while Jack stayed in the entrance hall holding George, waiting for the other two to go down ahead of him.

'I'm going up to fetch a book,' he told them. 'Be with you in two shakes.'

'Shall I take George?' Louisa asked.

'It's all right, I've got him,' Jack said. 'Poor chap's still calming down.'

Louisa started down, then stopped. 'Will you tell us what you know?'

'Everything,' Jack said. 'When we're all down there.'

He watched the old couple descend, then shut the door behind them.

It was the small things that were often the heartbreakers. The collapsed walls, roofs and ceilings, smashed tiles and crushed concrete were more than dreadful enough. Yet – the dead and terribly injured and the blood and burned flesh aside – it was their broken possessions strewn randomly around, the charred, soot-coated remnants of families' histories that also distressed those who searched the sites, scouring for signs of life.

Much of that gone from here by now, though Ashcroft would probably not have noticed or cared if he'd passed a baby's cradle as he heaved the unconscious woman over the wreckage, his target a house not far from the row of demolished properties, a structure still recognizable under stars that were suddenly emerging from the clouds along with a partial moon. Some walls still standing, signs of abandoned lives grotesquely visible: an unmade bed on an upper floor, a crooked painting on an inside wall, a toilet almost indecently exposed . . .

His hat had gone, fallen off somewhere along the trek, his hair sticky, his face wet with perspiration, pain-racked shoulders and throbbing back exacerbating his inner bitterness as he dragged his victim into the remains of what had days ago been someone's kitchen.

He let Harriet fall on to the broken stone-tiled floor, gave another groan of pain and relief, permitted himself a moment's respite, then took out his torch again, tore off the masking tissue and peered around.

His gaze fell, almost instantly, on a pantry, askew but bizarrely unscathed, tins and jars and packets still on sloping shelves. Only its door missing, and that just a few feet away.

'You'll do,' Ashcroft said.

Jack had swiftly changed into dark clothes, jammed a torch in one pocket, a folded cut-throat razor in another, and now, picking up the dog again, he made his way as soundlessly as possible down the staircase, passed the door that led to the basement, and let himself out through the front door.

The bicycle leaned against the side wall of the house.

'There you go, boy.' Gently he deposited George in the wicker basket Harriet had attached months ago, tucked the small blanket at the base over the dog, and mounted unsteadily.

It was a long time since he'd ridden the blasted thing, disliking the sense of imbalance his ruined eye and bad leg combined to create, giving it up as a dead loss, his excuse the potential danger to others on the road. If they'd only let him, he'd told himself as a salve, he'd have jumped at the chance of flying again, but the bike was such a pitiful conveyance beside a Hurricane it was hardly worth the bother.

The situation tonight vastly different because Harriet was in the gravest danger, and anyway, the blackout made him scarcely blinder than most.

Besides, anyone fool enough to be getting in his way in the middle of a raid deserved to be run over.

TWENTY

Harriet came round again to the sounds of ack-ack and distant bombing.

Not in the wheelchair anymore, which had to be a good thing, but she was sitting on cold ground, her hands still tied behind her with nylons, ankles bound too, and she seemed to be propped up against something hard and unyielding. Not a solid wall, she thought as it shifted a little; wood perhaps, but it was impossible to be sure. Of that, or of anything.

Except that she was still a prisoner. A murderer's captive.

It was still dark too, though she couldn't see much sky from where she sat, couldn't see much of anything, but the smell in the air, almost as much as the creak of shifting debris, told her where she was. At least, what kind of place Ashcroft had brought her to.

A bombsite.

It had taken hours after each post-raid WVS shift for her to get this horrid stench, a distinctive mix of smoke, blood, sewage and death, out of her nose and throat and, thereafter, out of her mind.

This was a bombsite, little doubt of that, and she wondered if it was the one in Fellows Road that had become poor Babs's grave or an older or even more recent one, and if it was the first, she could not now remember if she had told Jack where it was, or if she had not . . . and her brain was too foggy to think properly – and suddenly she recalled the awful pad of chloroform that Ashcroft had clamped over her face . . .

And where in God's name was *he*? Had he just left her here and vanished? Because if that was the case it meant she might stand a chance.

She tried to move and only just managed to suppress a cry. Every part of her, her head, her neck, her shoulders, her armpits, her legs, even her *bottom*, hurt so much that it was almost impossible to distinguish one pain from another, though nothing, she thought with some gratitude, seemed to be broken; and while a chilly breeze on the skin of her legs informed her that her slacks were torn, at least

Ashcroft had not, thank the Lord, taken them for burning, and wasn't that something else to be thankful for?

She heard him before she saw him.

The chemist – the killer – was heaving, straining, trying to move something – a table, no, a door, she decided, narrowing her stinging eyes and peering through the murk.

She had been aware of feeling sick again from the first moments of waking, but now, finding that he was still with her after all, and as everything else came back to her with more clarity – the monstrous photographs of those poor dead women, the hair – oh, God, her *hair* was gone, she recalled, he'd practically *scalped* her – a new and terrible sense of panic made the sickness so bad she thought she might vomit.

'Not as comfy as that old wheelchair,' Ashcroft called from where he still laboured.

Harriet did not reply.

'And no fish paste sandwiches on offer,' Ashcroft said.

The raid was audible but mercifully still distant as Jack steered the bicycle left into Belsize Park Gardens, heading for Fellows Road, cursing his appalling lack of fitness, since apart from his half-lost vision and feeble leg – which was *nothing* at a time when real men were daily risking and losing their lives, when civilians were being horribly maimed or blown to smithereens – he was fit and healthy, and he ought to be running now, he should be bloody well *sprinting* this puny distance.

'Useless,' he condemned himself out loud.

In the basket, George's ears stood to attention.

Worse than useless, Jack flogged himself, if he couldn't find Harriet.

Save her.

All that mattered now.

Ashcroft had completed his task, had dismantled the pantry shelves and tossed aside their contents before dragging that infernally heavy door into position, where it was almost ready to serve as a kind of extempore cell for his prisoner.

The bombing had paused a few minutes ago, but with no All Clear, they both knew it was likely to be no more than a lull.

'What now?' Harriet asked.

'Now you wait,' Ashcroft told her.

'For what?'

The chemist tested an upright chair he had found, checking to ensure it was safe to sit on.

He sat, placed his hands on his grime-covered knees.

'What am I to wait for?' Harriet asked.

'Are you certain that you want to know?'

Harriet's lips were horribly dry, her throat sore. Her heart was beating very fast, maybe a side-effect of the chloroform but more likely, she thought, of extreme fear.

'You haven't . . .' She licked her lips. 'You haven't done to me what you did to Miss Woodruff.'

'Or the others,' Ashcroft said. 'I told you I wouldn't.'

'Why not?' she asked.

Because it made no real sense for him *not* to kill her, she realized, given that she would obviously identify him the instant she was free. Though since he appeared to have believed that she had told others and that the police, therefore, would probably know that she was missing, maybe he accepted that the game would soon enough be up, with or without her, so maybe he was going to let her live after all.

'Because there's no need,' Ashcroft said. 'For me to kill you myself, that is.' He paused. 'I told you, I really don't enjoy that part of it, not at all, if that's what you still think.' He looked around. 'This is down for demolition. It's a dangerous structure. They have to finish the job properly in case children get in.'

Harriet's chest hurt when she breathed too deeply, that pain joining forces with the rest, and she realized now that he must have dragged her every which way over the site.

'They'll check around for people before they begin,' she said. 'Children might already have got in.'

'They'll have a bit of a look round, Harriet,' Ashcroft said. 'Shout a few warnings, that kind of thing. But they won't find you, my dear. No, they won't, my dearie dear.'

His voice had changed when he'd said that last bit, Harriet noticed, had become quite different, cloyingly sweet.

New fear crawled up and down her spine.

She prayed for him to leave.

The bombers were still silent, but the stars and moon had vanished again and the wind had picked up, rain starting to fall as Jack pedalled laboriously, swearing periodically at his painful knee, then leaned forward to try and pull the little blanket over George's head.

'Sorry about this, old boy,' he told the dog. 'Not much further now.'

Louisa, playing Massenet's 'Méditation', broke off abruptly.

'Should we go up and telephone the police station?' she asked Felix in German. 'Tell the inspector that Jack has gone?'

'Better wait till the All Clear,' Felix said. 'They won't search till then anyway.'

'But we could prepare them.'

Felix's shrug was helpless, frustrated.

'*Also gut.*' She gave in. 'After the All Clear.'

Jack was in Fellows Road, narrowing his good eye, trying to find the site.

The bombing began again.

'Damn and blast and sodding hell,' he said, wind and rain lashing his face.

He wondered if Harriet was out in this.

Prayed that bad weather was the greatest of her troubles.

In the basket, George huddled and complained.

'I know,' Jack said.

Ashcroft had moved her, yanking hard at her arms, threatening that if she did not help shift herself into position, he *would* kill her outright, and there was no remorse in him now, no regret, and Harriet sat, dumped on the floor inside what had been some poor housewife's pantry, terrified but hell-bent on not bursting into tears.

Ashcroft straightened up, groaned and rubbed his back.

'Not as light as you look, are you?'

'They'll hang you,' Harriet said. 'You do know that, don't you?' She flinched inwardly, aware of the folly of touching on his childhood tragedy.

He didn't answer, pulled something from his pocket.

Another black stocking.

'No,' Harriet said, courage deserting her.

'It's all right,' Ashcroft said.

'*No!*' Harriet shrank back, felt the wood hard against her bruised spine.

'For the last time, I'm not going to strangle you – I'm not going to kill you, you silly woman,' the chemist said. 'We've already agreed there's no need for that, haven't we?'

She saw that he was going to use the stocking to gag her.

'No need for that either, surely?' Harriet said desperately.

'Can't have you screaming when the demolition chaps arrive.'

She clamped her mouth tight shut, turned her head from side to side, but he was too strong and there was no escaping the disgusting thing.

'Now,' he said, 'let's get this job finished.'

He stepped back carefully, over to where he'd leaned the pantry door. 'This really is doing my back no good at all.' He stood, legs apart, bent his knees, gripped both sides of the door. 'Ah well, needs must.'

Harriet watched her view of the dark world steadily shrink and – as the murderer gave a final heave – disappear altogether.

She heard him groan again with pain.

Wished him pure agony.

'Uncomfortable, dearie?' he called.

'Go to blazes,' Harriet said behind the gag.

The wind gusted, and something in the wreckage overhead flapped.

'Hear that?' Ashcroft asked.

Harriet did not try to answer.

'The way this wind's blowing,' he said, 'this lot might come down without the demo lads.'

Harriet heard the weather, and then other sounds too, of Ashcroft moving away, planting his feet cautiously, heard his tread over planks, over broken stone and crushed glass.

Those sounds grew less distinct, became swallowed up in the rest of the clamour of the night.

And then were gone.

TWENTY-ONE

J ack dismounted, leaned the bicycle against the boards, close to a gap he'd spied near a warning notice.

'Right, George,' he said. 'I think this is our best bet.'

He picked up the dog, held him close as he widened the opening and squeezed through, then set him down, keeping a tight hold on his lead, took the torch from his pocket, removed the tissue paper – and if a sharp-eyed Nazi bandit up there spotted the small beam, that was just too bloody bad.

He shone the torch slowly around in a semicircle, saw nothing but desolation.

A bomb, dropped somewhere to the north, he thought, closer than the others, made George whine.

'What do you think, boy?' he asked. 'Do I yell for her or keep quiet?'

George whimpered softly.

'Quiet it is,' Jack said.

Ashcroft had gone. Leaving Harriet more alone than she'd ever felt in her life. Alone, bound, gagged, enclosed and exposed at the same time, to wind and rain and, quite possibly, to a bomb or incendiary or the same kind of parachute mine that had created the tragic wasteland around her.

The cacophonous noises penetrating her small prison were alarming enough even without the addition of explosions; the gale and the ack-ack and the creaks and groans of loose timbers and drainpipes and banging gutters and Lord only knew what else, all threatening to collapse at any time.

She tried out her voice, practising for when the team arrived to turn this surviving structure into rubble to match the other destroyed houses, but the awful stocking in her mouth muffled it almost completely and she knew that no one would be able to hear her.

Tears came, were swiftly dammed up by common sense. Because

if she cried, her nose would block up and she might die of suffocation.

She'd be damned if she'd do Ashcroft's work for him.

Jack and George made their way across the bombsite, and Christ knew it would be difficult enough to negotiate in daylight, but this confounded darkness made it potentially lethal, especially as Jack was concentrating the torch's beam in zigzags across the rubble, turning his head from side to side, searching for Harriet rather than lighting their own path.

Every second that passed heightened his fears for her, her description of the buried hand haunting him. He tried to focus only on this quest, tried not to think about the photograph of Babs Woodruff in Ashcroft's basement.

Tried not to think too much at all.

It was impossible, he decided suddenly, to stay quiet any longer.

'Harriet?' Tentatively at first, then much louder. '*Harry!*'

There was no human response, only the wailing of wind, the shifting noises of wreckage and debris, the booming of the raid – and the gale was making it harder to identify distance, though bombs had ceased to matter to Jack for now.

'Harriet!'

Nothing.

He limped on.

In the basement at Calla House, the tension was getting to Felix.

'We should go to look for them, Louisa. The raid is far away.'

Louisa shook her head, her expression grim.

'Waiting,' Felix said. 'All the time, waiting.'

Not just talking about Harriet and Jack now, thinking of those they'd left behind in Germany.

'I know,' she said.

'It's killing me,' he said.

'Me too, *Liebling*,' she said, and stroked his hand.

'Perhaps it's better not to have people to care for.' Felix paused, shook away that thought. 'We should be looking for them.'

'And if we get our heads blown off, how will that help Harriet or Jack?'

'*Dann spiel etwas*,' Felix said. 'Play something – play the Bartok.'

Louisa lifted her violin and bow.
And played.

In the cramped cell fashioned by Ashcroft, Harriet had renewed her
battle with the nylon knots around her wrists, but the chemist had
tied them even more tightly than before, so now she abandoned that
fight and directed her efforts to trying to shift the horrible gag by
rubbing the side of her face on the splintered edge of the pantry
wall, hoping to tear or at least ladder the stocking, maybe weaken
its resistance.

The wind whipped up into a shriek, sent what sounded like an
iron sheet crashing down nearby, making her prison tremble, and
Harriet too shuddered, then redoubled her struggle.

The droning of a plane stopped her again.

Too close for comfort.

Dying in an air raid was a possibility they'd all grown almost
resigned to. Dying in a raid like *this*, with a nylon stocking stuffed
in her mouth, was too intolerable to contemplate.

She went back to work.

Jack heard the same plane, thought, automatically, it was probably
a Junker, remembered, staring up into the blackness, his own idiotic
prang in the Hurricane, thought, as he did almost every day, of his
RAF comrades, competent, heroic men, some already killed in . . .

George's plaintive whine brought him back and he shone the
torch around, turning his head again to compensate for the blind
eye, and over to his right, some distance away, near the remains of
a destroyed row of houses, the beam caught on something.

Jack fixed on it, picked his way carefully over the uneven ground.

Froze as he realized what it was.

A wheelchair, a blanket on the rubble beside it. The wheelchair
old, as described by Harriet what seemed an age ago.

George growled, then gave a single sharp bark.

It was *hopeless*.

Harriet had all but given up, was resting, eyes shut, drained.

The sound, amid all the rest, was different, impossible to identify,
yet still it was enough for her to open her eyes and listen. To bombing
and wind and rain and creaking and . . .

Nothing.

Get on with it, she ordered herself, tried yet again to shift the gag, winced as a splinter from the pantry wall dug into her cheek, but the pain was *nothing*, so she went on, struggling harder than ever.

Jack left the wheelchair where it was and, with George still on the lead and pulling hard now, they were heading not towards the flattened buildings but to another house, a little further away, ruined but still standing.

The terrier was panting, agitated.

'Is it Harriet, boy?' Jack asked him. 'Is it her?'

The dog whined, pulled harder and Jack went with him.

They reached the house and Jack lifted up the squirming animal as he climbed cautiously across the remains of a pulverized outer wall. He put George down, then shone the torch beam over a collapsed ceiling, a half-fallen inside wall, across the depressing detritus of someone's home, on into another space beyond. A living room, without doubt, a sofa grey with plaster, but still right side up.

George barked again.

It was. It *was*!

Harriet knew that she was probably clutching at straws, that it was just some stray with a bark like George's. Yet there was such a thing as instinct, and surely a person could know the sound of their own dog . . .

She tried to cry out through the gag, and it reverberated loudly in her own ears, but she knew that no one else, probably not even a dog, even with their ability to zone into higher pitched sounds, would hear her through the stifling nylon gag and the rest of the clamour of this wartime night.

She cried out again, tried lifting her voice an octave.

George went suddenly mad, his tail wagging crazily, yanking on the lead, and Jack's heart began racing like a Supermarine Spitfire.

'Harriet?' he called, kept his voice low, *too* low in all the racket, but any louder and Ashcroft might hear.

George yanked harder suddenly, ripped the lead out of Jack's hand and vanished into the dark.

'Bugger,' Jack said, then hissed, 'George!'

No choice but to go after him.

He climbed over a wrecked internal wall, shone the torch around again, and the beam reflected off a triangular chunk of broken mirror on the ground, dazzling his good eye, startling him.

'George?' he called, warily.

The dog, sure now of his mistress's scent just feet away, found a gap in the door of her cell, pushed and squeezed through it – *found* her, leapt on her, whimpering, trying to lick her face, pawing at her, whining, not comprehending why Harriet wasn't speaking to or stroking him.

'George,' she tried to cry out, still distraught, though tears of relief were spilling down her cheeks because if he was here, dirt-covered but with his lead trailing behind him, that had to mean he was not alone.

George barked again, shrilly now, joyously, tail wagging wildly.

'George, where are you?' A male voice – *Jack's* voice.

She cried out again.

In the remains of a kitchen, in the torch's beam, Jack saw a kind of crooked cupboard, a door propped against it.

George's barking was coming from behind it.

Hope surged wildly. '*Harriet*?' He clambered over more rubble to the lopsided door. 'Harry!'

George's frantic barking seemed suddenly, to Jack's ears, to be blotting out everything else, even the gale and far-off explosions, and he could see now that the door had been wedged tightly in position except for one gap, through which George had squeezed his small, stocky self.

Jack stuck the torch between his teeth, freed his hands, gave the edge of the door three mighty wrenches and it fell with a crash.

The terrier flew out from the dark space beyond, barking excitedly.

'Harriet?' Jack took the torch from between his teeth, dropped it, saw a shape – her shape – on the floor. 'Harry?'

'Jack!' The word was muffled but thrilled.

Another sound – of broken concrete shifting behind Jack – and George's bark changed, became shriller, fierce. Jack turned, but a shove from the side sent him headlong and his forehead struck jagged stone.

'I knew you'd join us eventually,' Ashcroft's voice said.

George growled, then snarled.

'Shut up,' Ashcroft said. 'Tell him to shut up.'

'Harriet.' Dazed, Jack put out a hand, feeling around for a rock, *something* to use as a weapon, but the other man stamped on his fingers, Jack yelped in pain and Harriet shouted hatred behind her gag.

The dog's barking became frenzied.

'I said shut *up*, you little rat.' Ashcroft bent, tried to catch him, but George darted away and the chemist went after him.

Jack pushed himself up with his uninjured hand, felt dizzy. 'Harriet,' he said. 'Are you all right?'

She said something unintelligible.

Jack twisted around, saw her more clearly for the first time.

'God, Harry—'

Even in the dimness he could see she was bound and gagged, could see too that the murderer had hacked off most of her hair, and rage filled him, and he tried to move towards her, but he was still dizzy.

'Gotcha.' Ashcroft's voice came from somewhere, and they both heard George's protesting squeal.

Harriet cried out in distress. Jack turned, saw the looming figure of Ashcroft on his way back, holding the dog by the scruff of his neck.

'Leave him alone, you scum!' Jack said.

George snarled, twisted and bit Ashcroft's arm and the chemist gave a howl of pain and threw him into the rubble.

George gave one shrill yelp, then lay still.

'You *bastard*!' Jack got to his feet and launched himself at Ashcroft, who punched him hard on his left temple.

Harriet knew before Jack hit the ground that he was out cold.

'That's your rescue party scuppered, dearie dear,' Ashcroft said.

TWENTY-TWO

Daylight was breaking as Jack came round just after Harriet had finally succeeded in dislodging the nylon gag.

She spat, breathed in the foul bombsite air, saw him start to stir.

'Jack.'

Ashcroft had bound and gagged him too, but he made no sound, and fresh fear seized her. 'Jack!'

He let out a groan.

'Jack, it's OK,' she said quickly. 'He's gone.'

He groaned again, tried to move, but it was impossible, his feet and hands tied, wrists strung to the knob of the door he'd yanked down earlier.

'Darling,' Harriet urged, 'just nod your head if you can.'

He nodded, grunting with pain as the site of Ashcroft's punch flared back to angry life inside his head.

'I think he's really gone this time.' Harriet peered at the desolation around them and listened hard, heard only the sounds of the raid, more distant again, and of the wind, still gusting. 'Jack, he said this house is down for demolition. Which may be true, so we really need to get out.' She looked down at George, who had, just minutes before, crawled closer to her, but had not moved since. 'He's completely mad, Jack.' She spoke quickly. 'He blames everything on some awful things that were done to him, but whether they're true or not, he's definitely a very twisted murderer now. And I'm so sorry to say that he did kill Babs – I saw photographs, of her and of some other poor women.'

Jack nodded again.

'You know?' Harriet said. 'Poor Babs.' She took a gulp of air, swallowed tears that were threatening. 'And I think George is in a bad way.'

Jack stared down at the dog, then back at her, seeing the bruising and scratches and dirt on her face, and the ragged remains of her lovely hair, and began, with a sudden surge of violent strength, to try to free himself.

'Go steady,' Harriet said. 'He's awfully good at knots. I only just got rid of my horrid gag.'

For an instant, Jack was still, and then his struggle began again, but the hand Ashcroft had stamped on hurt badly, and the door he was bound to – or the section of wall it was leaning against – groaned alarmingly.

'Careful,' Harriet warned.

He stopped.

'Bloody hell,' Harriet said. She had another go at her own bonds, then sagged, near to tears again. 'Bloody, *bloody* hell.'

As the All Clear sounded, Louisa, ahead of Felix, hurried up the steps and through the basement door, on her way to the telephone in their flat.

Moments later, in Hampstead Police Station, DI Greenaway, grim-faced, was yelling for Constable Miller, a car and one more body.

'And make sure he's good and strong,' he shouted.

He took his hat and coat from the stand, looked balefully at the phone.

'Bloody amateurs,' he growled.

The All Clear had blotted out the dawn chorus that had sweetly erupted a while before, yet the siren was a most welcome sound to Harriet and Jack, both still grappling to free themselves.

And then new sounds began. Engines, distant at first, coming closer.

They stopped to listen, knew, almost instantly, what they were.

'Oh, my God,' Harriet said.

The sounds grew louder.

With a violent renewal of effort, Jack yanked at the stocking tying his hands, and the door behind him rocked, the wall groaned again, alarming them both, but this time he did not stop fighting and at last, with one final wrench, he was free of the door and, hands and feet still tied, he hauled himself the short distance across to Harriet.

'Fantastic,' she urged. 'Now wriggle around and try to get your face close to my hands so I can pull out that awful gag.'

They managed it, and Jack took a huge gulp of air. 'Jesus,' he said. 'Filthy thing – and you must have been like that for hours.' He squirmed around to look more closely at her face.

'Don't,' she protested. 'I must look hideous.'

'You could never look hideous,' Jack said. 'But I'm afraid I guessed about your hair because there was some on the floor in Ashcroft's basement, and we saw the photos of the other women . . .'

'You must have thought I was dead.'

'No,' Jack said firmly. 'I just knew I had to find you.'

'You said "we".'

'A detective inspector named Greenaway – good man. I told him about this place, so I think he'll be bringing the cavalry.'

The sounds of engines and now voices, too, grew louder, crushing his burst of optimism.

'Let's get on,' he said. 'I'm going to try and untangle your hands first, and then . . .'

'I'm very worried about George,' Harriet said.

The dog's tail wagged, once, weakly.

'He'll be fine,' Jack said and made a start on her wrists, wincing with pain.

'Your poor hand! I'd forgotten he stamped on it. Bastard!'

'Just bruised,' he said, carrying on.

'But this is all my fault and I'm so, so sorry – if I'd listened to you all and not gone out alone with George, but it was the middle of the night and I wasn't going to wake you up, so—'

'*Blast* these knots,' Jack said, then paused. 'I've just remembered I stuck a razor in my pocket, so if you can manage to reach it . . .'

Just arrived in Fellows Road with his two men, Greenaway saw a man's bicycle propped against a section of loose boarding, glanced into the handlebar basket and picked a dog hair off a small blanket.

'Sir.'

Greenaway looked up to see PC Miller pointing at a big lorry loaded with heavy equipment and at a large demolition ball swinging towards a bombed house not yet flattened, but plainly at risk of collapse.

'Oh, bloody hell,' he said. 'If that's his game . . .'

'They might not be there, sir,' the constable said.

'Get that stopped, Miller,' Greenaway ordered.

Harriet had freed Jack's hands and was cutting the bonds around his ankles when a deafening crash much too close for comfort shook the debris around them and made their own bodies vibrate.

'You now.' Jack flexed his fingers painfully, took the razor from her.

'Don't cut yourself,' Harriet said.

A thundering noise from some large vehicle out of their line of vision rattled their nerves along with the remains of the house.

'Bit of blood's the least of our problems,' Jack said, 'if we don't get out of here.' He cut her hands free, lifted his head and yelled, '*Hey!*'

'Waste of breath,' Harriet shouted, and helped him release her ankles. 'They'll never hear you.' She winced. 'Ouch.'

'Christ, have I cut you?'

'No, it's just my blood starting to flow again.'

The policemen's shouts had not stopped the demolition, nor their waving of arms, so Greenaway, puffing hard, cursing his lack of fitness, had ordered Miller and the driver to run like hell to where the lorry was moving back and forth, altering position to improve aim, but then the PC tripped and fell, and Greenaway could hardly bear to look as the demolition ball swung back again, and there was no telling if Jerome and Miss Yorke were even *in* that house, but Christ help them if they were.

'Come on,' Jack told Harriet. 'Take my hand and let's get out of here.'

She started to stand, but the world spun around her and she sank down again. 'Sorry,' she said. 'Dizzy.'

Jack took her right arm, helped her back up.

The new sound – like a giant's growl – made them both look up in fresh alarm.

'That beam –' Jack pulled at her arm – 'it's not going to last.'

'I'm not going without George.' Harriet pulled out of his grip.

The growl ceased, there was a sharp whipcrack, and then a tearing noise, and the beam crashed down on to the wall beside them, delivering a final blow to the unstable brickwork, which now crumbled and collapsed.

Onto Jack.

Seeing the abandoned wheelchair confirmed things.

'Miller!' Greenaway bellowed.

The constable stopped, wheeled around. 'Sir!'

'I'd lay odds they're in there,' Greenaway yelled. 'Make them stop *now*!'

'Jack!' On her knees, half hysterical, Harriet scrabbled wildly at the rubble around his head, fought to clear dirt from his face. 'Jack, *spea*k to me!'

His nose was clear, then the eye patch, then his good eye, blinking furiously, streaming, then his mouth.

'Jack, please *breathe*!'

'I'm all right.' He coughed, spat. 'Sorry.'

'Don't be an idiot,' she told him. 'You spit away.'

'Harry,' he said, and spat again.

'Yes?' She began scooping handfuls of shattered brick off his upper body, freeing his arms. 'What is it, darling?'

'I want you to get out of here,' he said.

'We will,' she said. 'Just as soon as—'

'Now,' Jack said. 'Get out *now*, Harriet.'

'I'm not going anywhere without you.' She went on digging.

'You *have* to get out –' his voice was hoarse – 'to stop them.'

Greenaway saw Miller gesticulating with a workman, realized that no one else had understood, that the heavy equipment was on the move again, the giant wrecking ball being readied for another swing.

'There are people *trapped* in there!' Greenaway bawled.

Miller was yelling too, and finally the workman grasped the gravity of the situation, shouted an order for work to stop.

But the huge ball was already swinging.

Harriet was up on her feet, searching around, wild-eyed.

'Harry, for God's sake!' Jack's arms were clear, and he was lifting pieces of rubble off himself. 'You have to stop them *now*!'

'I can't find George!' She was frantic. '*George*!'

The remains of the house descended like an avalanche, the noise deafening as a small mountain of wall and roof beams and tiles and plaster slid rapidly towards them and landed.

Dust clouds rose silently into the air.

Beneath them a fresh double grave.

On the bombsite all work and noise had ceased.

Greenaway and the others stared.

'Oh, dear God,' the DI said softly.

A small scraping sound startled them all, followed by a whining, and then, emerging from the debris, limped the terrier, dust-covered, still trailing his lead.

'Good grief,' Greenaway said. 'George.'

The dog's bark was feeble, and Greenaway stooped to pick him up, but George had other ideas, evaded him, limping straight back to the great mound of wreckage, digging at it with his front paws and whining piercingly – and then, abruptly, he was on the move again, running dementedly back and forth until suddenly he turned, ran around the mound and disappeared behind it.

'After him, Miller,' Greenaway ordered. 'He may know a way in.'

The constable was already off and running, the driver following.

'We need Heavy Rescue,' Greenaway told the other two demolition workers, 'and Christ knows we're going to need an ambulance.'

PC Miller spotted George's tail just in time, squeezed himself through the gap that the dog had sniffed out, saw nothing but dust fog and destruction.

'Can't see them, sir!' Miller stuck his head back out and called back to the driver. 'We need shovels!'

Greenaway arrived, took in the scene, saw George scrabbling at the mess, his whining shrill and desperate. 'If they're under this lot, we can't wait for anyone else.'

'I've called for shovels, sir,' Miller said.

Greenaway turned around and bawled to anyone within earshot, 'Shovels, lifting gear, gloves, whatever you've got, at the *double*!'

'Sir!' Miller was on his knees, digging with his gloved hands. 'Over here!'

Greenaway joined him, dug with his bare fingers, and a second later they'd exposed a man's hand, and then the top of his head was visible, and their digging became frantic.

'Hold on, Jerome,' Greenaway shouted. 'We've almost got you.'

Miller dug away more carefully and first Jack's patch-covered eye, then his nose and good eye and finally his mouth were free of the worst of it.

'He's not breathing, sir,' Miller said desperately.

Jack coughed, gasped for air, choked on dust, coughed some more.

'Harriet!' he managed.

The driver returned. 'They're bringing shovels, sir.' He got down beside Jack's head, joined in the digging.

'Not me, for fuck's sake,' Jack told them. 'Find Harriet!'

They heard a bark, looked around, saw that George was digging a little way away. Miller got there first, Greenaway and the driver right behind him.

'Good boy,' Miller said.

The dog's barking grew more high-pitched.

'Have you got her?' Jack called frantically, using his free hand to try and push weighty rubble off himself, aware of pain in his good leg but not giving a damn. 'Have you *got* her?'

'Doing what we can, sir,' Miller gasped.

Greenaway looked around, saw a man running towards them waving three shovels. 'Over here!' he yelled.

Four of them after a moment, all silently, resolutely digging.

'I've got something,' the driver called.

An arm was exposed.

'Oh, Christ,' Jack said, still half jammed.

The men worked silently, cautiously, unearthed Harriet's head.

'Is she breathing?' Jack asked, began coughing again.

Greenaway worked rapidly, gently clearing dirt from Harriet's nose and mouth while the others paused, waiting in suspense.

'Is she *breathing*?' Jack was beside himself.

Greenaway felt for a pulse in her neck.

'Oh, God,' Jack said, close to tears. 'Oh please God.'

'The DI's a first-aider, sir,' Miller called to him. 'Knows what he's about.'

'Get the rest of this off her chest,' Greenaway ordered, checked Harriet's airway as the other men dug on, found her wrist, felt again for a pulse. 'Got it,' he said.

'Is she *breathing*?' Jack demanded again.

Harriet gave a choking gasp, began to cough.

'That's it,' Greenaway said, gently. 'That's the way.'

She coughed again, struggling for breath, opened her eyes and lashed out with both arms, striking the DI across the face.

'You're all right, Miss Yorke,' Greenaway told her, then looked across at Jack, smiling ruefully. 'At least we know her arms aren't broken.'

Jack collapsed back weakly.

'More than can be said for my bloody leg, I think,' he said.

They were, at last, being carefully carried by a Stretcher Party crew over the bombsite to their waiting ambulance, Greenaway walking alongside carrying George under one arm, when the terrier gave another low growl, and his hackles rose.

'Stop,' Harriet said urgently. 'Please. It's Ashcroft.'

The stretcher-bearers looked at the DI, saw his nod, stopped, lowered them to the ground.

'It has to be him,' she said.

'Unlikely,' Greenaway said. 'I'd say he's long gone.'

'I'm with Harriet.' Jack winced as he looked around. 'He hung around waiting for me to turn up after he'd abandoned her.'

'He's a watcher,' Harriet said. 'He told me he'd been watching us.'

'From right across our road,' Jack said.

'I'll bet he's been waiting to see the walls collapse,' Harriet said. 'Make sure we were goners.'

Greenaway looked down at the dog's alert eyes, felt its deep, continuous growling against his chest.

'Put George down,' Harriet said quietly. 'Hang on to his lead, see where he goes.'

'Miller, you go on with the stretchers,' Greenaway directed the constable, and the stretcher-bearers began to lift their burdens again.

'I want to stay,' Harriet said.

'Harry,' Jack said.

'You're both going to hospital,' Greenaway said.

'Not till I know you've got him, please.' Harriet reached over and grasped at the inspector's coat. 'Anyway, if we disappear now, George will get confused and Ashcroft will get away.'

'She's right there,' Jack said.

The dog was still growling.

Greenaway made a decision, beckoned Miller over, spoke quietly into his ear, and the constable moved off towards the demolition workers still standing around, waiting, aware now that they were dealing with some kind of murder case.

'Now then,' Greenaway said to Harriet and Jack, 'you have to play this my way, all right?'

'Absolutely,' Harriet said.

'Mr Jerome?' he checked.

'You have my complete confidence, sir,' Jack said.

Greenaway smiled. 'Wouldn't have said that a few hours ago, would you?'

It unfolded perfectly.

The two stretchers were carried sedately over the rubble to the ambulances waiting in Fellows Road, Greenaway, still holding George, following behind. Constable Miller, with the police driver, hanging back, chatting to the demolition workers.

All smooth and natural, looking like the end of an operation.

And then, one at a time, every single man bent and picked something up – one a shovel, one a pickaxe, another a chunk of broken stone and so on – and began to move quite casually, fanning out across the site until they were close to the perimeter.

Nearing the ambulance, Greenaway handed George, briefly, to Harriet.

'All right, my darling.' Harriet planted a kiss on his furry head. 'All up to you now, brave boy.'

She unclipped his lead and handed him back to Greenaway.

The inspector set the terrier down on the ground.

For a moment, George hesitated, looked up at Harriet.

'Go on,' she urged him. 'Go *on*, George.'

The dog went fast despite his bruised leg and the rubble, his target a low, still intact wall on the far side of the part-demolished house.

'Right, matey,' Greenaway said, and raised his right arm as a signal.

The men moved in as one, swiftly now, encircling the wall.

Closing in on their man, inexorable and determined.

Greenaway waited another moment.

And then he stepped forward to join them.

PART TWO

June 2019

'Safety and the assurance of safety are things of the past.'
Bram Stoker

TWENTY-THREE

'What's it like, Ms Jerome, living with ghosts?' the journalist asked Libby Jerome almost eighty years later.

'I don't live with ghosts,' she replied. 'Just family history.'

'Yet you surround yourself with it. Living with these paintings in your grandparents' house. Haven't you ever felt like moving on?'

'Never.' Libby smiled. 'I love the house. And it belonged to my great-grandparents originally.'

'Your mother lives in Hong Kong, doesn't she? Something in fashion?'

'Yes.'

'Leaving you with a house in Hampstead. Lucky you.'

'It's still her house,' Libby corrected. 'In Belsize Park.'

'*Idióta*,' Marika Szalet muttered – a Hungarian-born friend of Libby's and her longest tenant, an archaeologist by profession, in her mid-thirties, though presently stacking shelves at Waitrose in Finchley Road.

'Elizabeth's more than a match,' Beatrice Newby reassured. Another of Libby's tenant friends – Marika's neighbour on the first floor – eighty-five years old, silver-haired and fine-boned, a former magazine editor, still blessed with a keen mind and an eye for style.

'Libby can cope with most things, I'd say,' Reggie Brownlow said, passing.

'Like you, Reggie,' Beatrice said.

Reggie smiled, and went to refill her glass.

'She's very glamorous out of overalls,' Marika said admiringly. 'How old do you think she is?'

'No idea,' Beatrice said. 'That is a beautiful dress.'

'So slim, too.' Marika sighed. 'Maybe I should retrain to be a builder.' She sighed and patted her stomach. 'All my fitness gone. Too many pies and cakes.'

'Luckily for me I'm past caring about such things,' Beatrice said.

Marika smiled at her. 'You're not past anything, Beatrice.'

* * *

They had come this evening – journalists, local regulars, a few students and Libby's Calla House 'family' – to the Fine Gallery in Hampstead to celebrate the posthumous mounting of Harriet Yorke Jerome's 'Private War' collection; a black-and-white painted journal into which Harriet – Libby's grandmother – had poured her personal and intensely dramatic wartime experiences.

It was the gripping tale behind the paintings that had pumped the lifeblood of publicity into an exhibition over which Libby had procrastinated for years. Mostly because the works had been a part of her home for ever, an integral part of her life, making their removal, even temporary, a quite wrenching experience.

She hoped that Harriet would not have minded. She had painted and sold other works post-war, after she and Jack had married, but the 'Private War' series had never been for sale. Grandpa Jack, always proud of his wife, had urged her to show them, but Harriet had been reluctant, and while she was still alive he hadn't challenged that, and then, after her death, he'd lacked the emotional strength to go through with it; and Sylvie, their daughter, born seven years after the war, had never been all that interested in the paintings.

Sylvie had studied at the London College of Fashion, had wanted neither marriage nor children, had never much liked Calla House, had moved to Notting Hill and been irritated at being caught out by pregnancy aged thirty-eight, the father a one-night stand instantly forgotten: Elizabeth, known by most as Libby, the result.

'We just couldn't *be* more different, could we, Dad?' Sylvie had said to Jack one day when Libby was fifteen. 'I mean, yes, we both draw, but she doesn't give two hoots for fashion, she's tall like you, she has Mum's red hair and she's a complete homebody.'

Libby adored her grandparents' house and the war paintings. She had begun drawing cartoons when she was about nine, soon developing a real deftness and – when dumped for convenience at Calla House by Sylvie – she was often to be found standing absorbed before the monochrome works. When Jack had asked Sylvie if she'd mind if he bypassed her and left Harriet's works to Libby, Sylvie had been relieved. And then Jack had died, by which time Sylvie was thriving in Hong Kong and had entrusted the management of the property to Libby, who'd been overjoyed to move in to Calla House lock, stock and drawing board.

The journalist's question about ghosts had not been entirely invalid, Libby privately allowed, for she did sometimes fancy that she could feel Harriet's and Jack's essence seeping out of the old walls and – most definitely – from the paintings, especially those scenes recreated by her grandmother of that most terrifying wartime night; a short distance and two generations away from Calla House.

Now, with the works removed, albeit temporarily, Libby thought that the house felt quite different.

Naked. Almost – irrationally, she realized – *vulnerable*.

TWENTY-FOUR

The attack on Beatrice and Nelson, her ten-year-old West Highland Terrier, on Hampstead Heath a few mornings later was the first harbinger.

They had been walking on the East Heath and had just turned away from Pond No. 2, heading back towards the main path when a man in a dark hoodie darted out from the trees on their right and forced a thin chain over Nelson's head, tightening it around his neck. Beatrice cried out loudly and struck the man hard with her walking stick, and he shoved her down on to the stony ground. Stunned and winded, Beatrice lay still, steeling herself against worse to come, but a horrified middle-aged couple came running and the man bolted.

'I'm all right,' Beatrice argued tearfully – angry with herself for showing weakness – as the couple telephoned for an ambulance and police. 'It's Nelson who needs the vet.'

'You're bleeding,' the female Samaritan said.

'And you're in shock,' the man added.

Beatrice submitted, comforting the trembling dog, then asked if they might be kind enough to call her friend Elizabeth, who worked at home in nearby Belsize Avenue, and who would, she was certain, drive over and take care of Nelson.

According to the Hampstead Heath Constabulary, the Royal Free Hospital's A&E department, and a kind vet in Belsize Village, Beatrice and Nelson had both been very lucky, because she had suffered nothing worse than scratches and bruises, and Nelson's collar had possibly saved him from serious injury because the attacker's chain had caught on one of the gilt Westies decorating its blue leather, whereas two other dogs similarly attacked over the past several months had been less fortunate and one woman trying to rescue her dog had been badly battered.

'Now perhaps you'll get a mobile?' Libby asked hours later, because Beatrice loathed the devices she considered the death knell to civilized human interaction. 'You do know this really might have been far worse?'

Both victims safely home now in the living room of Flat C on the first floor of Calla House, the dog snoozing on Beatrice's lap as she sat, recovering, on her couch, a cup of strong tea in front of her.

'I hardly think that monster would have waited while I took out the phone to report him,' Beatrice said.

Libby sighed, and went back upstairs to her top-floor flat.

More than ready for a large glass of cold Chardonnay as she settled down on her small patio roof garden to start work on the next *Dr Ellie* cartoon in her weekly series for the *Hampstead Chronicle Online*.

More than a little shocked, too, when a chimney pot came crashing down from the roof above, missing her by inches.

The second harbinger.

'*Jézus Krisztus!*' Marika was horrified. 'It could have killed you.'

'Only a chimney pot,' Libby dismissed.

'More than enough,' Marika said, 'if it had hit you on the head.'

Calla House was one of the more modest villas in the avenue; a late nineteenth-century paired red brick and stucco structure, ten steps up from the small front garden, three main storeys plus a basement, first divided into flats before the war. As the first tenant after the completion of its second conversion, now hosting two flats per floor (Libby having kept the top floor for herself as Harriet had before her), Marika had originally intended her London flat to be her oasis of tranquillity during gaps between overseas archaeological digs; but two years ago while working in Peru, she had suffered a nervous breakdown, after which Libby had slashed her rent to enable her friend to remain in familiar surroundings until she was ready to return to her profession. Now, though vastly improved, Marika was still stacking supermarket shelves, still doubting her ability to cope in more challenging environments.

'You must get Reggie in,' she said now. 'The roof might be next.'

Libby picked up the phone.

Reggie Brownlow had a solid team of all-rounders and, since the day almost a decade ago when they had been working next door and a high wind had blown down an old satellite dish, smashing a fence, trellis and a cluster of white lilies in the garden, the firm had taken care of all Calla House's building, plumbing and electrical needs. Reggie, rake-thin, tough as tungsten, unsentimental and pragmatic, had inherited her skills along with her firm, Brownlow & Daughter, from her father; his best advice to her, she had told Libby years ago, to be sure always to employ experts in every field.

Libby was not anticipating any need for experts for this job.

Just a chimney pot, after all.

Live and learn.

TWENTY-FIVE

Asbestos.

Only a suspicion for now, but the word itself enough to keep Libby from peaceful sleep any time soon.

Asbestos.

Reggie hoped to be wrong, she said, but she had recommended testing, and Libby had never known her to exaggerate a risk. Reggie was no cowboy builder.

Not just herself to worry about, of course. Her tenants' well-being was Libby's priority, and she had been determined, when undertaking the house's conversion, that no corners be cut when it came to comfort, safety and taste, and everyone since then had been content with their homes.

Until now.

The residents' meeting held that evening, with Reggie and her foreman, Mal Evans, present, bearing leaflets and willingly answering questions, was showing no signs of doing anything to alleviate Libby's stress.

'Bottom line –' Mack Kennedy, tenant of Flat B, the garden flat, and Libby's least favourite resident, was first to speak – 'this stuff is lethal, right?'

'Not, in general, if it's left alone,' Reggie answered, 'but if asbestos-containing-material is handled or moved or damaged, it can become hazardous.'

'But it's moved itself already,' Kennedy said.

'Do you know if the chimney pot actually fell because of this asbestos, Reggie?' Beatrice asked.

'It's likely.' Mal Evans, a tall, broad man with a tough, slightly scarred face, answered for his boss. 'Nothing to do with the pot. Probably down to the cement used to fix it – though that kind of cement only contains ten to fifteen per cent of asbestos – a lot less than you'd find in insulation or lagging materials.'

'But if the same cement was used in other parts of the house . . .' Libby's stomach twisted with stress.

'Let's not get ahead of ourselves, Libby.' Reggie's smile was kind.

'So what do we do?' asked Lucas Hendriks, the quiet physiotherapist who lived in Flat A, the smaller front flat on the ground floor.

'First we take samples for analysis.' Evans answered again, his voice deep and resonant. 'If they're positive, decisions will have to be made whether to seal the asbestos in or remove it altogether.'

'And your firm would do all this?' Marika asked.

Reggie took over from the foreman. 'If Libby wants us to.'

'So what I want to know –' Kennedy turned to Libby – 'is how you could have had all the conversions done and not found out then about this asbestos.'

'Obviously I can't speak for anyone involved back then –' Reggie stepped in quickly – 'but Mal and I can give you umpteen examples of buildings worked on any number of times before the presence of asbestos was detected. If the chimney pot hadn't—'

'Are you even qualified to deal with this at all?' Kennedy interrupted.

'My firm's certificates are available for viewing,' Reggie said equably. 'Brownlow & Daughter is a member of the Asbestos Removal Contractors Association. You can all search for us online – any queries, you have my numbers.'

'Still, finding asbestos and having to deal with it wouldn't do your bank balance any harm, would it?'

'Oy,' Evans said.

'That's enough, Mack,' Libby agreed.

'Why so aggressive?' Marika asked.

'Because it's our health at stake. Not to mention the costs.'

'The cost's not your problem as tenants,' Libby said.

'Goodness, Elizabeth,' Beatrice said. 'What a worry for you.'

'Will you be covered by insurance?' Marika asked, concerned.

'I'm not sure,' Libby said.

'What if it isn't?' Kennedy said. 'Can you afford it?'

'I think that's Libby's business,' Lucas Hendriks said.

'Not if she goes bust,' the other man said. 'These are our homes. *Our* fucking health and safety. What if we have to move out?'

'I have a duty of care,' Libby said. 'If necessary—'

'Let's all stay calm.' Reggie stepped in again. 'Though depending on exactly what we do find, I will be suggesting Libby compares quotes from other firms.'

'I'd rather you do it,' Libby said, 'since we know your firm is qualified.'

'Jumping the gun again,' Reggie said. 'I still hope to be wrong.'

'But if it turns out to be bad news . . .' Libby looked around the room. 'I'll obviously do all I can to make life easier during any upheaval.'

'That's kind of you,' Hendriks said.

'Least she can do,' Kennedy said.

'Do you think Reggie has a thing for you?' Marika asked later over a glass of wine upstairs in Libby's flat.

Libby was startled. 'Why would you say that?'

'I think she has a soft spot for you.'

'We go back a long way,' Libby said. 'I don't think Reggie does "soft spots", at least not at work.'

'But you're a beautiful artist – who could blame her?'

Libby laughed. 'I'm just a passably gifted cartoonist and you're the beauty in this house.' She poured more wine. 'Along with Beatrice, of course.'

'What do you know about our dishy physiotherapist, Mr Hendriks?'

'Not much.' Libby smiled. 'He's Dutch, he pays his rent on time, doesn't complain, wraps his rubbish, makes no noise.'

'I thought it was charming the way he defended you.'

'He seems a nice guy,' Libby said.

'And single, handsome – very clean.'

Libby laughed, shook her head.

'And about thirty, your age,' Marika continued. 'Any girlfriend?'

'I wouldn't know.'

'He's straight, if I'm any judge.' She chuckled. 'Maybe you should ask him for a back rub to help with all this stress.'

'You're obsessed with sex, Marika,' Libby said.

Libby's worst fears were confirmed. Suspect cement had been used in various parts of the house at some time in the past. Safety being paramount, agreement was reached for Brownlow & Daughter to carry out the work of removing every trace of asbestos, preparations getting rapidly underway for the major operation that lay ahead.

Mack Kennedy, the belligerent tenant, had departed, Libby waiving his one month's notice, returning his rent deposit in full, agreeing to pay reasonable costs, frankly relieved to see him gone. Beatrice's niece, Alison Keyes, had invited her aunt to stay in her family's Maida Vale flat until Calla House was fully habitable again – though with a No Pets regulation in the niece's building, Beatrice had declined the offer till Libby had volunteered to look after Nelson.

Just Libby and Marika remaining now, and the Westie. And Lucas Hendriks, who said he saw no reason to leave until it became unavoidable. A nice man, Libby agreed with Marika, no doubt about that.

And attractive, she was right about that too.

TWENTY-SIX

Learning at the *Chronicle* that there had been another attack on a dog and female owner on Hampstead Heath, Libby phoned Beatrice at her niece's to reassure her that she and Nelson were safe and staying away from the Heath.

Lucas Hendriks, having heard the news too, knocked on her door soon after to offer his company on walks until the man was caught.

'You're very kind,' Libby said, 'but it's really unnecessary.'

'It would be a pleasure for me,' he said. 'I grew up always keeping dogs in Amsterdam. I miss having one, and Nelson's a lovely little guy.'

She saw no reason to argue.

Next afternoon, however, everything changed.

Harriet's 'Private War' paintings had arrived home that morning from the gallery, and Libby was downstairs in the entrance hall preparing to carry them up to the top floor, when she heard a crash from the basement.

She put down one of the paintings and went to open the door beneath the main staircase. 'OK down there?'

'Fine,' Reggie called. 'Just dropped something.'

'How's it going?' Libby asked.

'Come see for yourself – and d'you mind bringing down the tool bag I left in the hall?'

'No problem,' Libby said.

Except there was, because she'd never liked going down to that dark basement, despite it having provided safe shelter for her grandparents and their refugee lodgers during the Blitz.

Heaven knew Calla House had known far worse threats than asbestos.

Still, basements were, Libby felt, a little spooky.

She found the tool bag, started down the steps, but a jagged stair edge caught the sole of her right sneaker and – already off-balance because of the weight of the bag – Libby tried to grab the handrail . . .

Long way down when you're falling.

The ugly snapping sound as she collided with the concrete at the bottom told her, even before the pain, that her left leg was broken.

The hours that followed were traumatic, but blurred. Later, she remembered being given Entonox gas by the paramedics and appreciating its effect; remembered too that Mal Evans, Reggie's foreman, had come to help while she was still in the basement, and that Lucas had ridden with her in the ambulance, offering calm reassurance from his seat by the doors, and she vaguely remembered liking that. Before that, she thought she recalled Reggie – while they were both still below – being deeply upset and full of self-recrimination for having asked Libby to bring the tool bag and angry with herself, too, for failing to notice the faulty step.

'Not your fault,' Libby remembered telling her. 'My step.'

'My site,' Reggie had said.

'I didn't notice it either, Reg,' Evans said.

Mild concussion diagnosed as well as a fractured tib and fib, so they'd kept her in at the Royal Free, surgery scheduled for next morning.

'Shit,' Libby had said, close to tears. 'Oh shit, shit, *shit.*'

'Now, of all times,' she said to Marika when her friend visited late the following day. 'I'm such an idiot.'

'No good time to break your leg.'

'What am I going to do? I can't drive, can't bloody *walk*, can't keep an eye on the works.' She paused. 'And I'm not going to leave Calla House, so don't bother suggesting it.'

Marika smiled. 'Lucas said you'd say that.'

'Did he?'

'He also said that he's happy to take care of Nelson, and we both think you should move into Flat B.'

The abandoned garden flat.

'I'm not moving,' Libby protested. 'All that hassle.'

'Just till you're OK,' Marika said. 'You can't climb all those stairs and Reggie says that B is safe for now, and you'll tell us what you need and Mal and one of the men will bring it down for you.'

'It would be nice for Nelson,' Libby had to agree.

After the surgery, Libby settled into the garden flat, relieved of stairs and glad to still have the dog's company, somewhat consoled too, after a time, by feeling just about fit enough to return to work on *Dr Ellie*, surrounded in the living room and bedroom by her grand-mother's paintings, propped for the time being against a different set of walls and another blessing in the circumstances, and by some of her favourite family photographs – all but one that was missing: of Harriet and Grandpa Jack posing with a very old George and a very young Sylvie, squeezed into the handlebar basket of her parents' bicycle.

'I can't understand where it's gone,' she said to Marika, feeling upset.

'It'll turn up. These things always do.'

'I hope so. I'm especially fond of it.'

'When you find it, you should photograph it and keep it on your phone,' Marika said.

Libby didn't know what she would have done without her Calla House friends, and Sylvie had been wonderfully pragmatic, albeit all the way from Hong Kong, transferring emergency funds and helping to sort a bank loan while Libby waited to learn if her land-lord insurance would cover her. Libby was very lucky, she told herself regularly when worries and her leg brought her close to tears; she was *bloody* lucky.

'I don't understand why you won't claim against the builder's insurance for your injury,' Sylvie had said during a phone call. 'I mean, you said she suggested it herself.'

Reggie had, but Libby had refused.

'My house – well, your house – but my step, absolutely *my* clumsiness, and I'd feel horrible for sending her premiums rocket-ing.'

'Very generous of you,' Sylvie had said dryly.

'At least I can still work,' Libby had said.

Reggie was passing the open door to Flat B a few days later as Libby was ending another conversation with her mother.

'Sorry,' she said. 'Didn't mean to eavesdrop.'

'It's all right,' Libby said. 'Nothing secret.'

'Your mum staying put in Hong Kong?'

Libby nodded.

'Long way to come, I suppose.' Reggie shook her head. 'My father could never stand being separated from me.'

'That's nice.' Libby smiled. 'I've always thought the name of your firm is lovely. Brownlow & Daughter. Still unusual, even these days.'

'We were together every minute we could be.' Reggie paused. 'And then he died.'

'You must miss him very much,' Libby said.

'He was the best,' Reggie said.

Marika was being amazing between her Waitrose shifts, shopping, cleaning, running errands and cooking for Libby. Reggie was being both efficient and considerate, doing her best to ensure that she and her team maintained a safe core within the house, though Libby couldn't help wishing that Mal Evans – strong and experienced and clearly of great importance to his boss – was not quite as omnipresent as he seemed to be. Whereas Reggie tried to bother Libby as seldom as possible, purchasing materials upfront and waiting, wherever she could reasonably do so, to bill her, Evans was noisy about it, seeming to want Libby to be aware of the special treatment their firm was affording her.

'I don't like the man,' Marika said to her one evening. 'I've never liked him.'

'He's not my favourite,' Libby agreed, 'but I can see how vital a tough foreman must be to Reggie.'

'He looks at you too much,' Marika said.

'Can't imagine why.' Libby grinned ruefully.

Lucas had been the most surprising gift since her accident, his help unexpectedly, quietly, lightly offered. Everything from appearing as if by magic to pick up her crutches a moment after she'd dropped one or both, to cleaning up after Nelson in the garden, to starting her car now and again, to driving Libby to and from hospital visits in his old Hyundai Jazz, collecting her art supplies and, frequently, cooking dinners for her. And enjoyable, delicious dinners they were, sometimes in her temporary home, sometimes in his own snug flat next door, Balinese incense sticks burning, relaxing music playing because Lucas felt it was healing.

'*Not* romance,' Libby repeatedly insisted to Marika.

Not yet, anyway, she thought, but failed to add.

'I'm just his landlady-cum-patient,' she said. 'And friend, now.'

'You're not his patient,' Marika pointed out.

'He's offered to give me some physio,' Libby said, 'after the plaster comes off.'

'I hope you'll accept,' Marika said, smiling broadly.

Time passed. Libby's heavy first cast was changed to a lighter one. Under more normal circumstances, she might have become more independent at that stage, but the combination of her still weighty, still painful leg, and the house gradually mutating into a foreign landscape, familiar lines cloaked in heavy plastic, workers in protective clothing moving back and forth – her own *real* home still unreachable – meant that she remained heavily reliant on others.

She lay awake some nights in the dark, trying to push away anxiety, hearing unfamiliar sounds from below, and maybe the noises had always been audible in this part of the house, hidden from her on the top floor. Though Mack Kennedy would surely have complained, unless he just slept more soundly than she did.

Faint bumping and scrabbling, nothing worse than that, but still, Libby didn't like the sounds, and the thought of rats scurrying deep inside Calla House upset her, and maybe the building works had disturbed a nest in a wall cavity . . .

'It's mice, not rats,' Reggie said after Libby had nabbed her one morning as she was heading down to the basement where, apparently, a structure had been built as a temporary storeroom. 'Mal's set traps.'

Libby winced. 'Can't we find some kinder way?'

'They're vermin, Libby. Last thing you need is sharp little teeth gnawing through our materials.' Reggie paused. 'And please don't get any ideas about going down to the basement yourself.'

'Hardly,' Libby said wryly, leaning on her crutches.

Mal Evans came to the garden flat soon after, his expression grim.

'Reggie meant what she told you about the basement, and you need to pass that on to Miss Szalet.' His pronunciation of the name was excellent to Libby's ears, and she felt surprised, then annoyed with herself for being quite offensively judgemental. 'She's agreed to carry on as long as possible with you and your tenants on site, but everyone really needs to stick to the rules for safety's sake.'

'Of course,' Libby agreed. 'We all understand that.'

'Last thing she needs is another accident.'

'She's not the only one,' Libby said, sharply.

TWENTY-SEVEN

August arrived. Libby rejoiced to be plaster-free, with permission granted by the hospital for Lucas to help with her physio at home. Not yet able to drive, but expert by now on her crutches, she looked forward to being allowed short walks with Lucas and Nelson. No more attacks on dogs or owners had been reported locally, though Beatrice had phoned from her niece's to let Libby know that she'd heard of a similar spate of crimes in South London. No comfort to dog walkers there, but it felt good to know that the Heath was probably safe again.

The friendship between Libby and Lucas had been gently building. Something more, she felt, in the air, something deliciously promising, but on a slow and careful simmer.

They were still learning about each other, neither rushing, spending more and more time together, talking occasionally about their pasts, about their history, though it was, perhaps, Libby was aware, a rather one-sided disclosure. She had no issues with being open with him about her family, about her lack of a father – and, to an extent, of a mother too – but she felt that Lucas never really wholly reciprocated. He was a fine listener and sensitive to her needs without ever overly encroaching on her privacy, but there were some things, she supposed, that he did not feel ready to share.

He had told her about Anouk, his late wife, who had died five years ago riding her bicycle to the school where she had taught art and design, when a van had swerved into the cycle lane and killed her outright. His grief in the retelling had been palpable, but he had said little more, and Libby had respected his silence until one warm summer's evening, sitting outside on the garden bench, enjoying the remnants of a bottle of wine.

'Do you mind if I ask you about Anouk?' she asked, gently.

'What do you want to know?' Lucas asked.

'Anything.' She paused. 'If you don't mind, that is.'

He picked up his glass, gave a small sigh, set it down again. 'She was lovely.' He smiled. 'What can I tell you? She was born in Nederland, grew up in Rotterdam, but moved to the UK when she was eighteen after her parents and sister were killed in a train crash.'

'How terrible,' Libby said.

Lucas nodded, took a drink. 'She couldn't bear to stay there after that, decided to finish her studies here.' He gave a little shrug. 'We met at a Dutch expats event in the City, fell in love very quickly, got married six months later.' He put down his glass. 'We didn't have very long.'

'I'm so sorry,' she said.

'Long time ago,' he said.

'Not so very long,' Libby said softly.

Lucas started to say something more, but hesitated and stood up. 'Feel like a little stroll around the garden? I need to stretch my legs.'

'I'm fine here,' she said. 'Take your time.' She picked up her own wine glass. 'If you want to go out for a proper walk, don't worry about me.'

'This is fine.' He smiled down at her, crinkles forming at the corners of his eyes, then turned away and proceeded slowly along the left side of the small square garden, stopping to look at the calla lilies, now in full bloom, then moving on.

Libby sipped her wine, wondered how much pain she might have caused with her probing, knew she couldn't possibly fully imagine that kind of grief, knew that the loss of her grandparents – however deeply she'd loved them – was not the same thing at all.

She watched him gaze up at the sky for a few moments, then turn and start back towards her.

'Legs stretched enough?' she said as he sat back down on the bench.

Lucas nodded. 'I was going to say that I thought that Anouk would have liked you. Things in common: art, though of a different kind. And me, I guess.'

Libby stayed silent.

'But the truth is that if she were still here,' Lucas went on, 'I'm not at all sure she'd like you one bit.'

He looked at her, looked more deeply into her eyes, she felt, than ever before. And then he kissed her.

She kissed him back.

He drew away first. 'Should we? I'm your physiotherapist.'

'Only part-time,' Libby said. 'Not sure that counts as misconduct.'

'Except you only just asked if I could take over.'

Libby saw that his concern was real. 'I could ask to be referred back to the hospital.'

'It might take too long,' he said. 'I don't want to screw up your rehab.'

'Would you rather I didn't ask then?' Libby said.

'I'd much rather you did,' he said.

There was less than an inch of space between them now.

'I'll do it tomorrow,' Libby said.

'Do you think we have to wait till then?' Lucas asked.

'I won't tell if you won't,' she said.

At *last*. Simmer into burn.

They lay awake later, skin against skin, the duvet pushed away, both intensely glad of each other, Libby registering that she hadn't been even remotely aware of her bad leg since that first kiss.

They were in the garden flat's main bedroom. Still Libby's flat for the time being, though despite the presence of her grandmother's paintings and family photographs, it didn't feel at all like home to her.

Outside, a thunderstorm was brewing.

'On nights like this,' she said, 'I sometimes think about Harriet and Grandpa Jack here in the Blitz, in this very house, try to imagine how that must have felt.'

'Scary.' He held her a little tighter.

They fell silent again.

'I think I just heard your mice,' he said after a few minutes.

Libby didn't answer, had fallen asleep.

He lay very still, careful not to disturb her.

Lightning flashes illuminated the three paintings to his right, and Lucas tilted his face towards them, stared into that long-ago black-and-white world.

The 'Private War' paintings that Libby had said were so intensely important and personal to her grandmother that she had never wanted them to be sold.

Lightning flashed again, and Lucas felt he could see why Libby's grandfather had so admired them. Multi-layered fears, of bombing and madness and imminent death emanated from them.

A true-life story of horror and love and courage.

And sorrow, too, for so many.

Lucas closed his eyes, felt Libby's warm body curled beside him.

Thought for a few moments about that night in the Blitz, then turned his thoughts to Anouk.

And drifted off to sleep.

TWENTY-EIGHT

Five days later, while Libby was drafting out future ideas for *Dr Ellie*, hoping to get a little ahead of the game, her work having been rather 'eleventh hour' since she'd started back after the accident, she heard the front door of the house open and close, followed by a double knock and the sound of Flat B's door opening.

'Only me!' Lucas called. 'Mind if I come in?'

For obvious reasons, she'd given him and Marika keys not long after she'd come home from hospital and moved in downstairs, but she appreciated the fact that Lucas was continuing to call to her first, rather than just marching in, even though they had spent three out of the last five nights together. Not that she would dream of just walking in to his flat, even though, as his landlady, she did have a key.

'Not one bit,' she called back now.

He opened the living room door, waved a bouquet through the opening ahead of himself, and Nelson barked.

'Shush, you silly boy,' Libby said. 'Dahlias!' she exclaimed with delight. 'How gorgeous.'

Lucas came through, plainly pleased. 'Couldn't resist – I thought you'd like them.' He bent to kiss her, then stroked Nelson's ears. 'Just got time to put them in a vase and then I have another patient to get to.'

'I can do the flowers,' Libby said.

'Not easily,' Lucas told her. 'Too much balancing for you.' He went into the kitchen, found a vase, did the necessary. 'Not as artistic as you.' He ran water and brought them in. 'Where would you like them?'

'On the table, please.'

He set down the vase, fiddled with the blooms, then turned to look at her. 'You need a break and some fresh air.'

'I have work to do.'

'You look tired,' Lucas said. 'Why don't I help you into the garden? You could sketch out there for a while.'

'I need coffee,' she said.

He looked at his watch. 'Just enough time. Let's get you settled out there first and I'll bring you a cup.'

'You're not my carer,' Libby said.

Lucas frowned. 'Why say that?'

She watched him go back into the kitchen. 'Because you're spoiling me, and I really can make my own coffee.'

'Not as quickly as I can do it.'

Libby sighed and picked up her sketchpad and two graphite pencils, dropped them into the canvas bag beside her. 'I'm ready when you are,' she called.

He came back with a mug, set it down. 'OK, you take the bag, and lean on me. I'll come back for the coffee and crutches.'

She waited while he opened the glass doors, then let him help her outside to the bench. She leaned back, enjoying the afternoon sun. 'You were right about this. It's wonderful.'

'Do you need sunglasses?'

Libby held up the canvas bag. 'In here – plus a hat.'

Lucas stooped and kissed her mouth.

'Definitely not a carer,' she said. 'Sorry I said that.'

'It's fine. I get it.'

He went inside, returned swiftly, put the coffee on the small table in front of her, then produced her mobile from his pocket. 'You forgot this.' He dropped another kiss on her hair. 'I'm putting the crutches here, right behind you where you can reach them, OK? But I'll be back in just over an hour, so try not to go back inside by yourself, especially not with this boy to trip you up.'

'Thank you,' she said. 'For this and the flowers.'

He went back into the living room, Nelson wagging his tail at his heels, hoping for a walk. 'Phone me if you have a problem.'

'I wouldn't,' she said, 'not when you're with a patient.'

'You can,' he called, 'any time.'

She heard the flat door close, then, almost immediately, the front door.

Leaned back, raised her face to the sun again.

'You're getting spoiled, Libby Jerome,' she said.

Nelson returned, lay down beside her, gave a doggy sigh of satisfaction, and dozed off.

The loud clap of thunder jolted them both from sleep, Libby's right arm jerking in reflex, hitting the mug on the table – she tried to catch it, managed only to propel it further away, stretched towards it, overbalanced and only just stopped herself from falling.

'Shit,' she said as her leg twinged a warning, and manoeuvred herself back into a safer position.

Nelson stood up, went to sniff at the smashed pieces, licked at the coffee puddle.

'No,' Libby told him. 'Nelson, leave it.'

The terrier stopped, looked at her.

'Good boy. Come here.'

Nelson went back to the puddle.

'Nelson, don't – you'll cut yourself.'

The dog took no notice, and Libby remembered Beatrice saying that he excelled in selective deafness.

There was another bang of thunder, then a lightning flash, and the heavens opened. Libby swore again, then grabbed at her sketchbook and pencils, neither touched, and put them back in the canvas bag.

'Phone,' she said, and dumped that in the bag too, then twisted around and reached for the crutches.

They weren't there.

'For heaven's sake.' She twisted around again, holding on to the edge of the bench with her left hand and feeling for the damned things, which were far too big to be easily missed.

She was *sure* that was where Lucas had left them. Where she could reach them, he'd said.

The rain turned to hail, and Nelson stopped licking at coffee and came to hide under the bench. Libby put the bag over her left shoulder and struggled to her feet, but without the crutches or another body to hold on to, she lost her balance again, grabbed at the bench, hit her good knee hard but managed to land back on the seat.

'Shit,' she said again, took out her phone to see how long Lucas had been gone, but she had no idea of when he'd left.

He'd said she could call any time.

No signal.

'Great,' she said. Then, to Nelson, huddling beneath the bench: 'Sorry.'

For a moment, she felt like crying, and if she'd done any work and that was being melted away, she probably would have wept, but unless she – or worse, the dog – was struck by lightning, she could almost see the funny side of this, could only imagine what she looked like, and the hailstones had piled up around the lilies quite prettily, and anyway, it was already back to ordinary raindrops, and Lucas was bound to be back any time now . . .

'Libby!'

She heard his voice, raised with anxiety.

'Still out here,' she shouted.

And settled back to wait for rescue.

'Oh my God,' Lucas said as he reached her, Nelson emerging, wagging his tail and whining. 'You look half drowned.'

He bent, picked up the crutches, came round to help her up.

'Where were they?' Libby said.

'Just lean on me,' he told her.

'Where were the *crutches*?' she demanded.

'Where I left them,' Lucas said. 'Come on, let's get you inside.'

'But they weren't there,' Libby said. 'I looked.'

Inside, Nelson jumped on to the couch and rolled around, trying to dry his small wet ears, and Libby explained to Lucas what had happened.

'You must have got disorientated,' he said. 'Is he supposed to be doing that – he's soaking the cushions.'

'Nelson, stop that!' she told the dog. 'He needs a towel.'

But after that, as Lucas began to remove her waterlogged clothes, kissing her bare, damp skin as he went, then fetching a towel from the bathroom and slowly drying her, a little at a time, she forgot about the dog and the sofa and the mystery of the crutches, and decided that it was the best thunderstorm-soaking she'd ever experienced.

Lucas said, much later, that perhaps she'd accidentally kicked the crutches and moved them out of her reach without realizing, and Libby thought back to the moments of small chaos, and agreed that it was what must have happened.

But still, she couldn't quite picture how.

TWENTY-NINE

'Do you ever wonder,' Marika asked Libby, 'about the murdering chemist's wife and children?'

It was the last Sunday afternoon of August – it was sunny, with no rain forecast – and they were in the garden. Lucas was out walking Nelson, and Marika, in a restless mood – it seemed to be a residue of her depression that she often suffered from an edginess that made her pace around – was wandering about while Libby sat on the bench with her leg – more uncomfortable today than usual – up on a chair, her sketchpad resting on her knees, a small glass of white wine in one hand.

'Ashcroft.' Libby shrugged. 'Now and then. More often when I was younger.'

'I've sometimes thought,' Marika said, 'since you first told me the story, how hard it must have been for them.' She shuddered. 'What he did to those poor women – and then for him to drink *bleach*, of all things. I can't imagine a more agonizing death.'

'Grandpa Jack thought he was escaping the hangman and wanting to torment his wife into the bargain, which perhaps made some kind of sense, considering how much he hated her,' Libby said. 'But my grandmother believed he was looking for the most self-destructive kind of punishment.'

'His family better off without him, that's for sure,' Marika said.

'I suppose so,' Libby agreed. 'Though, who knows, if they loved him . . .'

'Could anyone,' Marika asked, 'love that?'

Libby shrugged again. 'That old cliché. Love being blind.'

'And dumb, maybe.'

'Sorry to disturb.' Mal Evans stood in the doorway in full coveralls with shoe covers. 'I did knock. Doors all open.'

'I didn't think you were working today,' Libby said. 'Come out and have a drink.'

'No thanks,' Evans said. 'Just came in to tell Miss Szalet we'll be ready to start your floor next Monday.'

Marika pulled a face. 'That's me out then.'

'You've got a week,' Evans said.

'I thought we'd agreed you'd camp in here with me,' Libby said. 'In the second bedroom.'

'I don't know.' Marika was dubious. 'What about Lucas?'

'What about him?' Libby said.

'Miss Szalet might not want to play gooseberry,' Evans said.

'Is there anyone who doesn't know about us?' Libby said, suddenly irritated.

'Sorry,' Evans said.

'It's fine,' Libby said.

'It won't be too long till we have to boot you all out.'

'I know,' Libby said.

'And then no coming back till the whole job's done.' Evans saw Libby sigh. 'HSE rules,' he said. 'You've known it was coming.'

The following Tuesday, her memories about her grandparents' nightmare time having been triggered by her conversation with Marika the other day, and in pressing need of an excuse not to get to grips with her work, Libby sat down at the dining table – currently her desk – opened her laptop and googled the Ashcroft family; not for the first time, of course, but she had found in the past that search results changed over time, and she had suddenly remembered that Grandpa Jack had once told her that Ashcroft's son had moved away from his mother and sister and gone to live in Holland.

She ransacked her memory for the son's name and Frederick popped into her mind. Nothing doing, though, with her search, all relevant mentions of the Ashcroft name relating to the murderer, but then again, she supposed that if the son had left the country, it had probably been to escape his family's past, so no search results would be just what he must have hoped for.

She couldn't blame him, she thought, closing the laptop, picking up her current sketches and ordering herself to focus.

Except that hours later, after some reasonably successful cartoon work and a therapeutic massage session with Lucas, she noticed that the laptop was not where she'd left it. Or at least, it was still on the dining table, but not in the same spot, which was only surprising because no one else had been here since Lucas had gone next door to catch up with paperwork.

Imagination, she supposed, and in any case, her memory wasn't always at its sharpest these days, especially when she'd taken pain pills – just a couple of paracetamol now and then, something that Lucas told her was no bad thing if it meant she could continue with her normal activities.

All the same, she opened the laptop and found her usual wallpaper and the sign-in bar that normally meant she'd previously sent the computer into sleep mode.

Except she hadn't shut down after her search for Ashcroft's son, so shouldn't it have been her *Dr Ellie* screensaver on there?

Still puzzled, she signed in, went to Google and checked the day's search history – and found nothing. Not just nothing since her last sign-in, but nothing at all. Which had to mean, presumably, that her searches had been deleted. And maybe this was something that computers did automatically for some reason, or maybe there had been one of those annoying updates – she never really under- stood the way those things worked.

The only reason she was at all troubled, she supposed, was that with so many strangers in the house she probably needed to consider security a little more than she had been. Just because Reggie trusted her team didn't mean they were all beyond suspicion.

Suspicion of *what*? She shook her head, aware she was stressing about nothing at all: a laptop a couple of feet away from where she thought she'd left it.

Besides, everything of any consequence on there required pass- words or log-ins, and no one had those. Though Lucas had been with her when she'd logged on in the past, and she'd never hidden her details from him because there was nothing to be secretive about – and, in any case, she trusted him – and Lucas had been next door for hours today, so end of wholly non-existent mystery.

Then again, the builders were in the house – at least, she'd seen Mal Evans earlier heading down into the basement – and even when she and Lucas did lock their own front doors – which they often did not bother to do these days, with Lucas coming in and out so frequently – she knew that Reggie had keys to all the flats . . .

So, theoretically, she or Evans might feasibly have been in here, and both probably knew about computers – Reggie certainly did, but Libby knew she would never snoop – but just because Mal Evans was a builder didn't mean he might not be a computer geek in his spare time. Not that he or anyone else would bother with a not-especially-successful cartoonist's personal stuff.

Yet still, just in case, Libby did check her bank account and her Calla House business spreadsheets to make quite sure, and of course nothing was out of place, and after that she felt thoroughly ashamed of herself for her unworthy and completely unfounded suspicions.

She confessed the whole absurd business to Lucas over supper, and for a few minutes she worried that she might have upset him, because he felt it necessary to tell her that he would never dream of looking at her laptop or at anything private.

'I know that,' Libby tried to reassure him. 'Any more than I would poke my nose into anything of yours. I think I'm getting a bit paranoid.'

'It would be easy to understand why,' Lucas said.

'Would it? I'm not so sure.'

'Did you find out anything?'

'About?'

'The man's family. Ashcroft.'

'Nothing.'

'What made you start looking?'

'Just something Marika said which sparked an old memory of my grandfather telling me that the policeman who'd saved him and Harriet got in touch when he retired from the force, and he said that the killer's son had moved to Holland.'

'Nederland,' Lucas said. 'At least, depending on where he went, it might still be called Holland now, which is actually one of twelve provinces in the country.'

'But there's nothing offensive about my calling it Holland?'

Lucas grinned and shook his head. 'But from next January, the government is "rebranding" the whole country as The Netherlands, or Nederland.'

'I'll try to remember,' Libby said, and paused. 'But I think you said that your family are from Holland.'

'Amsterdam is in the province of North Holland – Rotterdam and The Hague are in South Holland.' Lucas leaned across the table and kissed Libby's head. 'Lesson over. Too dull.'

She couldn't argue. Except that she had noticed again that he never wanted to talk much about his background, and she did wonder why that might be. So much she didn't know about the Hendriks family. She supposed he would talk more about such things when he was ready, and having just assured him that she would never snoop into his private business, this was probably not the right moment to push further.

They washed up together, Lucas still insisting on doing most of the work, even though he had shown Libby how to carry things like plates while still on crutches, and sometimes it irritated her when he did more than his share of household stuff – but other times it was frankly wonderful, especially when she was extra tired, which she was that night.

'I'm a lucky woman,' she said, when they'd finished and were getting ready for bed. 'Please know that I do realize that.'

'Masseur and chief washer-up,' Lucas said. 'Pretty damned lucky.'

He took away her crutches, rested them where she would be able to reach them, and put his arms around her.

'Too tired to make love?' he asked.

'I was a bit too tired to argue about washing up,' she said. 'But strangely, I do seem to have got my second wind.'

'That is strange,' he said, and kissed her.

'Best ever,' she said, when she could breathe again.

'Best ever washer-upper?' he teased.

'Now you're fishing,' she said.

THIRTY

Libby was starting to worry about Nelson.

They'd all noticed it, and at first she had been concerned that getting caught with her in the downpour in the garden might have sparked a chill, but he was eating as usual and Lucas reported that he was frisky enough on their walks.

'It's only when we get back that he changes,' he said. 'His head goes right down between his paws.'

'I know,' Libby said. 'He looks really glum.'

'Missing Beatrice,' Lucas supposed.

'I am too,' Libby said. 'Poor Nelson.'

'He'll be fine.' Lucas was reassuring. 'We'll all spoil him even more than usual, and Reggie and co will finish the job and Beatrice will come home, and your leg will be healed and you'll be back upstairs.'

'Simple as that,' Libby said, wryly.

'Best way to look at it,' Lucas said.

She didn't really feel in the least bit rational, generally speaking, Libby told Lucas over dinner at Hazara in Belsize Lane two weeks later.

'It all still feels surreal, though I'm not sure why it should, considering there's nothing much *more* real than building works. But every time I get used to one thing, something else changes, and I can't seem to picture ever getting back to normality.'

'Loss of control is always tough,' Lucas said. 'Your injury and the house all in one hit.'

'Mm,' she said. 'Probably.'

'But everything is not bad, I hope.' Lucas smiled into her eyes.

'Far from it.' She returned the smile. 'But even this – us – is a little surreal. Getting swept up into something so lovely when everything else is falling apart.'

'Only your house,' Lucas said. 'Not everything.'

Libby ate some of her *samosa chaat* and warmth filled her. 'Oh my goodness, this is amazing.'

It was the twelfth of September, Lucas's birthday, and this was her treat and thanks for all he had done for her and was still doing.

'I'm sorry Marika didn't feel like joining us,' he said.

'I'm actually worried about her too. It's good that she finally agreed to move in with me, but I'm still not sure how well she'll cope when we all have to get out.'

'Do you know yet where you'll go?'

'No. And Marika won't talk about it.' Libby put down her fork. 'I feel so responsible.'

'You worry far too much,' Lucas said.

'I can't help it.'

Their starters were removed.

'Is it all right for me to ask about Marika's breakdown?' Lucas asked. 'I know that it happened in Peru, but do you know what precipitated it?'

'She's never told me that,' Libby said. 'And I've never asked.'

'And it's none of my business,' Lucas said. 'Except that I see how you care about each other.' He paused. 'I've actually wondered if she might be in love with you.'

'Definitely not.'

'Why the smile?'

'Because she once asked me much the same thing about Reggie – said she thought she might have a "thing" for me.' Libby shook her head. 'Which was absolute nonsense.'

'Why nonsense?' It was Lucas's turn to smile. 'It's not hard for me to understand why anyone would fall in love with you.'

Their main courses arrived and they ate in satisfied silence for a few minutes, sharing their Murgh Makhani and Rogan Josh, and then Lucas put down his fork.

'Something I think it's time I shared with you,' he said.

Libby set down her cutlery too. 'You look very serious.'

'It's nothing,' he said. 'But in a way, it is, for me, at least.' He took a drink of his wine. 'It's just something about my family history that's always been a source of awkwardness – even a degree of shame. Which is ridiculous, I realize – have always realized – but my father's an old-fashioned man.'

Libby waited, intrigued.

'His father's . . . my grandfather's *onwettigheit* – that's Dutch for illegitimacy – has rarely been mentioned, but when it was spoken of, it was always in low whispers.' He paused again. 'Which is why I've been concerned not to cause you any embarrassment.'

'Because of my own non-father? My goodness.' Libby smiled. 'Is that really what you've been worried about?' She saw gravity still in his eyes. 'I do get it – of course I do. And it's lovely of you to have been concerned about it for my sake, but you needn't have been. The subject has never worried me, though I understand if it hasn't been as easy for you – or rather, for your father.'

'Your family's obviously more liberal than mine.'

'No family left to speak of now,' Libby said. 'Only my mother, and Sylvie is very much the "liberal" one and the reason I was born "out of wedlock".' She half-whispered the words, a slight tease in her tone, instantly regretting it. 'She hardly told me anything about my father – she didn't actually know anything about him, she was very honest with me about that. She said he was exceptionally attractive and that he'd modelled for one of her life drawing classes – and that he'd been rather sweet.'

Libby also remembered that Sylvie had never referred to him as her 'father', but as the man who'd 'got her pregnant', adding that he had been very good in bed, but in the circumstances, Libby thought that might sound too flippant for this conversation.

'But the point is,' she went on quietly, 'my grandparents never made a thing of it, or certainly not with me, and though others may have gossiped about my being illegitimate, I've honestly never been fussed about it. I've never had to be. Which makes me very lucky, I realize.'

'I'd say so,' Lucas said.

She noticed that he glanced at the nearest tables, as if wanting to check that no one was eavesdropping.

They both returned to their food, but their appetites had waned.

'I'm glad you've told me,' she said presently.

He nodded. 'I am too.'

'You've been quite reticent about your home life. It made me feel you didn't want to get too close to me.'

'On the contrary,' Lucas said, then hesitated.

'What?' Libby asked, then smiled. 'Let's not stop now.'

'OK.' He put down his knife and fork. 'I've felt a few times lately that you thought I was overstepping.'

She frowned. 'In what way?'

'Mostly when I've tried to take care of you,' he said.

'That was just me getting ratty because I hate being dependent.'

'You'll be fully independent soon enough,' he said. 'Though . . .'

'Go on.'

'Even tonight, a little earlier, you said you thought our relation-ship seemed surreal. Which makes me feel that maybe you're the one who doesn't want to get too close.'

'Something else we have in common, then,' Libby said. 'We're both over-thinkers.' She picked up her wineglass. 'Can we remember why we're here tonight, please?'

She gestured to him to pick up his glass.

'Happy Birthday,' she said.

'You're not going to sing, are you?'

'Only if you're very unlucky,' she said.

THIRTY-ONE

Lucas hurried into the flat two days later, Nelson in his arms. 'He's OK, don't worry, but his collar snapped halfway up Rosslyn Hill. If he wasn't such a good old boy . . .'

He set the dog down carefully on the rug, stroked his ears. 'Where's the nearest pet shop, do you know?'

'Not sure, though I'll ring Village Vet – near the restaurant we went to on your birthday.' Libby thought. 'But in the meantime, my grandmother's dog's last collar is in that old nostalgia case I asked you to bring down for me.'

Except that, when she went to find the collar, it wasn't there.

Which was silly, because it had to be there, which spurred her on to pull everything out of the case, and she knew its contents more or less off by heart, because only a matter of a few months ago she'd had to open it to find some papers proving provenance of the 'Private War' paintings.

George's collar had definitely been there then, together with a whole load of other items: photographs; Harriet's painting smock; Grandpa Jack's piano recordings, on tape and 78s and vinyl; Libby's mother's first booties; a sketchpad of Sylvie's early fashion designs and some of Libby's own first cartoons; the original front door key to Calla House; and numerous other items of personal value to Libby.

'I don't understand it,' she said to Lucas now.

'Maybe it dropped out of the case when you were going through it before the exhibition?'

'I don't think so, and I'm sure that missing photo didn't,' Libby said. 'The one I think I told you about – of my grandparents and Mum and the old bicycle.'

'It's probably all down to the chaos,' Lucas consoled. 'When you're back upstairs in your own place, I expect they'll both magic- ally reappear.'

'Don't do that, please,' Libby said.

'Don't do what?'

'Make me doubt myself. I've told you that two important things have gone missing, and you're acting as if I'm imagining things.'

'I only wanted to make you feel better,' Lucas said.

'Well, you're not,' she said.

One week later, when the house was empty – a rare event these days – because the builders had finished for the day, Lucas was out on appointments and Marika was working late at the supermarket, Libby, unable to settle to work, decided to wash her hair instead.

Lucas had installed – temporarily, and that only after she had raised multiple objections – a seat in the shower so that she could wash and shampoo her hair in relative safety for the duration of her physical limitations; and when she was being honest and less defensive, Libby had to admit it was a very sensible idea that had enabled her to maintain a little more independence.

'Always have your phone with you though,' Lucas had said after she had agreed to the seat.

'It was my leg I broke, not my brain,' Libby had said scathingly, and then she'd shaken her head. 'Sorry. I'm feeling very touchy.'

'Understandable,' Lucas had said.

'And please don't be so understanding.'

'Even when I do understand?'

'Especially then,' she had said. 'It makes you sound like a carer.'

'I thought you wouldn't say that again. I'm your lover and I care *about* you, which is very different.'

'I know,' Libby said. 'But please, just remember that I do still possess a degree of common sense.'

She did not, however, always remember to take her mobile phone everywhere she went, which was why, on that occasion, while she was all alone in the house and in the middle of shampooing her hair when the lights went out, she froze.

'Shit,' she said.

It was an indoor room with no window.

The extractor fan had gone silent too.

She groped for the taps and turned off the shower.

'It's OK,' she told herself. 'Stay calm.'

Which she might have, if she had not always had a mild *thing* – not as extreme as a phobia, but not a happy state of mind – about being in pitch-darkness. As a small child, if her mother had turned out the lamp in her room and closed the door, Libby had cried until Sylvie had relented and opened it again so that she could see the light from the landing.

Right now, sitting naked on Lucas's plastic bath seat, gripping its sides, feeling that her balance had gone askew along with her leg, she felt incredibly vulnerable – far more so even than on that stormy afternoon in the garden stuck without her crutches.

'Just wait,' she said, hoping the lights would magically come back on.

Which was unlikely if a fuse had blown and there was no one to fix it.

'OK,' she said after a minute or two, shivering a bit because she was soaking wet and on the fringes of being scared. 'Towel.'

She closed her eyes – which seemed easier for some reason than staring into blackness – pulled aside the shower curtain and reached for where she knew the towels were hanging.

'Ouch.' The rail was hot, but the good news was that the bath towel was nice and warm when she wrapped it around herself.

Still no light.

If she'd had her phone with her, she'd have had a torch.

An old memory came to her, of Grandpa Jack telling her how stubborn Harriet had been, never listening to warnings against late-night walks on her own.

Stubbornness clearly another inheritance, along with her small talent for art and her red hair.

No choice now, but to step out of the shower as carefully as possible, pick up her crutches and get to the door, just a few feet away.

She closed her eyes again, swivelled around on the seat, then felt for the metal outer edge of the walk-in shower – then, keeping her towel-wrapped behind as firmly as possible on the seat, she reached further for the crutches . . .

'Gotcha.'

One of them, at any rate.

She slid her right arm through the cuff of the crutch, then felt for the second one with her left hand – and knocked it over.

'Of course,' she said wryly.

The effort of staying seated while bending to retrieve the fallen crutch, using the right-hand one to stabilize the process was hard work – plus it made her leg twinge.

'Ouch,' she said again, as she located the infuriating crutch.

She sat still for a moment or two, finding herself ridiculously breathless, and Lucas had been trying to persuade her for some time to keep up with her exercises to help her maintain core strength, but of course she'd known better, and from now on, she was going to treat his professional advice with more respect . . .

She stood up, shut her eyes again, concentrating on not falling over the narrow lip where the shower enclosure met the main floor, then turned towards the door.

Her towel, having been kept in place till then by her upper arms, now predictably fell to the floor, and Libby swore softly, glad that the house was empty so that she could open the door, then, with the light from the hallway, retrieve the towel and get decent.

The door would not open.

She groped for the small sliding lock, but it was in the open position because being alone in the house, not to mention in the privacy of Flat B, she hadn't bothered with it – wasn't even sure why she'd shut the door in the first place, because she never did upstairs in her own flat.

But this wasn't her flat.

She sighed, tried the handle again.

'Oh, come *on*.'

She wiped her palm against her body, gripped the door handle more firmly.

It would not budge.

'Not funny,' she said, aware that she was fending off panic.

Again, she tried, more forcibly, dumped the right crutch, pitched up to full-strength and jerked the handle up and down – then, realizing she might just break it, she stopped.

'Hello?!' she called.

Which was pointless, because she knew no one was there, neither in the flat nor anywhere in the house, but she called anyway, because what choice did she have, and at some point Lucas or Marika would come home, so she was just going to have to keep calling until they did. And she wasn't in any danger, she could sit on the loo and drink from the tap, and Lucas would be home before dinner, so she wouldn't starve.

And she'd probably get used to the dark.

'Help!' she shouted.

More decibels needed.

'*Help*! I'm locked in the shower room.'

Nothing. Of course.

'*Help!*'

She thought she heard a sound.

'Hello!! I need some help in here!'

She heard the sound of a key in the front door lock.

'Oh, thank God,' she said, waited an instant. 'Lucas?'

She heard footsteps entering the flat.

'I'm stuck in the shower room,' she called. 'The light went out and the door won't open.'

'Libby?'

Not Lucas. A man's voice, but deeper than his.

'Miss Jerome?'

Mal Evans.

She remembered with a start that she was naked. She dropped the second crutch, splayed one hand against the wall to keep her balance, bent as low as she could without falling to reach the dropped bath towel, and she was warm now, with relief and embarrassment – or rather, she was *hot* now, and probably sweaty and red-faced, in more ways than one.

'Oh, thank goodness, Mal,' she called. 'The lights have fused and the bloody door won't open.'

'Sure you haven't locked it?' Evans asked from the other side of the door.

'Quite sure,' she said, trying not to sound annoyed. But just the same, she felt for the slider again, and it was definitely in the open position – luckily, she thought, for her reputation as a half-intelligent adult. 'It's just decided to jam, for some reason. Could you please get something to open it with?'

'No problem,' Evans said. 'Are you decent?'

Libby felt herself grow redder and, irrationally, more annoyed. 'Yes, thank you.'

'Stand back,' he said.

And opened the door.

'I don't believe it,' Libby said. 'It wouldn't open from in here.'

She started to emerge from the dark room, then swayed and remembered the crutches.

'Let me,' Evans said, politely, and stepped past her. 'Sorry,' he said as he brushed against her towel and picked up both crutches. 'Here you go.' He handed them to her, then backed out of the room. 'Can you manage now? Are you OK?'

Her annoyance evaporated, and gratitude took its place. 'I can't thank you enough, Mal. I thought you'd all finished for the day – I thought I was going to have to wait for Lucas to get home.'

'Light's fused, you say?'

He flicked the switch, and for a second Libby froze, worried that it would spring into life the way the door had, but nothing happened, the room remained dark, the extractor fan silent, so at least her credibility was partially intact.

'I'll go and deal with it,' Evans said. 'If you're sure you're all right.'

She nodded. 'I'm wonderful, now that I'm out of there. Not keen on the dark,' she added.

'Plenty of people feel like that,' the foreman said. 'I wouldn't worry about it. And I'll check on that door later.'

He headed off to the kitchen, where the fuse box was located in a cupboard, and in less than two minutes the power was restored.

And that was that, except that Libby was starting to wonder again if she really might be becoming a little paranoid, because everything was getting to her in a way that was quite unfamiliar to her. She was a practical person, she easily managed ordinary things like jamming doors and blown fuses, she'd looked after Calla House for years, only resorting to Brownlow & Daughter when absolutely necessary.

Evans came back to check on her a half-hour later, knocked on the front door, came in with unusual discretion when she called to him to come in.

'Just want to make sure you're OK after your fright.'

'I'm fine, thank you.' She was actually very tired, because the foolish panic she'd got herself into had taken it out of her, and what she wanted was a little peace and quiet until Lucas came home. 'But I really do thank you, Mal, for helping me.'

'It was nothing,' he said. 'Shall I deal with the door now or let you rest a while?'

'I wouldn't mind a rest, if that's OK,' she said.

'No problem,' he said. 'Maybe don't close it for now.'

He came a little further into the living room, and Libby saw that he was looking at one of the 'Private War' paintings: the largest of the series, almost a panorama of the bombsite and, somehow cleverly focused on by Harriet, the house in which she and Grandpa Jack had been trapped by Ashcroft.

Evans was looking at it very intently, took a step closer, apparently fascinated.

'It's one of my grandmother's,' Libby said. 'I mean, she painted it.'

'I know,' the builder said, and looked away from the painting, back at her. 'Everyone knows.'

And she thought, for just an instant, that she detected a frisson of hostility, as if he thought, perhaps, that she was bragging.

'She was very good,' Evans said.

'She was,' Libby said.

'They lived here,' he said. 'Didn't they? In this house.'

'They did.'

'Nice, being able to keep it in the family,' he said. 'Pity about all this.' He looked back towards the front door. 'The asbestos, I mean.'

Libby nodded, gave a small sigh of agreement.

'Oh well,' Evans said. 'I'll leave you in peace.'

'Thank you,' she said. 'And thanks again for everything. If it hadn't been for you, I'd probably still be stuck in there.'

'Not nice,' he said. 'Being in the dark.'

He left, closed the door quietly behind him, and Libby let out a longer sighing breath of relief, hadn't realized quite how tense she'd been while he'd been in the room.

Something about him.

'More paranoia,' she said, out loud, but quietly, as if she was worried that he might be out in the hall, might hear her.

This was nonsense, she told herself, and it had to stop – especially this uncharacteristic suspicion of others, about *nothing*, especially those who had been perfectly helpful.

Then, more gently, she reminded herself that – up to a point – it was probably understandable, as Lucas had said. The asbestos. Her broken bones. Things going missing. Her beloved house, now this increasingly alien territory, not feeling like *hers* any more. Being trapped in the dark room.

This would all pass, she reassured herself. A little oil on hinges, a mended fuse, a helping hand or several for a while longer.

And then all would be well.

THIRTY-TWO

Work was getting harder, too, Libby found, cartoon deadlines seeming tougher for her to meet. She had always had abundant energy, but lately she'd been dozing off over her drawings; and she remembered Marika once talking about her own battles, during her depression, with alternating insomnia and the struggle to stay awake in daytime, and Libby wondered again if perhaps she might be far more psychologically thrown by events than she'd realized.

'I've even begun thinking that the reporter at the gallery might have been right when she asked what it was like living with ghosts,' she said one evening to Marika. 'I don't mean actual ghosts – not the people – just this house.' She waved a hand vaguely. 'Maybe the asbestos was a sign. Telling me to sell up.'

'You just need to bring down your stress,' Marika told her. 'Like you've told me in the past.'

'I'll try.'

'Have you been drinking the relaxing tea I bought you?'

'Not really,' Libby confessed. 'I don't like the taste.'

'It's very good,' Marika said. 'You should make a cup.'

Libby said that she would, and that same evening Lucas had pointed out to her the pointlessness of getting so worked up over things that were completely out of her control. And then he'd gone into the kitchen and had made a cup of Marika's herbal tea, and it was all Libby could do not to scream at him for conspiring with her friend over her stupid *tea*.

And whatever they both said, there were matters she needed to be dealing with, like working and making arrangements for the leaving of Calla House, but the only thing she really seemed fit for was procrastination, which was why the following afternoon, when she had promised herself that she would get to grips with her next cartoon – Dr Ellie and the patient who believed he was invisible – she was just too sleepy, and maybe, she decided, a short power nap might help to restore some creativity . . .

* * *

A monk in a hooded cloak stood over her, his face obscured in shadow, so close to her own that she could feel his breath on her mouth.

'No!' Terror propelled her arms from her sides, hands thrust palms out to shove him away as she struggled out of her chair. '*No!*'

'Take it easy, Libby,' a woman's voice said.

Libby sank back against the seat, her heart pounding furiously, trying to blink sleep away, knowing right away that she'd been dreaming, that it had been some kind of daytime night terror, and of course there was no monk, just Reggie in her hooded coveralls.

'Sorry,' Libby said, embarrassed. 'Must have dozed off.'

'No, I'm sorry.' Reggie held up Libby's coffee mug with Dr Ellie's face printed on it, a gift from her editor at the *Chronicle*. 'Your coffee was right on the edge there and your leg jolted and I didn't want it spilling over your work.'

'I've hardly done any work.' Ashamed, Libby took the mug. 'I'm meant to be drawing, not sleeping.'

'The perils of working at home,' Reggie said.

'I was dreaming.' Libby laughed. 'I thought you were a monk.'

'My hood,' Reggie said. 'Very sinister.'

Libby was in bed late the following night, dozing fitfully – Lucas sleeping next door in his own flat as he had since Marika had moved into the second bedroom of Flat B – when she heard a tapping on her door.

'Come in.'

'I'm so sorry,' Marika said. 'Were you asleep?'

Libby shook her head, and Marika, a boho patchwork robe wrapped around her, came in and sat at the end of the bed, and Nelson, his sleep disrupted, jumped down and curled up in the corner of the room, grumbling.

'Are the mice keeping you awake too?' Marika asked.

'Just life.' Libby paused. 'I can't hear anything.'

'They just stopped.' Marika sighed. 'As soon as I got out of bed.' She shook her head. 'I don't know how you've ever managed to get any proper sleep down here.'

'I seldom do, but I think maybe I've started to get used to the sounds.'

'I'm going to take a look,' Marika said. 'It's driving me mad.'

'In the basement?' Libby shook her head. 'Definitely not. Reggie's rules.'

Marika sighed again. 'Is it only me looking forward to life without Reggie and her gang and their *rules*?'

'If you mean to the work being finished, of course.'

'I don't think I do mean just the work,' Marika said. 'She and Evans are always *around*, you know? They apologize for intruding, but they always seem to be listening.'

'I don't think that's fair. Short of wearing ear plugs, none of them can really avoid hearing us some of the time.'

'It's probably just my mood,' Marika said. 'All kinds of things creeping me out.'

'What kind of things?' Libby asked. 'Want to talk about them?'

Marika shook her head, then stood up and wandered restlessly around the room. 'I could wear one of the masks I take on digs to go down.'

'Absolutely not,' Libby said. 'It's not safe.'

Marika shrugged.

'Promise me you won't,' Libby insisted, 'or I won't get a single wink of sleep, and my leg's really hurting tonight.'

'I won't go down tonight,' Marika said. 'I promise.'

'You won't go down at all.' Libby was firm. 'I'll have another word with Reggie about the mice.'

'I thought she said Evans was going to set traps.'

'I thought he had,' Libby said. 'I hate the idea, but Reggie said it had to be done.'

'Then they must have come back,' Marika said. 'Or perhaps they were wrong – maybe there are rats, after all. You need different sized traps.'

'Stop, please.'

'I'm just being practical,' Marika said. 'And you should start drinking my tea.'

'You're the one not sleeping,' Libby said.

THIRTY-THREE

It really was the last straw.

Another thing had gone missing. And not just a *thing* this time, nothing so small or insignificant as a dog's collar or even a photograph.

One of her grandmother's paintings – one of the 'Private War' series, the one of Harriet tied to the ghastly wheelchair – and Libby believed she really was losing it for a while, that fatigue and her generally fraught state of mind were making her imagine things. She made herself stop looking for the painting for a time, tried to convince herself that if she got on with other things, the next time she looked for it, it would be there.

But it was not.

'Do you think someone may be stealing your stuff?' Lucas asked.

'I don't know.' Libby felt upset. 'I hope not.'

'One of Reggie's people?' Lucas kept his voice low. 'Coming and going all the time. It's not impossible.'

'But I've known most of the team for years,' Libby said. 'And they're never here without Reggie or Mal, and I know he's not my favourite person, and Marika really dislikes him, but I've asked Reggie about him, and she totally trusts him and I trust her judgement.'

'Still, in theory,' Lucas mused, 'an outsider could nip in to the house when they're all here. I've seen the front door left open a few times.'

'I haven't,' Libby said. 'That's not good. But it makes no sense. The painting has some value – though not without the rest of the series – but who on earth would want an ancient dog's collar or one of my family photos, which wasn't even in a decent frame?'

'It's certainly very odd,' Lucas agreed. 'Could someone be playing tricks on you?'

'Like who?' Libby frowned. 'I think I hate the idea of that even more than someone stealing.' She shook her head. 'I'm going to try to forget about it.'

'Can you?' Lucas asked. 'Now that the painting's gone missing?'

'I'm still hoping it'll just reappear,' Libby said. 'Maybe I am going bonkers and I did put all the things somewhere and I've just forgotten where.' She saw his doubtful expression. 'I'm certainly not going to start interrogating people. Quite frankly that's more than I can face right now.'

'Maybe you should at least report it.'

'Absolutely not.'

'It's your painting,' Lucas said. 'Your decision.'

The next day, a Saturday, with time to spare before an orthopaedic hospital check-up, Libby met Beatrice for lunch at Café Laville in Little Venice, nabbing a table with a view of the canal. Watching her friend, who'd always had a good appetite, pick half-heartedly at her risotto, Libby knew that all was not well with her.

'I'm simply missing Nelson,' Beatrice insisted. 'And you, of course.'

'You should have let me bring him along,' Libby said. 'They're dog-friendly here.'

Beatrice shook her head. 'It would just have confused him.'

'Are you sure that's all that's wrong?' Libby persisted. 'Things are working out with the family?'

'My niece is being very kind,' Beatrice said, 'and it's a lovely opportunity to spend time with the children. But I confess I am looking forward to coming home.'

'You're not ill?'

'I really am perfectly fine, Elizabeth.' She was firm. 'Missing you all, but otherwise fine.'

'And you would tell me if there was anything I could do for you? This whole upheaval is my responsibility, after all.'

'I'm a very satisfied tenant, and I would tell you.' Beatrice went briskly on. 'Now, your turn to tell me what's wrong with you. Aside from having your house bulldozed around you.'

Libby laughed. 'Not exactly, thank God. But I can't wait to have all this disruption over and done with.'

'Leg feeling better?'

'Much.'

'The lovely Mr Hendriks still looking after you well? As friend rather than physiotherapist?'

Libby smiled. 'Very well.'

'So there we are, both untroubled,' Beatrice said dryly.

'Nothing a good dose of normality wouldn't cure,' Libby said.

With Libby lunching with Beatrice, Lucas on the Heath with Nelson, and the builders off until Monday, Marika, alone in the house, still suffering sleep deprivation because of the marauding mice or rats and all the other issues that were gnawing away at her, decided to take advantage of the rare opportunity to ignore rules and to do some checking up of her own.

She rummaged through her storage boxes and found one of her archaeological face masks, then opened the basement door, felt around inside for the light switch and flicked it.

No light.

'*Szar!*' Marika swore, went back to the same box, grabbed a torch.

And hurried down the steps.

Arriving home in good spirits, Libby knocked first on Lucas's door, then went into Flat B to look for Marika.

Deflated at finding no one home, she flopped on to the couch, but moments later, hearing the outer front door open, she went back into the hall to find Lucas and Nelson returning from their walk, the dog panting.

'Look!' She hugged Lucas, then stood back and struck a pose. 'No crutches.'

'That's fantastic.' Lucas unclipped Nelson's lead and kissed her.

'I thought I'd cook us all a chilli this evening to celebrate,' she said.

'So long as you don't overdo it.'

'You can be my sous chef,' Libby said. 'I thought it might cheer Marika up. She's still quite low.'

But by nightfall there was still no sign of her friend, and Marika's phone was on charge in her room – which was not of great concern to Libby since Marika regularly forgot to take it with her. By Sunday morning though, Libby was more than a little troubled. She'd taken a look at her friend's belongings, and though she was not sure exactly how much stuff Marika had brought down here from the first floor, it did seem to her that there was a little less than usual in the wardrobe.

'She's probably taken a break somewhere,' Lucas said.

'But where? Anyway, she'd have left me a note,' Libby said. 'This isn't a bit like her. Though—'

'What?'

Libby hesitated. 'Just something else that's not like Marika. Something I found with her things.' She pointed to the corner table – to a framed black-and-white photo that had not been there before.

It took Lucas a moment. 'Is that the one you lost?'

Libby nodded. 'I was checking to see if she'd taken her make-up and hairbrush – which was actually not that easy to judge, because it's all in a jumble. But there it was. The missing photo.'

Lucas took another moment. 'Nothing else? Not the collar, or—'

'I didn't look for anything else,' she said sharply. 'Nor will I be.'

'Don't get upset, Libby.' Lucas was gentle. 'There'll be a good explanation.'

'All I'm upset about,' she said, 'is not knowing where she is.'

A letter arrived on Tuesday morning, picked up off the mat by Lucas and brought straight to Libby, who tore it open eagerly.

'It's OK,' Libby said as she read. 'She says she had a call –' she scanned the handwritten letter – 'about a last-minute place opening up on a dig in Peru . . . says it was just the spur she needed.'

'That's great,' Lucas said.

'She's desperately sorry not to be able to wait to see us,' Libby read on, 'but she had to leave right away, and she tried my mobile but couldn't get through.' She frowned. 'I know she can be scatty about her phone, but if she was going to fly to Peru, that would have been right up there along with her passport and credit card.'

'She'll have been in a state,' Lucas rationalized. 'Having to rush like that. She probably put it on charge and then forgot. And you said you couldn't find her passport.'

'But I'm not sure where she kept it,' Libby said. 'Maybe she always had it in her bag – I don't know.' Her stomach was in knots. 'And why a *letter*? She says she was writing it at Gatwick. She could have gone to a payphone. She could have bought a cheap phone.'

'Maybe she couldn't face talking to you.' Lucas paused. 'Why aren't you more relieved? At least you've heard from her.'

'I don't know. Except Peru was where she had her breakdown, which was why she buried herself in the depths of Waitrose, because that was all she felt she could cope with – and that's another thing

I still don't understand: it isn't like Marika to leave a job without notice. None of it makes sense.' Libby lifted the letter. 'This reads like a declaration of recovery, doesn't it? But what if it's the opposite?'

'Another breakdown, you mean?' Lucas said.

'The start of one, maybe,' she said. 'I'm really worried.'

'Maybe it truly was just too good an offer to resist,' Lucas said.

'I hope so,' Libby said.

Most of the interior of Calla House now resembled a weird kind of moonscape, the only areas not shielded from view – the only remaining pockets of normality – the two ground-floor flats.

'Almost time to go,' Reggie reminded Libby and Lucas one morning, finding them both in Flat B's kitchen. 'A week today. That OK?'

'Most of my stuff's already packed,' Libby said.

'Know where you're going yet?' Reggie asked.

Libby and Lucas looked at each other.

'More or less,' Libby said.

'*Tempus fugit*,' the builder said.

Lucas waited till the other woman had gone downstairs.

'More or less?' he repeated. 'I thought you decided you were going to meet your mum in Paris.'

'She's not sure now if she can leave Hong Kong,' Libby said. 'Nothing's fixed.'

'Are you OK?'

'More or less,' Libby said.

Lucas looked at her. 'Do you have a problem with me?'

'Why would you think that?'

'Because you're being a bit cool.'

'Can you blame me?' Libby said.

And then, awkwardly, she changed the subject and would not be drawn back to it, because though she knew that he was right, that despite his explanation about his family issues on his birthday, something was still spoiling the sense of ease between them, and she was unsure if it was just her own stresses getting on top of her – or if perhaps she had been sensing something negative going on in Lucas's head.

And she *knew* it would be better to talk about it, get it out into the open, and the normal Libby, the one not still feeling so wretchedly beleaguered, would do just that. But she did not feel normal, was not at all sure, frankly, if she could cope with hearing the truth.

Especially if the truth was that Lucas had had enough of her.

THIRTY-FOUR

'I have *got* to know what's bugging you.'

It was Lucas, at last, who tackled the problem head-on, two afternoons before they were due to move out.

'Is it me?' he said. 'Or us getting kicked out, or what?'

They were in his flat because Lucas had baked brownies and suggested an old black-and-white movie for a little relaxation, but even *All About Eve* was failing to break the tension in the room.

'I could ask you the same,' Libby said.

She heard her own belligerence, felt annoyed with herself for that, but attack felt safer right now than confessing her vulnerability.

'Why?' He was puzzled. 'Am I different in some way?' He turned off the television.

'Am I?'

A stand-off. Both confronting the other, neither responding.

'I think,' Lucas said carefully after a moment, 'it's been strained for a while. Just worse since Marika left.'

'Maybe.' Libby didn't want to be this distant. She wanted to be honest enough to do what she felt like doing, which was bursting into tears and begging him for a hug.

'What does "maybe" mean?' Lucas was getting frustrated. 'Please talk to me, Libby, tell me what you're feeling.'

'Isn't it obvious?'

'Some of it,' Lucas said. 'I get your being upset about Marika leaving the way she did, but sometimes it's true what they say about knowing when to let go.'

'It's not a case of letting go.' She was bristling. 'If she'd called or answered just one of my emails or messages – and she must have access to a phone or tablet by now – I'd be fine about it. I'd be very happy for her, but not a single *word* – something's not right.'

'We don't know what the conditions are like where she is.' He saw she was unconvinced. 'But this isn't just about Marika, is it? It's this whole mess, the house, the things going missing, the loss of control—'

'So now I'm controlling?' Libby broke in.

'I didn't say that.'

'It's the second time you've used the word.'

'Is it?'

'You used it the other day, at lunch.'

'Oh, Libby.' He tried to reach for her, but she pulled away. 'I'm not blaming you – you're a very independent person, and one minute you're running a houseful of people, and the next everything's been ripped out of your hands, and you were already fretting about Beatrice, and now, with Marika—'

'I'm not that fragile,' Libby said.

'On the contrary, you're very strong. But things mount up.'

'Don't patronize me,' she said.

'I'm not.' He tried to take her hand, but again she pulled away.

'I was going to suggest we take a place together.' Finally, she let the truth fly, close to tears now, furious with herself for feeling so insecure. 'Even though you haven't mentioned anything like that, which rather makes me assume you'd sooner not—'

'Because I thought you wanted to meet your mother.' Lucas was startled by her outburst.

'I told you it might not happen and it isn't. Sylvie can't get away, and anyway, I've got Nelson to look after and you said you were going to stay with your mate from college.'

'I only arranged that because I thought Paris sounded wonderful for you, and I supposed you'd have to put Nelson into kennels, but I didn't bring that up in case it sent you off on another guilt trip. If I'd known—'

'Anyway, I can see now –' Libby couldn't seem to stop – 'that if I had suggested our staying somewhere together, you'd probably think I was being controlling.'

'Now you really are overreacting.'

'Oh, fuck off,' she said.

Mal Evans was out in the hallway carrying one of their big H-Class vacuum cleaners towards the basement door as Libby exited Lucas's flat and stalked into Flat B, ignoring Evans and slamming the door hard behind her.

Lucas, still in his doorway, saw the foreman's sympathetic smile.

'Couldn't help overhearing,' he said. 'Sorry, mate.'

'Not your fault.'

'We do try to keep out of our customers' private lives.'

'Libby's just a bit upset,' Lucas said.

'Not my business,' Evans said.

The door of B opened again, and Libby came out, carrying a jacket. 'Talking about me again?' she asked acidly.

'Libby—' Lucas said.

'Nelson's fine,' Libby said. 'I won't be too long.'

As the front door shut behind her, Evans gave Lucas another commiserating look.

'It'll blow over,' he said.

Having visited a B & B behind Swiss Cottage (a place her editor had once recommended when his flat had been flooded) and made a reservation, Libby knew that was a knee-jerk reaction, but still, it pleased her to do it at that moment. And with no other plans for the morning except packing, and definitely in no mood for *Dr Ellie*, Libby decided to pay Beatrice a visit at her niece's, but arriving at Alison Keyes's mansion block in Maida Vale, Libby learned from her young au pair that Beatrice was no longer staying there.

Now she was seriously perturbed – *two* friends missing – perhaps three, she added gloomily, if she counted Lucas; though at least the young woman had given her an address for Beatrice, to which Libby now hurried.

And was further dismayed to find a tiny, shabby and objectionably noisy flat over a bar in West End Lane, with Beatrice plainly embarrassed at being found out.

'Why didn't you tell me?' Libby asked, standing in the small sitting room, feeling upset for her friend. 'This is horrible.'

'Because I didn't want a fuss, and I knew you'd make one, albeit with the best of intentions, but there's really no need because I'm perfectly all right and it's only for a little while and it's not so bad.'

'Do you want to tell me what happened?' Libby was gentle.

'Nothing much.' Beatrice sighed. 'Alison did want me to stay on, but I'm afraid the others were finding it all a bit much to cope with. So we had to find me something rather swiftly, and here I am.'

Libby could smell damp, guessed that the clamour from the bar below probably continued into the small hours and reached a snap decision.

'Not for much longer,' she said. 'Reggie's finally booting me out, and I've found somewhere I think you might like, so you and I could stay there together.'

'What about Lucas?' Beatrice asked.

'Plans of his own,' Libby said shortly. 'So it's just you and me. If you don't mind too much, that is.'

'Elizabeth, it's completely unnecessary for—'

'It's just a really nice B & B –' Libby over-rode her – 'behind Swiss Cottage, and they'll take Nelson – it was the first thing I checked. And don't look like that, Beatrice. The mood I'm in right now, I deserve a treat, and there's no one I'd rather share it with than you.'

Libby let herself quietly back into Calla House, but the instant the front door closed, Lucas's door opened. For a moment they looked at each other, and then she was in his arms, their relief mutual and intense.

'I'm really sorry.' She was the first to pull away.

'Me too,' Lucas said.

'I was awful, you were just being kind, as usual, and I swore at you. I am honestly so sorry.'

The hostility was gone, but the awkwardness was still there.

'I think, maybe,' she said, 'it's all been a bit rushed. Us, I mean.'

'Rushed?' Lucas's dismay was palpable.

'Magnified,' Libby said. 'By the situation.'

She walked ahead of him into B, where Nelson greeted them both with enthusiasm.

'My leg is partly still to blame, I think. Or rather my just being a grumpy cow.' Libby opened the glass door to the garden, much of the grass now filled with builders' materials, let the dog out, watching as he cocked a leg against the calla lilies, always mindful of their toxicity were he to nibble any part of them. 'You having to take care of me.'

'Not having to,' Lucas said quietly. 'Wanting to. I hoped you knew that.'

'I did.' She managed a smile. 'I do.' She took a breath. 'Still, I think it might be a good idea if we use this bit of time, give each other a little space.'

'Very overrated,' Lucas said. 'Space.'

She said nothing.

'I wonder . . .' He stopped.

'What?'

'Your mother – Sylvie – is obviously a woman who likes her "space".'

Libby bridled at the suggestion. 'So what? I'm like her?'

Lucas stood his ground. 'Could be your father. Perhaps you've inherited traits from him – you wouldn't know.'

She stared at him, silent with anger.

'That wasn't nice, I know.' He tried to smile. 'Not so kind, after all. Just human. I apologize.'

Nelson came back inside, tail wagging, and Libby bent to pet him.

'All right.' Lucas gave in. 'Maybe space is a good idea.'

'I'm going to take Nelson and stay with Beatrice,' Libby told him.

'That'll be nice for her.'

'And you're still going to your friend's flat?'

'Tom Brent. Off Edgware Road.' He paused. 'If I may, I'll leave you his address. And you can call me day or night on my mobile.'

'Likewise,' Libby said.

'So, Maida Vale. We'll almost be neighbours.'

'I'm not . . .' Libby stopped, too tired and stressed to start explaining Beatrice's move now, and she was glad he hadn't queried Nelson being allowed to stay at the niece's.

'What?'

'Nothing important,' she said. 'It can wait.'

Lucas eyed her a little warily for another moment, then stepped closer.

'Our first fight,' he said softly.

'Not really,' she said. 'We've had a few spats.'

'Just differences of opinion,' Lucas said. 'This was worse. I was nasty.'

'It was inevitable, I suppose,' Libby said. 'And you weren't so nasty. You might even have a point about inherited traits. I don't know about my father, obviously, but my mother and I have been distant from each other for years, and not only geographically.' She paused. 'I hope that isn't a thing, genetically.'

'I haven't met your mother, but she doesn't sound at all like you,' Lucas said. 'And I'm afraid I wasn't being nice when I said that.'

'Just a bit insensitive, perhaps.'

'At a very sensitive time.' He touched his hand to her cheek, very gently. 'Still, you know what they say about fights. And making up.'

Libby managed another smile.

'I look forward to that,' she said.

THIRTY-FIVE

M oving-out day – the first of October – was upon them, and Lucas was leaving first, not before offering, several times, to stay and help Libby.

'Reggie and Mal are both going to be here for me,' she'd told him. 'And even without Mal, Reggie's probably as strong as you.'

'Wounding, but true,' Lucas agreed.

Time now for him to go.

'You sure about this?' he asked her softly as they kissed, surrounded by crates and Harriet's carefully stacked, well-wrapped paintings – bar one, still missing.

'Not remotely sure,' Libby said.

'I'll only be up the road from you,' he said. 'I can always bring the car if you need a lift somewhere.'

Libby hesitated. She still hadn't told him of her changed plans, had thought, perhaps, that he might have wanted to join her and Beatrice, had told herself that it would be wrong to mess up his plans with his friend at so late a stage. Though maybe she really did just want some time out. Perhaps she was more like Sylvie than she'd ever thought; if she were a better person, or at least a more 'natural' daughter, she might not have felt so perfectly fine with her mother thousands of miles away.

She shut off that train of thought, decided that hopefully, when all this was over and Calla House was restored to normality, she would feel more equipped to move on wholeheartedly with their relationship.

'What?' Lucas drew away, peered into her eyes. 'Of course. Space. I forgot.'

'We'll speak,' she said. 'I'll call you.'

'Beatrice gave me her niece's number before she left.'

'Best to use my mobile, though,' Libby said, trying to sound casual, guilt clutching at her, and she didn't like this deceit, hated lying, hated liars even more, and she wondered if they could ever come back from this.

'Is lunch once or twice an option?' he asked. 'With Beatrice, of course.'

Libby smiled. 'I'd love that,' she said.

With her packing completed and a few hours still to kill before check-in time at the B & B where she had arranged to meet Beatrice, Libby decided to take Nelson for a walk to try to calm herself – and then afterwards, she decided, a dose of Beatrice's common sense and positivity would kick out the remnants of her blues. And she couldn't think of anyone she'd rather be with this evening. Except Marika, of course.

And Lucas.

And why on *earth* had she thought she needed space, when she was already missing him?

'I'm an idiot,' she said to Nelson, clipping on his lead.

Received no argument from him.

She became aware of the footsteps behind her, crunching autumn leaves, about twenty yards or so from Viaduct Pond where Nelson had, moments before, been barking at ducks.

'Nelson!' she called, and he came, more swiftly obedient than usual, and as Libby reattached his lead, she thought he seemed a little anxious, and suddenly she realized that she'd brought him very close to where the thug had attacked him and Beatrice back in June. Though they'd all believed the attacks were now safely in the past, and Lucas had walked him on the Heath several times – but then again, the crimes had always been against women alone with their dogs . . .

The footsteps were still behind her and it was hard to stop herself looking back over her shoulder, and maybe – almost certainly – they were innocent, but the tread did seem to be moving in time with hers, brisker now as if someone was mimicking her steps, and it was quieter here than usual too, no other walkers about, with or without dogs. And right now there was absolutely no one in sight ahead of her either, but East Heath Road wasn't far, so all she had to do was stay calm, keep moving . . .

Her grandmother sprang into her mind: the story of the night Harriet had been abducted by Ashcroft—

Don't think about that.

The road was getting closer, which made her feel better, and it

would be fine in a minute, had just been her imagination anyway
– again – she was sure of that.

Almost sure.

Except that the footsteps sounded closer too now, reminded her
of the old children's party game, Grandmother's Footsteps, and now
she couldn't help herself, she *had* to look, but even as she swivelled
around quickly to see, the steps were silenced and there was nobody
there, which was somehow even creepier with bushes and trees still
around, and her heart was pounding uncomfortably and Nelson was
whining.

'OK, boy,' she said softly. 'Let's go.'

She started running, as best as she could, felt her leg protest
strongly, but adrenalin pushed her on and she didn't stop until she
and the little dog, panting hard, tail wagging with excitement, had
crossed East Heath Road and were halfway up Downshire Hill with
a reassuring number of other people on the pavement and cars
moving steadily back and forth in the road.

Perfectly safe now, feeling a total fool and exhausted into the
bargain, the leg more painful than it had been in a long while, and
serve her right.

Though at least the fright had taken her mind off Lucas and the
leaving of Calla House.

And by the time she'd had a sit-down and changed her clothes,
it would almost be time to go.

A sound woke her.

Libby sat up, muzzy-headed, realized she'd fallen asleep. She
looked around, feeling disorientated because the furniture in Flat B
was all covered in dustsheets, and she'd been so tired when she'd
come in from their walk that she'd just pushed the sheet on the sofa
to one side and flopped down to rest.

The sound was Nelson – who'd been beside her when she'd sat
down.

She stood up, stretched, looked around.

'Nelson?'

He barked.

'What's up, boy?' she called.

Realized that the dog was in the outer hall, and she'd thought
she'd closed the front door when they'd come in, but it was open
now, so she must have left it ajar.

'Nelson, come.'

She heard him bark again, then whine, went out to get him.

He was at the basement door, scratching at it, not growling, his little tail wagging hard, apparently determined to get to something.

'Nelson, stop that,' Libby told him.

The dog looked up at her, barked again, then scrabbled at the base of the door with both front paws.

'All right, now get back.' She stepped between him and the door, told him to sit – an order he usually only obeyed when food was involved, and Libby wondered what was tempting him now.

Not rats, she prayed silently, opened the door and wavered.

Nelson shot through the gap and down the steps.

'Nelson, no!'

She heard a familiar sound then, knew that the dog was gobbling down something delicious.

Which left her no option but to go down after him.

She felt for the light switch, flicked it on, but it remained dark.

'All I need,' she muttered.

She stepped gingerly through the doorway. There were a few lacelike flickers of light coming from somewhere below, but they were of no use in helping her to see the steps.

'Nelson, please come,' she told him. 'I really don't want to come down there. You know what happened last time.'

Like that was going to help.

She needed a torch, but her phone had been out of charge when she'd got back, and she couldn't remember if she'd plugged it in, and with everything now packed up or covered up, she wouldn't have a clue where to look for a real torch, and she couldn't just leave Beatrice's beloved dog down there where there might be untold dangers . . .

She started down very cautiously, feeling her way, then stopped.

The builders always wore masks or even respirators and she had nothing.

'*Nelson!*' she hissed.

He was still munching on something – she dared not think what.

'You're a horrible hound.'

She reached the bottom and, peering through the dimness, saw his shape, just feet away, still tucking resolutely into something, and she would damned well tell Reggie to make sure none of the crew left their lunch packs lying around down here or anywhere else in the house.

'Oh, really, Nelson.' She bent down. 'You greedy boy.'

She fondled his ears, debating the best way to carry him safely back up the steps.

She heard something – someone – behind her and straightened up.

'Who's that?'

No one answered and it was silent again except for the dog's panting.

Not silent. Someone – human – breathing.

'Who's there?' Libby's heart began to race.

Nelson growled.

The breathing seemed to shift to her right. She turned, squinting to peer through the darkness.

'This isn't funny,' she said sharply.

Now she saw a faint shape – moving around her, behind her.

'Nelson, come on now. We're going up.' She bent back down, grasped his stocky body, lifted him.

Two strong, thickly-gloved hands snaked around her, one pinning her arms, the other choking off her windpipe. Nelson's bark was high-pitched with alarm as Libby had to let him go, terror and disbelief swamping her, and she struggled, tried to scream, but the other person was far too strong.

Libby felt the pressure on her throat intensifying.

Gave up.

At the small, pretty B & B in Eton Avenue, Beatrice, filled with pleasurable anticipation, was checking in.

'My friend, Miss Jerome, should be here presently.'

'There's tea in your room. And custard creams,' the pleasant receptionist said.

'That sounds perfect,' Beatrice said.

Libby came to with a jolt, momentary confusion followed swiftly by abject horror stampeding wildly through her chest and throat, and she tried to scream, but something was taped over her mouth.

She was seated, unable to move her arms or legs, in a small cell-like space, and in the light from a single naked bulb overhead, she saw that her ankles had been bound together with black zip ties, her wrists fastened to the arms of a chair.

Not just any chair. A wheelchair.

A very *old* wheelchair.

Frantically, her heart pounding, Libby scanned the space around her, trying to make sense of it. The walls and ceiling – the light bulb screwed into a fitting right above her – were covered with padding. A metal stool stood between the door and the wheelchair.

And less than a foot away, just to the left of the door, propped against the wall, was her grandmother's missing painting: the one of Harriet, her hair horribly cropped, tied with nylon stockings to that other ancient wheelchair.

Libby, almost too shell-shocked to register what she was seeing, became aware of something else. Around her neck. Not all the way around, for it was not long enough, but it had been sticky-taped to her skin at the nape, she thought, could feel it pulling on the hairs there.

She could not see it, yet she knew with icy certainty what it was.

George's – Harriet's dog's – missing collar.

Libby's moan of horror was muffled by the tape over her mouth.

In the twin-bedded room in Eton Avenue, Beatrice had unpacked her small case and, waiting for Libby and Nelson to arrive, was pouring herself a cup of tea and eyeing the small dish of custard creams and shortbread biscuits.

'Lovely,' she said, contentedly.

And settled back in her chair.

THIRTY-SIX

C alla House was hushed, the strange, plastic world deserted, abandoned.

The door to the basement closed.

Down below, the only visible lights came from the outside world, daylight darting in snake-like flickers through air bricks beyond the sealed polythene enclosures.

Barely enough light – were anyone there to see – to make out the box-shaped concrete storage structure.

About six feet high, five or six feet square.

A small, closed door cut into the front.

Faint sounds coming from within.

Libby.

Her panic rose at irregular intervals, peaked horribly, then ebbed again, as she knew it had to if she was to endure this – whatever *this* was. Clearly its links travelled all the way back to Harriet and Grandpa Jack's horror story of their own struggles and survival – and they *had* survived, Libby needed to fix her constantly surging, eddying thoughts and terrors on that fact. And she would probably have been thinking of them now even if the 'Private War' painting had not been placed in here with her – especially given that she was stuck to this awful wheelchair.

Which could not – *surely* – be the actual chair, since according to Grandpa Jack's tales that one had been dumped by the murderer but must have been taken by the police as evidence.

But her grandmother's dog's collar was around her neck, she was as sure of that as she could be.

But why in God's name was the painting – why were any of these things – *here*? Had they been stolen just for this purpose? To terrify her – terrorize her?

Biggest question: who was doing this to her?

First into her mind: Mal Evans.

She didn't like him, Marika didn't trust him. Always hanging around. In the house when she'd been so mysteriously trapped in the shower room – there when he had not been scheduled to be working. He'd opened the jammed door and fixed the fuse so easily.

Her brain clicked back to the summer afternoon in the garden when the thunderstorm had struck and her crutches had been out of her reach, though Lucas had said he'd put them where she could get them easily. Maybe Evans had been in the house that day too. She had fallen asleep, hadn't she – and he could have come out, gauged the situation, seen her sleeping, seen the sky turning dark, moved the crutches just too far away.

Like a malicious child's trick. Not someone capable of doing this.

Whatever *this* was.

Only one other person was spending as much time in Calla House as the builders.

No! Not Lucas.

Fiercely, she wiped the thought from her mind, wanted to scream that denial to the rafters.

No rafters here. Just a box.

Or a cell.

Holland.

Ashcroft's son – Frederick – had gone to live in Holland.

Lucas had come here from Holland.

Coincidence, she told herself – except then she remembered a Sherlock Holmes quote about coincidences: 'The universe is rarely so lazy'.

For pity's sake, she thought frantically, she couldn't start quoting detective fiction about something as potentially devastating as this nightmare.

Irrelevant, anyway.

Not Lucas.

Not!

She remembered Mal Evans in the garden flat's living room, staring at the bombsite painting.

'She was very good,' he had said.

And just before that, when she had identified Harriet as the artist, he had said, 'Everyone knows.'

She'd thought then that he had sounded hostile.

And it was already clear that this was connected with her grandparents. And therefore – not conclusively, but what else could it be? – linked to Ashcroft. Serial killer of women.

Could Evans possibly be a descendant of the murderer?
Frederick's son, perhaps?

But Evans was more probably Welsh than Dutch . . .

Holland again.

Only one person with a link to Holland.

'Nederland,' Lucas had corrected her, then lectured her about the
Dutch government rebranding the country.

It hadn't been a lecture, she rebuked herself for the thought.
Lucas was not remotely pompous.

Not Lucas.

Panic was rising again, making it hard to breathe, and she ordered
herself to calm down. She would find out soon enough when they
– *they* – came back. Evans or maybe another of the Brownlow &
Daughter crew. And she hadn't really got to know any of Reggie's
team as well as she might have, because asbestos precautions had
made it virtually impossible to communicate with people always
wearing masks or respirators . . .

So, still Evans the most likely.

Another possibility – *impossibility* – flashed through her mind.
Marika.

Her very first tenant. Who had become, over time, a dear friend.
With a complex back story that Libby had never thought of ques-
tioning, a tale of archaeological digs in faraway places, of nervous
breakdowns, and who would invent anything so sad? And of course
Libby had not questioned it because she knew – *knew* – that Marika
was telling the truth, that she was the most honest of women . . .

But the missing photograph had been in her room.

And Marika had, out of the blue, vanished, gone. Run away.

To Peru, for a dig. Libby reminded herself of the letter.

Except who wrote letters these days?

And what if she hadn't run away or flown to Peru? What if she'd
slipped into the shadows in order to wait for this moment?

Libby shook her head violently, because that was as insane as
suspecting Lucas, and what next – *who* next? Perhaps she'd decide
that Beatrice was actually some lunatic mastermind.

If she hadn't been so terrified, so intensely in shock, she might
have laughed at herself, but she couldn't even *speak*, was lucky to
be able to breathe with this tape over her mouth.

What if whoever it was did *not* come back?

What if she had been abandoned in this bizarre cell, maybe left to die if no one came to rescue her, if no one could hear her because of the padding enclosing her. To die without knowing why. Or even *where*, come to that? She might have been moved anywhere while she was unconscious.

And how had she been rendered unconscious? Back in Harriet's time of trial, it had been chloroform, the chemist's chosen method, easy for him to come by and administer. But Libby didn't feel that she had been drugged, neither did she feel pain in her head, so she didn't think she'd been struck by a blow. Her neck hurt, and she thought she remembered pressure on her throat, so perhaps she had been squeezed into unconsciousness, partially strangled? And just the thought of that made her feel she was being choked again, and she needed to *stop* the line of thought.

As to where she was or might be, she did feel, somehow, that she was still at home, still inside Calla House – or perhaps that was just wishful thinking? Because if she was going to die, she would rather it be here, because she would at least, eventually, be found, and people would *know*, Lucas and Beatrice and Marika and Sylvie, and she would hate so much for them to be left guessing . . .

The one responsible for this wouldn't need to guess.

She remembered hearing, either from Reggie or Evans, that a structure had been erected in the basement as a temporary storeroom, and she hadn't gone down to look, it had been against the rules, and anyway, after her accident, and even before that, she'd come below only out of necessity because she'd never liked basements or cellars, had always preferred buses to the tube, had always hated it when her Northern Line train had stopped for a while – presumably at a red light or for some other innocent reason – and people in the carriage had always gone a bit quieter, emphasizing unspoken unease, or maybe that was just her, and she'd thought what if the lights went out? And then a train had come in the opposite direction, flashing past, so close, much too close, and her heart had sped up, but then moments later, their train had begun to move, and she had always felt stupid, wanted to smile at her fellow passengers to share her relief, but that would have been embarrassing.

Libby dragged herself back to her predicament.

Probably this cell was that 'structure' – though surely this wasn't big enough to store anything much.

Maybe it was simply big enough to store *her*.

Maybe it was her coffin.

Too morbid.

She was letting her thoughts grow wilder, madder, and she forced herself again to bring them under control, told herself that she was *not* going to die, whether or not her captor came back. Because she would, of course, be missed. By Beatrice, primarily, who would already be wanting to know where she was. Though Libby didn't know what time it was, had not been wearing her watch when she'd been woken by Nelson out in the hall scratching at the damn basement door.

When she had so *idiotically* gone downstairs after him.

She suddenly realized that she hadn't thought about Nelson or what had happened to him. At least he wasn't trapped in here with her – but what if the bait he'd been tempted with, the food he'd been devouring at the base of the steps – what if that had been poisoned?

She heard her own whimper behind the tape.

She couldn't hear him barking, but she looked again at the padded, more than likely soundproofed, structure – 'structure' a nicer description than *cell* or even box, certainly better than coffin – and realized that if it had been made to stop anyone hearing her scream – if she ever had the chance – then maybe poor Nelson was still nearby barking his head off.

He was probably in the flat, she tried to reassure herself, shut in but safe – and the idea that someone might have harmed that sweet animal was intolerable, and rage rose and, parallel with that, fear, for Nelson as well as for herself.

She thought about Beatrice and how much time might have passed since she had been scheduled to meet her at the B & B, thought about what that remarkable old person might do to try to find out where she was; hoped that Beatrice would not decide to come here to find out, would not put herself in danger.

If 'here' was Calla House.

Another name sprang abruptly into her mind – another suspect dragged into Libby's mad frame. Mack Kennedy, the disgruntled former tenant of Flat B, the garden flat that he had seemed to enjoy before the asbestos scare. Maybe he was far angrier than she had known when he had moved out – maybe this was his idea of punishment for her – maybe he was a complete psychopath, had been in their midst for years, never exposed . . .

That, she knew, truly *was* ridiculous.

She remembered her walk with Nelson earlier, the footsteps behind them seeming to mimic hers, wondered suddenly if that really *had* been pure funk on her part or if perhaps that had also been a deliberate ploy to throw her off-balance. And maybe it had been the same person who had attacked Beatrice and Nelson in June – though that made no sense at all given the other attacks going on at the time.

But how often had she said that lately? 'Makes no sense.' When the photograph had gone missing, and then the collar and then the painting. And then the photo had shown up amongst Marika's things, and however wild her current imaginings, she could *not* picture Marika as any kind of villain. Which meant that the individual behind this must have planted it there – except, of course, if it had not been planted at all, if Marika herself had taken it and left it there to be found . . .

No sense at all.

Tears erupted suddenly, of fury as well as fear. She shook her head, did not want to cry, wanted to find a means of getting *out* of here, and the tears were making her nose stuffy, and suddenly she couldn't breathe because of the tape on her mouth, and she couldn't blow her nose, and oh God, oh God, she was going to *suffocate*.

Panic surged again, but Libby blew out through her nostrils to clear them, and the terror level lowered again.

She heard a sound. Faintly. From outside the box.

So not totally soundproof.

The light went out.

Terror soared to new record heights.

She cried out behind the gag.

Another sound.

A key in a lock.

Libby's brain clicked despite the fear. No keyhole visible on this side, but the door was locked with a key.

And what earthly use was that knowledge to her now?

In the *dark*.

The door opened, and for one instant she saw faint light from beyond – but then a flashlight was turned on – an incredibly bright, probably ultra LED beam – and she was totally blinded by it, squeezed her eyes shut for protection.

She felt a movement of air, knew that someone had entered, tried opening her eyes, had to close them again.

'Who . . .?' The word scarcely emerged from behind the tape.

She heard something being put down on the floor near her feet, felt the air move again as the person bent, then straightened, and she listened intently, trying to tell if it was a man or woman, but they were holding their breath, she thought, and she had no sense of size or proportion.

She forced her eyes open again, saw the dazzling light recede, knew that the person was backing away – and then the light went out, only the vivid imprint on her retinas remaining, and the door was shut.

And locked.

She blinked several times, afraid she'd been blinded, wondered if one could be blinded by a strong enough light?

The overhead light bulb was turned on from outside.

She was not blind.

On the floor stood a glass carafe of what looked like water.

And a loaf of bread.

Unreachable.

A means of torture, perhaps?

And yet, the door had been opened, and her tormentor had brought her bread and water, and Libby had not been able to see anything except the faint light beyond when the door had been unlocked, and though she didn't know why, she felt quite strongly that she was still in Calla House, presumably in the basement, almost certainly in the so-called storage structure.

She allowed herself a glimmer of hope.

Not just being left to die then.

She realized another thing – the closest to comfort that she had experienced till now. She would have known if that had been Lucas who'd brought the bread and water – she had learned his personal scent over the weeks of their sleeping together, making love, even showering together, she sitting on the wretched plastic chair, Lucas soaping her back and her breasts, then afterwards, drying off together . . . She knew his smell.

And that had not been Lucas.

She could have sung with joy. Until shame barrelled into the joy, for how could she, even for one second, have allowed herself to suspect him? And then, following the shame, came a terrible bleakness, because the door had been locked again and she was entirely alone, and most probably no one but her captor knew that she was here.

She tried to recall whether Mal Evans had a personal scent.

Made herself return to the afternoon when he'd saved her from the dark shower room. He had brushed close to her, she remembered, when he'd had to pass her to pick up her crutches and hand them to her.

She had no recollection of his smell, good or bad. There had been no body odour, she would have remembered that; probably just the general whiff of the building works that they had been living with for so long that they had become scarcely noticeable – sawdust, plastic, soldering, chemicals . . .

She had not noticed any trace of that just now.

Her vision restored to normal, she noticed something else.

A piece of paper taped to the carafe. A note.

She had to strain her eyes to read the writing.

Black handwritten capital letters on a small sheet of white paper.

CAUTION. FLOOR IS ASBESTOS.
PROBABLY BEST NOT TO SPILL WATER.

Fresh alarm struck, followed by the realization that whoever was behind this was playing a game with her. Vicious, sick and perhaps ultimately deadly, but there was a sardonic kind of humour behind it.

Another realization. The person who had put her in here, who had brought in the bread and water and note, might not be the one behind the game. That person might have employed someone or several people to carry out their instructions.

Anger hit her hard again, almost blotting out the fear.

And then a huge wave of fatigue came, forceful as a vast rolling wave, and suddenly all she wanted to do was *sleep*, and she understood that this new desire was probably a survival mechanism, her brain telling her to shut down, even for a short while, to give her a better chance of regrouping, gathering her strength, perhaps her intelligence, to give her some prospect of getting out of this nightmare.

Libby closed her eyes again.

And slept.

THIRTY-SEVEN

In the bedroom at the B & B, Beatrice looked for a number in her small, age-scuffed leather-bound address book. Finding it, she went to the telephone on her night-table and dialled.

Inside Flat B in Calla House, Libby's mobile, charged now, but abandoned by her when Nelson's barking had woken her earlier, began to ring.

No one to answer it.

Not even to hear it.

Not even a dog.

Down below, in the almost total darkness of the basement, the ring tone sounded distant.

Inside the box, it was completely inaudible.

Libby slept on.

Until another sound woke her.

Key in lock again.

Libby steeled herself.

The door began to open.

A voice.

Familiar.

'Sorry about the wait.'

The door opened fully.

Reggie entered.

Stooping to pass through the frame.

Reggie Brownlow.

Wearing coveralls and a surgical mask.

Reggie!

She sat down on the stool, leaving the door open behind her.

Darkness beyond.

'Bit of a shock for you,' Reggie said.

Libby felt as if her world had tilted. Registered, numbly, that she was truly seeing this woman for the first time.

Reggie Brownlow. 'Daughter' of the previous Brownlow, the builder, as posted on her van and letterhead.

A complete stranger.

At least now she knew.

'First things first,' Reggie said. 'This little room. Concrete and steel externally. Internally, walls and ceiling as well as the floor all padded with asbestos fibres. As you may or may not have guessed. Your very own Calla House asbestos, found by me years ago. Well-sealed, it could have been left alone, presented no risk to anyone.'

Libby stared, not sure what she would say if she could speak.

'The minute I found it, though, I knew it was perfect.' Reggie's eyes were smiling, and Libby noticed for the first time that they were light brown, one iris slightly flecked, and she knew that she had never looked that closely at her, because why should she have looked into her builder's eyes?

'I rigged the chimney pot,' the stranger went on, 'and after that it was pretty plain sailing. By the way' – she interrupted herself – 'in case you're worrying about being late for Beatrice, I left a message on her niece's phone saying you've been called away, won't be staying with her after all.'

Libby managed – she hoped – to blank out that instant glimmer of optimism, and then her captor leaned forward and ripped the tape from her mouth, and it stung, but the relief was immense. Libby sucked in air, stared hard at Reggie for another moment, then said the word uppermost in her mind.

'*Why?*'

Inside Flat B, Libby's mobile began to ring again.

Inside the concrete box, with the door open, it was muffled, but audible.

'Now you hear it.' Reggie stood, stooping again, and closed the door, cutting off the sound. 'Now you don't.' She opened the door again as the ringing stopped. 'Never mind.' She sat. 'If it's important, they'll call back.'

'It's probably Lucas,' Libby said.

'If it is,' Reggie said, 'he'll assume you've gone to Beatrice's niece.'

'That wouldn't stop me answering my mobile.'

Reggie shrugged and returned to Libby's question.

'You asked me "why"?' She looked at Harriet's painting. 'Doesn't that give you a clue?'

Something in Libby toughened up a little.

'Either tell me or don't,' she said.

'It's a long story,' Reggie said, 'but I'll edit it where I can.'

'Could you release these ties first?' Libby said. 'My arms are numb.'

Reggie ignored her. 'I've mentioned my father to you in the past. Frederick Brownlow. All this, though, is as much about his father as it is about my dad.' She paused. 'My grandfather's name was Ashcroft,' she said. 'Alfred Reginald Ashcroft.'

So Libby had been on track trying to research Frederick – not that it had got her anywhere. Holland just a coincidence after all. Nothing whatsoever to do with Lucas. Of course.

'Perhaps you've already guessed that.' Reggie looked at the painting, then the wheelchair. 'I gave you enough clues.'

At the B & B, Beatrice was looking for another number, momentarily vexed with herself for her stubbornness over mobile telephones, because if she had one now she would perhaps decide to send one of those annoying text messages. She did *know* about such things, was not at all helpless with computerization, indeed found many technological advances fascinating, but she simply refused to be ruled by an electronic device.

Though it might, she supposed, have proven convenient now.

She found the number.

Inside the concrete box, its door still open, the new ringing from above had a different tone, fainter than the last. Lucas's landline. Libby knew its sound intimately, associated it with cosy suppers and the essential oils of soothing massages during her recovery – and *why* in God's name had she pushed for this separation? Might this call be from Beatrice, perhaps trying to find her in Lucas's flat, though she doubted if her friend even *had* Lucas's number . . .

'Frederick – his father called him Freddy' – Reggie was telling her tale – 'was the only person in the family who stayed loyal to his dad. Emily, Alfred's wife, my dear, cold-hearted bitch of a grandmother, had turned her back on him long before his arrest, but after the trial, with the help of her father, who despised my grandfather, she changed her name to Brownlow and, after the war, moved with Freddy and his sister, to the seaside.' She paused. 'You already know that my grandfather killed himself before they could hang him. Stole bleach from the prison laundry and drank it. My dad was just a child when it happened. Younger than Alfred when he found his mother's body hanging and his monster of a father with half his head blown away by his own gun. Young, but old enough to understand grief and injustice.'

'That's all awful, and terrible for your father,' Libby said, 'but Ashcroft became a murderer.'

Reggie ignored her. 'Freddy grew up hating his family and England, so when he was old enough, he went to Holland, hoping for more liberal attitudes. He'd abandoned his education, took the only work he could get, labouring, met my mother, Anna. Who turned out to be another narrow-minded bitch. She found out about her father-in-law two years after I was born, and dumped us both.'

'I'm sorry,' Libby said.

'Really?' Reggie said. 'We came back to the UK. Not much choice.'

'I am sorry,' Libby said, 'for your father. It must have been incredibly painful for him. But I don't understand what this has to do with me. Why you're doing this to *me*.'

'Old sins come to visit you, Libby,' Reggie answered. 'Very unfair, I know. But life is fucking unfair. And someone has to pay.'

Beatrice had come down to the small reception desk, asking if they'd heard from Miss Jerome.

'Only I was rather expecting her to be here by now.'

There had been no call or message.

'That's very out of character,' Beatrice said.

And asked for a taxi.

'We lived in a flat in Palmers Green,' Reggie told Libby. 'Dad cooked for me, took me to school and picked me up every day, told my teachers and other kids' mums that Anna was dead, and they were nice to us. He found work with a big building firm, then took out a bank loan and set up on his own. All my dad wanted me to do was study hard and enjoy life. And to trust only him.'

Libby shifted in the wheelchair, trying to get more comfortable.

'I wouldn't do that,' Reggie said. 'Every time the wheels move, they disturb the asbestos on the floor.'

'Christ, Reggie,' Libby burst. 'This is mad.'

'Maybe,' Reggie said.

'Then can't we stop—'

'When my dad thought I was old enough, he told me about my grandfather and what he'd done. It was bad, he said, of course it was. But he knew what Alfred had been up against his whole life because he'd written a kind of history – on scraps of paper, sometimes – while he was in prison, waiting for trial, and he'd given it to his solicitor to give to his son. Only to Freddy, no one else. And the solicitor carried out his instruction when my dad tried to find out if he could visit his father's grave – which he couldn't, because it was unmarked and in the grounds of Pentonville and relatives weren't allowed to visit. Which my dad felt was very cruel, whatever he'd done. He also said that when you considered Alfred's whole story, on balance he'd been more sinned against than sinful.'

'Did you believe that?' Libby asked. 'Do you, even now?'

'He was mad when he killed those women,' Reggie said. 'He admitted it himself, but he said he'd been driven to it over time. He wrote that he'd had an ability to compartmentalize his life, which was how he was able to continue his work as a pharmacist. The part that kept him sane enough for a long time, to pay his bills and stick two fingers up to his wife and his father-in-law.'

'My grandmother said he was obsessed with red hair,' Libby said.

'He was always looking for his lost mother, my dad told me.'

'That's really sad,' she said.

'Harriet was bloody lucky he didn't kill her,' Reggie said. 'And if he could see you, he'd probably have gone after you too.'

Libby didn't answer. Safer, she thought, not to, in this bizarre nightmare of a situation, in the midst of this surreal conversation. Nor did she want to say anything to stop Reggie Brownlow's flow, because the door of the cell was open, which meant there might be hope of rescue if Lucas came looking for her – though why would he when he believed she was safely ensconced at Beatrice's niece's home? But perhaps Mal Evans might come to work, might come down to the basement, might see what was going on. Unless Evans was in league with Reggie, which was still a possibility, given how many years they'd worked together.

'It was other people, my dad said – and I believed him – who screwed Alfred up. Fucked with his mind till he couldn't take any more.' She took a breath. 'Think of it from my dad's – his kid's – point of view.'

'It must have been ghastly for him,' Libby said.

'Understatement,' Reggie said. 'Fucking understatement.'

'But at least your father had you. He must have loved having you working with him.'

'He hated it. He wanted me to achieve the things he couldn't. Alfred had been a pharmacist, but Freddy wanted more for me, he wanted me to be a doctor at least, wanted me to be respected. But all I wanted to do was work with him. I was strong and I loved building sites. I loved watching brickies building walls, watching scaffolding being put up – listening to it all, the hammering and drilling and singing and cursing and banter – seeing houses grow up out of foundations. I loved learning how to fix things. So we compromised. I got a degree in engineering, which helped my dad's business. We got bigger contracts, employed a bigger workforce – we did bloody well for a long time.'

In Eton Avenue, Beatrice climbed into the Uber that the receptionist had organized for her on her own mobile, the cost to be added to Beatrice's bill, and it was no problem at all, the young woman said, suggesting that she borrow her umbrella as it was raining rather hard, and it warmed Beatrice that people could still be so thoughtful when you needed a little help.

'So what went wrong?' Libby asked, knowing that she did now need to ask questions, to keep Reggie talking, keep the door of this box open.

Besides, she *wanted* to know what had happened to sever this woman she'd thought she had known, this *stranger*, from so much promise; she wanted to listen, maybe even understand, if that was remotely possible, because maybe that would help get her out of here.

'My mother – dear Anna –' Reggie's mouth twisted with scorn – 'came crawling out of the woodwork and held my dad to ransom. Freddy had everything, she said: the firm, money, a good name – and me. She wanted twenty fucking years of backdated maintenance or else she was going to tell our clients, the bank, our colleagues, our workers, all about his father and see what that did to our business.'

Libby felt her heartbeat accelerating again, because this tale seemed to be nearing some kind of climax, and she needed it *not* to end, not before someone came to save her.

'I watched the strain making him ill,' Reggie said. 'If I'd been in his place, I think I might have killed the bitch, but he didn't. He was too good, too decent. He gave her as much as he could reasonably manage, but Anna wanted more, or else. And of course, it wasn't his own good name my dad was afraid for. It was mine.'

The Uber driver told Beatrice there had been an accident near Swiss Cottage tube, turning the already busy rush-hour traffic into total gridlock, the heavy rain and an increasingly blustery wind not helping.

'Our firm, as it was, went under,' Reggie said. 'My dad believed he'd ruined my life. I tried everything to put his mind at rest, reminded him that I was a bloody good builder and that I'd never been scared of hard graft. So long as I had him, I said. But all his strength was gone.' She paused. 'He took rat poison, died as his father had, in agony.'

'Oh my God.' Libby felt true shock. 'I'm so sorry.'

'Not good enough, Libby. Not nearly good enough.'

'I don't know what else to say.'

'That's not all.' Reggie's eyes were steady on hers. 'When he died, I was pregnant.'

Libby was silent.

'I found his body.'

'God.' A whisper.

'The horror killed my baby.' Reggie paused again. 'Our baby.'

She kept watching Libby's face, her own expression blank now.

'That's right,' she said. 'His and mine.'

The Uber finally turned into Belsize Avenue and, a two-pound coin in her gloved right hand, Beatrice checked that her handbag was closed, placed it on her lap, expressed sympathy to the driver, saying she could imagine how stressful this kind of driving must be, and readied herself for arrival.

'Don't know what to say, do you?' Reggie said. 'Too scandalized. Probably thinking "poor Reggie", abusive bastard dad, and just as well the baby didn't make it.'

'I'm not thinking anything like—'

'Shut up,' Reggie said.

'Right,' Libby said quietly.

'I wanted the baby. It was all I had left of him.'

Libby shut her eyes.

'Don't do that.'

Libby opened them again, stayed silent.

'You don't really get it at all, do you?' Reggie said. 'You don't get that he loved me, really, truly loved me. That it was never disgusting. That there was nothing wrong with it. It was perfect. Pure.'

Libby's exhalation slipped out before she could stop it.

'Don't you dare,' Reggie said. 'Don't you *dare* judge him.'

'I'm not judging anyone,' Libby said.

'He loved me, and I loved him, and I always knew he was right, that I could never trust anyone else, that as long as I was with him there was no danger, no risk of being hurt or betrayed.'

Libby waited, not daring to speak.

'People use words like abuse, *incest*, load them with righteous disgust, like they're spitting out dung, even when they're completely ignorant of how it can be. Freddy knew all about betrayal, so he wanted me to know how beautiful love could be with someone who'd never let me down.' Her eyes filled. 'And then he was gone. And then our baby was gone, too.'

'I am sorry,' Libby said again. 'Reggie, I'm—'

'I am Regina Brownlow, daughter of Frederick Brownlow, and very proud of that.' Reggie was trembling. 'Granddaughter of Alfred Reginald Ashcroft, and not stupid or unrealistic enough to be entirely proud of *that*. But my father was.'

'I think I can understand—'

'I don't give a fuck what you understand. My father was everything in the world to me, and I was all that mattered to him. So what he wanted is what I want. And what Freddy wanted most was revenge for his father.'

Running out of time, Libby sensed suddenly.

'What happened to Alfred Ashcroft was not Harriet's fault,' she said. 'Nor what happened to your father, however much of a tragedy.'

'But without Harriet and Jack,' Reggie said, 'my grandfather might have stood a chance. He might have stopped, might have been helped.'

'He *killed* all those women.' A burst of anger fuelled Libby's courage. 'He plucked them off the street and murdered them because of their *hair*. And I realize how terrible that and what happened after must have been for his son, but you must know, Reggie, you *must*, that none of that's down to my family.'

The Uber pulled up outside Calla House, behind the Brownlow & Daughter van. The rain was heavier, the wind heightening, and the driver got out to help Beatrice.

'And anyway, Harriet and Jack are both long gone,' Libby said.

'After their long, happy, respectable lives,' Reggie said.

Libby stayed silent again.

'This must be tough for you to take in, Libby. Good old, down-to-earth Reggie, obsessed with revenge? Not really her style, is it? Not Reggie Brownlow. Good old dependable, turn-her-hand-to-anything, no-home-life-of-her-own-so-we-can-always-call-on-her Reggie.'

'I've never taken you for granted,' Libby said.

'Perish the thought,' Reggie said. 'You're too fucking well-mannered to do that.'

'Then clearly,' Libby said, 'I can't win.'

'You're complacent, Elizabeth Jerome,' Reggie went on. 'At least your mother chose to move on, leave the past behind, but not you, still smugly holding Grandma Harriet up as some kind of heroine. Her precious house – and isn't it *wonderful* that a family can go on living in the same home for generations?'

'God, Reggie,' Libby said, overwhelmed by so much bitterness.

'Harriet's paintings – not much better than your cartoons, a bloody comic strip, but "so clever", they all said at the art gallery, while you preened in your quiet, well-dragged-up way. And then one afternoon, Mal heard you talking so blithely about how the murderer had drunk bleach, and I think you said that Harriet – who'd testified against him in court, who'd heard him being sentenced to be hanged by the neck until he was dead – that she thought he was probably looking for the most self-destructive kind of punishment – and wasn't Grandma compassionate to think—'

'What have you done to Nelson?' Libby's question cut through the rant like a slap. 'I'm sorry,' she said, 'but I can't listen to this any longer, and I can't do anything about Alfred Ashcroft or your

father, and if you want to kill me because of them, I can't really
stop you, but I do want to know why Nelson's stopped barking.'

'He's fine,' Reggie told her. 'You don't have to worry about him.'

'Was it you?' Libby asked. 'This afternoon, on the Heath?'

A hint of a smile lit Reggie's eyes. 'I hadn't planned that, but
you decided to go walking, and I found I couldn't resist a little
appetizer.'

'And back in May? Did you do that to Nelson, to Beatrice?'

'Of course not.' Indignant now. 'I've nothing against the animal
– he's a nice little chap – certainly nothing against Beatrice. Except
perhaps the patronizing way she admired my beautiful dress at the
gallery.'

How the slights, real or imagined, must have piled up over time,
Libby thought. Then looked over at the painting, then back down
at the terrible old chair she was pinioned to. 'What about this chair?
This can't be the one—'

'It can,' Reggie said. 'It wasn't a weapon as such, more part of
a crime scene, I suppose, so after the judicial stuff was over, it was
returned to the family. My father said Emily wanted shot of it but
didn't know how, and her father said she should dump it in the
garden shed until he got around to getting rid of it. But one day,
when she found Freddy trying to polish it, she tied him to it with
string and left him there all night. So much for Emily Brownlow
being better than my grandfather.'

From above, muffled but unmistakable, came the sound of Calla
House's front door bell.

Reggie stood quickly, took a roll of sticky tape from a pocket,
tore off a strip. Libby saw what was coming, fought to evade her,
but Reggie slapped the tape across her mouth, stooped, went out
through the door, closed and locked it.

The light bulb went out.

'No!' Libby protested through the gag.

Not so much as a sliver of light visible now.

Her panic soared.

THIRTY-EIGHT

On the doorstep of Calla House, Beatrice, clinging to the receptionist's umbrella with one hand and being pushed sideways by the gale, finally found the key which had slipped down into the depths of her handbag, inserted it into the lock and—

The door opened before she'd turned it, Reggie there, smiling an apology, her surgical face mask around her neck.

'Sorry I took so long,' she said. 'I was upstairs.'

'My fault for troubling you.' Beatrice stepped inside, shut the door behind her, leaned the soaking umbrella in the corner. 'I know you didn't want us coming back, and I did ring twice, but—'

'Why are you here, Beatrice?' Mild, polite reproach in her tone.

'Is Elizabeth still here by any chance?'

'She left a long while ago,' Reggie said. 'She was in a rush, so she asked me to leave a message for you on your niece's phone.'

Beatrice frowned. 'I haven't been at my niece's. What was the message?'

'I was to let you know that Marika had called,' Reggie said. 'She has a big problem, apparently, something she needed help with urgently. Which was why Libby asked me to call you.' She saw Beatrice's frown become confusion, added, 'She had no time to call you herself.'

'Elizabeth asked you to call me at my niece's?' Beatrice asked.

'Yes,' Reggie said patiently.

'And when was this?' Beatrice asked.

'Quite a while ago.' Reggie paused. 'Problem?'

'Only that . . .' Beatrice changed her mind. 'Never mind.'

Reggie took a step forward, placed herself between the old lady and the door. 'What were you going to say, Beatrice?'

'It wasn't important.' Beatrice felt unaccountably uneasy.

'Humour me,' Reggie said. 'What was it?'

'Only that I thought Libby and I were going to spend a few nights at a B & B, but clearly I've got the wrong end of the stick. Must be getting scatty in my old age.'

'Nothing scatty about you, Beatrice.'

'Still,' Beatrice said, 'if she's not here, I'd better be going.'

'No,' Reggie said. 'I don't think so.' She leaned forward, pulled Beatrice's bag from her hand and dropped it on the floor. 'You won't be needing that.'

'Whatever are you doing?' Beatrice stooped to pick up the bag, but Reggie kicked it away.

'I'm sorry about this, Beatrice.' She took her arm. 'I really am.'

'Reggie, what is this? Let go of me.'

'Nothing for you to worry about.' Reggie pulled Beatrice towards the staircase. 'Come on.'

'You said we weren't supposed to *be* here.'

Reggie didn't bother answering, just pushed Beatrice ahead of her up the stairs and into Flat C, her own flat, the door propped open, the polythene walls shifting with the movement of air as the women passed, rustling as Reggie propelled the old woman to the sofa.

'Let *go* of me,' Beatrice said again.

Reggie gripped her arm harder with one hand, used the other to strip plastic off the sofa. 'Least I can do, make you comfy while you wait.'

'Wait for what?' Beatrice tried to struggle free. 'You're *hurting* me. I don't understand. What about the asbestos?'

'Don't worry about that. Just sit down and be quiet.'

'I will *not*!'

Reggie shoved her down, hard. 'I don't want to hurt you, Beatrice.'

'Then let go of my arm,' Beatrice said angrily.

'Will you sit still if I do?'

'Certainly not.'

With her free hand, Reggie pulled the roll of silver sticky tape from her pocket, and Beatrice's eyes widened with fear. Reggie let go of her arm and Beatrice scrambled to her feet, but Reggie was too fast, too strong, and in seconds Beatrice was back on the sofa, hands taped together on her lap, Reggie starting on her ankles.

'What on earth is happening? Where's Elizabeth?' Beatrice demanded. 'What have you done to her? And where is Nelson?'

One floor down the front door banged, and Beatrice opened her mouth to shout, but Reggie covered it with her hand, slapped more tape over it, and was swiftly out of the flat, quietly closing Flat C's door behind her.

'Reggie?' Mal Evans called from the hall. 'Reg, you up there?'

'I thought you weren't coming in,' Reggie said on her way down.

'Football was cancelled,' Mal said. 'Thought you could use a hand.'

Reggie walked through the hall, moved smoothly between him and Beatrice's handbag and yawned. 'I'm just about done for the day. Wasted journey, but kind thought, Mal.'

'No biggie,' he said.

Down in her pitch-black concrete cell, Libby's panic had morphed again into rage, and she was making blind but furious attempts to free herself – and then the wheelchair jolted, and she thought she heard it knock against the carafe and held her breath, praying she wouldn't topple over on to the asbestos floor.

The chair righted itself.

Libby stopped struggling.

Panic surged again.

Then gave way to despair.

'See you Monday.'

Out in the road, Reggie waved Mal off, then went back inside, double-locked and bolted the door, picked up the umbrella and handbag and, grim-faced, started back up the stairs and into Beatrice's flat.

'I really am sorry, Bea.' She checked the bag for a phone, then dumped it and the brolly on the floor, then, quite gently, tucked two cushions behind her back. 'This is just temporary. There's no question you'll be found quite soon.'

Beatrice's eyes implored her. To no avail.

'And just so you know,' Reggie added, 'your landline's been disabled, so no point even thinking of trying to reach it.'

She left again.

Returned to the basement.

To the job in hand.

In Tom Brent's irritatingly untidy flat off the Edgware Road, Lucas, alone and unable to settle down to his overdue paperwork or anything remotely more satisfying, and growing fed up with getting voicemail on Libby's phone, looked up another number in his contacts. And called it.

The light bulb came on just before the door was unlocked, and

Libby's eyes squeezed shut for an instant before Reggie entered and peeled the tape off her mouth again.

'Sorry,' she said from behind her mask. 'I forgot you said you weren't keen on the dark.'

'Did I say that?' Libby asked.

'You told Mal. The day you got yourself stuck in the shower.'

'He told you about that.'

'Mal tells me most things.' Reggie looked down at the carafe. 'Water?'

'Who was at the door?' Libby asked.

'The man himself. Mal.' Reggie paused. 'He's gone.'

'Does he know about this?'

'No one knows.'

'How've you kept it from them all? This thing, this *cell*, they must have seen it.'

'Obviously,' Reggie said. 'But take away the padding and all this –' she looked at the painting, gestured at the wheelchair – 'and all you have is a storeroom. In plain sight, best way to hide something big.' She shrugged. 'Anyway, they're my team, they do what I tell them. I'm a good boss.'

She sat down on the stool, turned her head to the right and left and right again, easing away her tension.

'Beatrice came too, before Mal,' she said. 'You neglected to mention that you were both going to a B & B.'

It felt like a punch to her stomach. 'Where is she?' Libby asked.

'I got rid of her.'

'What do you mean?'

Reggie's eyes smiled coldly.

'What have you *done* to her?' Libby lost it, went a little crazy, thrashed in the wheelchair, straining against the zip ties while Reggie watched dispassionately.

Libby stopped, breathless, heart pounding.

'You really want to be careful,' Reggie said. 'You don't want to knock that water over, not with asbestos on the floor.' She smiled again. 'And, by the way, there's just a touch of ground calla lily in that bread. I remember you mentioning once that the roots are the most toxic part.'

Libby stared down at the loaf.

'I don't believe you.'

Reggie shrugged. 'Your choice.'

'So Mrs Newby's moved to this flat in West End Lane?' Lucas double-checked with Beatrice's niece's au pair. 'Do you know if her friend Libby – Mrs Newby calls her Elizabeth – is with her?'

The young woman had no idea.

But at least now Lucas had an address.

Something, he felt, was distinctly off, unless he was just ruffled because Libby hadn't been straight with him about the change of plan. Which meant that they still weren't back on track.

He considered doing nothing, just waiting for her to get in touch.

Waiting was something he'd never been much good at.

'Couple of things, before I leave you,' Reggie said, and took her phone from a pocket. 'I should take a photo, shouldn't I? For posterity. My grandfather took photos, didn't he.'

She set the camera to flash, briefly blinded Libby again.

'Another unlucky redhead.'

She checked the image, nodded, put the phone back in her pocket.

'And now, to give you a sporting chance.'

She took a penknife from another pocket, opened it and placed it in Libby's right hand, curled her fingers around the handle.

'If you're careful, you might find a way to cut yourself loose.'

'Sure,' Libby said, the word hate-filled.

'Bit too difficult?' Reggie said. 'Maybe you're right.'

She took back the knife, sliced deftly through the zip tie binding Libby's left wrist to the wheelchair's arm, then placed the penknife on the floor and watched Libby flex her numb fingers.

'You're a resourceful woman,' she said. 'Given enough time, you'll probably get yourself out of the chair. Which means you'll be able to eat the bread and drink the water.'

'Poisoned bread.'

Reggie stood up, stooped, went out for a moment, hit a switch somewhere in the dark.

Another light came on – very bright, but not dazzling Libby.

A spotlight directed on something behind her.

Reggie came back, sat down again.

'Can you swivel yourself around a bit? Take a look.'

It was to Libby's left. A long, bulky, black plastic-wrapped package.

'You might want to use the knife to cut that open. Though you might be wiser not to. It depends on your level of curiosity. Harriet seems to have been a very curious woman.'

'Harriet did not seek out your grandfather,' Libby said.

Reggie ignored her.

'The knife,' she said, 'won't actually help you get out of here, if that's what you're hoping. Firstly, cutting through asbestos is a very bad idea, as you'll know from all the bumf we gave you early on. Besides which, remember, the walls and ceiling under the padding are concrete and steel.'

Lucas exited West Hampstead tube station, checked the address again on his phone – which rang, startling him, and it was Alison Keyes, the niece, saying that since Lucas had called looking for her aunt, she felt she ought to pass on a rather odd voicemail that had been left for Beatrice by the builder working on her aunt's home.

'Something about Marika needing Libby's help,' the niece said. 'In case you speak to Aunt Beatrice or Elizabeth before I do.'

Lucas thanked her, then tried Libby again.

Straight to voicemail.

Frustrated, he left another message. 'What's going on, Libby? I heard about Marika – just please tell me you're not going to Peru without so much as a conversation. All this mystery's driving me crazy.'

Reaching the address he'd been given for Beatrice's rental flat, there was no response to his buzzing. Lucas took a look in the bar below, could not picture the elegant octogenarian in there, wondered where she and Libby might have gone.

They could, of course, just be out together, shopping, having tea.

But something seemed more than *off* to him now. Something felt wrong. Unsettling.

'Of course,' Reggie went on, 'there is another way you could make use of the knife. If you decide you can't take any more. But suicide's not really you, is it?'

'Sorry to disappoint,' Libby said, her mouth very dry.

'Chances are, anyway, that you'll be found long before you starve or die of thirst – even if you decide not to trust the bread or water.'

'They're going to catch you,' Libby said.

'I'd say that's a given,' Reggie agreed.

'Then *why*?'

'You know why.'

'Your father wouldn't have wanted you to go to prison,' Libby said.

'Maybe not, but if I have to . . .' She paused. 'I found his body, Libby. I miscarried our child.'

'Yes,' Libby said. 'And I'm desperately sorry for you about that, but if you accept that I will be found and that you will be caught, arrested, imprisoned, then what is the *point* of this?'

'Haven't you got it yet?' Reggie asked.

Upstairs, Beatrice had managed to struggle to her feet.

With no telephone, she needed to reach the door, hopping the only way – not really the thing for old knees – and *all* she needed now was a broken hip, but needs must, except that even shoving at the handle with her taped-up wrists didn't work, because of course Reggie had locked it from the outside.

A groan of frustration escaped her, and she hopped back to the couch, sank down, exhausted, then raised her bound wrists to start trying to get rid of the damnable tape over her mouth.

Though even if she succeeded, she wasn't at all sure that calling for help would not just bring a seriously angry Reggie to deal with her.

And that seemed a very bad idea.

'All they can do to me is lock me up,' Reggie said. 'But your sentence is going to be longer and probably harder.'

And finally Libby *did* get it.

'The asbestos,' she said.

'You're inhaling fibres as we speak,' Reggie said. 'A minor hazard for now, or else I'd be wearing a real respirator.'

'But once I cut myself loose . . .' Libby let the sentence trail away.

Reggie's eyes smiled again. 'Every move you make, you'll disturb more fibres. When you eat the bread, lily roots or not, or drink the water, you'll probably digest the fibres in the air.'

'You wicked bitch,' Libby said softly, incredulously.

'You may stay healthy for years. You may decide to have regular check-ups, or you may choose to try to forget about it. But any time you get a bad cough or get a bit breathless or feel a bit shitty, you'll remember. And then there'll be no escaping it.'

*   *   *

Libby's mobile was ringing out again. Walking back into West Hampstead tube, Lucas gave up on leaving messages, sent a brief, urgent text instead, then turned and went back outside to look for a taxi, wishing now he'd brought his car, but it had started raining again, the wind coming in great gusts, and traffic was crawling, his sense of things not being right growing more intense.

He had tried Reggie's number twice and that had gone to voice-mail too – but since it seemed to have been she who'd passed Libby's message to Alison, she had to be the person to ask. So he was going to head back to Calla House, ignoring Reggie's and Evans's rule of no-return.

Suddenly, Lucas was filled with an immense sense of urgency.

No taxis in sight. No Uber available.

He hustled back into the station.

'I don't understand,' Libby said, 'how you can turn actual, incontrovertible history on its head this way. Totally ignore the wicked things your grandfather did.'

'Killing isn't as terrible as you probably think it is,' Reggie said. 'It's actually much easier than you'd imagine.'

Libby absorbed those words, their meaning, the potential horror behind them. Had to force out the question suddenly exploding in her mind.

'Beatrice?' It was a whisper.

'No,' Reggie answered. 'Not Beatrice.'

And her eyes flicked, swiftly, to the black plastic bag on the floor, then back to Libby.

Lucas's Oyster card was playing up.

'Fuck,' he said.

Leaves and litter swirled around his feet in the wind.

At last the card obliged and he moved on.

Things flying back into his mind as he went. *Wrong* things.

Like Libby's missing possessions: the old photograph and the dog's collar and the painting. Like the photo turning up in Marika's room.

Wrong.

'You haven't asked,' Reggie said, eyes on the black bag again, 'what's in there?' She paused. 'Best not to, perhaps.'

She stood. Stooping again.

'You really are insane,' Libby said.

'Quite possibly,' Reggie said, reasonably.

Libby watched her turning away.

Last chance.

'Your father,' she said.

Reggie stopped.

'Did he know about the baby?'

Reggie turned back. 'Yes, he knew.'

Libby took a breath.

'Then I don't believe he swallowed rat poison because of your mother's blackmail.'

'Don't you?'

Libby read the dangerous glint in Reggie's eyes, but she felt she was finally fighting back, and this was probably her final gamble, her last chance to delay being abandoned.

'I think,' she said, 'it was because of the baby.' She licked her dry lips again. 'Because of what he'd done to you.'

The glint was of real rage now, and even with the face mask, Libby thought she could see it, physically *see* it even beyond the brown part-flecked eyes, like a moving force from within, taking over, smashing down the self-control this woman must have armed herself with for many years.

'He abused you,' she pushed on. 'Your father used and abused you in the worst possible way.'

'Shut up.'

'He raped you, Reggie,' Libby said. 'You were his child. There was no pure love – he filled your head with lies, and then he *raped* you, over and over again.'

'Shut the fuck *up*.'

'And then he found out you were pregnant, and *that* was what he couldn't take, Reggie. Not just Anna's blackmail, it was his own wickedness he couldn't live with.'

'Shut your stinking mouth.'

Reggie's fist struck the side of Libby's head.

Whirled fire through her temple.

The force of the blow sent the wheelchair toppling sideways.

Reggie watched it sway, then start to tilt back, to steady itself.

She bent over and pushed it the rest of the way.

Saw Libby land, face half down on the asbestos floor.
'Eat that, bitch,' she said.
And left.

THIRTY-NINE

Beatrice had tugged the tape off her mouth a few minutes before, but the effort had worn her out, so she was only just about ready for another attempt, had got herself up on her feet again, trying to decide if she stood any chance of getting across to the window . . .

She heard the key in the lock and the door opened.

'I had a feeling you might try something daft.' Reggie moved in and gripped Beatrice's left arm. 'Don't you know how dangerous bad falls are for the elderly?'

'Where is Nelson?' Beatrice heard the fear in her own voice, hated it.

'Safe and sound,' Reggie said. 'In my van.'

Beatrice steadied herself. 'And Elizabeth?'

'Having a lie-down,' Reggie said.

Libby was conscious, still dizzy, her head throbbing violently.

Alone now, staring, from this new, oblique angle, at the locked door.

At least Reggie was gone. And she'd left the light on this time. A double relief, even if her own jeopardy had sky-rocketed.

Tears sprang to her eyes, but she willed them away, afraid that even they might present a potentially heightened risk with her mouth and one nostril right against the asbestos.

Delayed instinct moved her freed left hand up, slid it between her face and the floor. Allowed her to dare to breathe again.

Harriet's black-and-white painting was closer now, reminding her of what her grandmother would almost certainly have done in her place.

Fight.

Libby took another minute, dizziness receding, and then she lifted her head a little, searching for the knife.

Gone. Reggie had taken it. Final payback for her last *stupid* provocation.

Stupid beyond belief.

But then she saw it. Still there after all, half stuck under one of the wheels of the chair. She reached for it, not quite managing, wriggled closer, resolute, trying not to think about inhaling asbestos.

Every move you make, Reggie had said, *you'll disturb more fibres.*

No other choice available. Libby's fingers groped for the penknife, got to it, rolled it into her grasp, tried not to suck in too much air, but it was impossible and anyway, all other bets were off, and it took valuable moments for her to saw at the horrible tie attaching her right wrist to the chair's arm, cutting the skin on the front of her wrist – better than the back, but blood and asbestos? – but she *managed* it, released her arm, flexed her painful fingers, then reached up for the awful thing around her neck, fumbled for the fastening, found it, undid it.

George's old collar looked so innocent back in her hands.

Libby wanted to cry again, controlled the impulse.

Asbestos aside, weeping was a waste of precious time.

Lucas got off the train at Hampstead Heath Station and headed for the exit, still hoping that his anxieties were just a product of his imagination working overtime. That maybe, as warm as their parting had seemed to him, Libby's talk about space and time had been more seriously considered than he'd realized. Maybe that was why she hadn't phoned to tell him about Marika, maybe she simply hadn't wanted to include him.

Except that didn't really sound like Libby.

Or was that just his idealized, romantic view of her?

No. Something was wrong. She had a problem, he was sure of it.

Though maybe, even if that was true, she didn't want his help.

But like it or not, she was going to get it anyway.

Finally free of the wheelchair, Libby pulled off her T-shirt and tied it over her face, covering her nose and mouth, felt oddly exposed in just her bra, though there was no one to see, and what the fuck, anyway . . .

She looked down at the big, oddly-shaped, black plastic package.

Knelt carefully beside it, penknife in hand, suddenly even more deeply afraid.

She gathered her courage, made a first cut, found the plastic thick and hard to slit, went at it with more strength and this time pierced it.

There was more plastic beneath.

Tentatively, she touched the bundle, then jerked her hand away, breathing hard beneath the makeshift T-shirt mask, a growing sense of dread tightening her chest.

Reggie had taped over Beatrice's mouth again, released her ankles and pulled her into the bathroom.

'Get in,' she said now, standing beside the bath.

Beatrice shook her head defiantly, though behind the tape her teeth were chattering, fear and outrage getting the better of her, sending her blood pressure soaring.

'Don't make me hurt you, Beatrice.'

It was a battle the older woman stood no chance of winning. She tried to put one foot over the side of the bath, but her skirt hampered her.

'Let me help,' Reggie said and ripped the fabric.

Starting, finally, to cry, Beatrice clambered into the bath.

Lucas was walking fast in the heavy rain as he turned into Rosslyn Hill.

Not fast enough, that sick sense told him.

His Tante Mirjam had had a kind of sixth sense, used to tell him as a boy that he had it too, and he'd scoffed at her, teased her about it.

Not so sure now.

He began to run.

Libby cut into the next layer of the plastic bag.

The release of stench rocked her back so violently that she knocked over the carafe of water.

Dropping the penknife, retching, Libby bolted into the furthest corner and huddled.

Escaping into herself.

Beatrice's ankles were taped together again and her wrists fastened to the base of the hand shower in the centre of the bath as Reggie, ignoring the furious glare of her blue eyes, found a cushion, tucked it behind her back, then covered the rest of her with a blanket.

'Best I can do, I'm afraid,' Reggie said.

She closed the bathroom door, exited Beatrice's flat, locked it and pocketed the key.

Libby, weeping now, all caution abandoned, sanity threatening to shred, pulled the T-shirt off her face, used it to wipe her eyes and cheeks. Then, shaking, she crawled back to the bundle, steeled herself – and ripped it a little further open.

Enough to see a piece of fabric, its bright, ethnic design familiar.

Libby cried out in wordless horror and grief.

Marika.

In the minutes that followed, new strength was born out of bitterest anguish and rage.

Libby tied the T-shirt back over her nose and mouth, found the pieces of sticky tape that had gagged her and fastened the old dog's collar to her neck, and tried, all the time weeping inconsolably, to reseal the plastic.

'I'm sorry,' she told Marika. 'I'm so, so sorry.'

Trembling violently, she went on resealing.

And finally, when she had done all that was possible, Libby rocked back on her heels, threw back her head, and screamed:

'*Reggie!*'

FORTY

Lucas, panting, neared Calla House and slowed down.

Libby's car was still parked in a resident's bay along the road. Which meant nothing since she hadn't driven in months, and meant even less if she'd gone to catch a flight to be with Marika.

Except he didn't believe that she had.

Reggie's van was right outside the house.

Lucas took out his keys, wiped rain from his eyes.

Walked up to the front door.

Reggie was halfway down the staircase when she heard the key in the lock.

She froze for a second.

Then turned back.

The front door was double-locked. Which was strange, Lucas thought, if Reggie was working inside – though he supposed it might be a safety precaution.

No coming back till the whole job was done, Evans had told Libby and Marika. 'HSE rules.'

He removed the Yale key from the top lock, selected the Chubb.

Libby was huddled up again, as far from the black bag as she could get.

Way beyond tears now.

Shivering, she had put the damp T-shirt back on over her bra.

Other than that instinctive bit of self-protection, she knew that she was in shock, felt almost grateful for that.

Without the numbness, she thought she might lose her mind.

Upstairs, at the window of Marika's living room, Reggie flattened herself against the wall and peered out carefully, saw Lucas down on the doorstep, saw his rain-soaked hair, saw him failing to open the door with the Chubb key. Saw his hand reach for the doorbell.

The ring was loud and clear even from here.

She watched as he waited, clearly impatient, then turned away, but then stopped again, looked towards the side gate.

'Shit,' Reggie said softly.

She ran down the staircase, went to her pile of belongings in the corner to the left of the front door, pulled off her mask, took a bunch of keys from her pocket, stripped off the coveralls, stood still for a moment in her combat pants and T-shirt, thinking.

And then she crouched, retrieved her wallet from her parka, stuffed it into one of her back pockets along with the keys, picked up a tool belt and put it on, then delved into a bag and drew out a Stanley knife and a claw hammer. She stood, tucked the hammer into the belt and the knife, blade retracted, into a front pocket of her pants, and moved swiftly and quietly into Flat B.

The side gate was locked, as it always was. Lucas hesitated, looked around, then, using the narrow ledge of the wall beside it as a foothold, he climbed up and over – made a mental note to alert Libby to the security defect – and dropped down on to the far side, knocking into one of the wheelie bins.

In the garden flat's living room, Reggie heard the noise of his landing, took two deep breaths, readying herself for explanation if a neighbour should come looking.

Or for a confrontation with Lucas.

No one came.

Reggie backed well away from the garden doors, moved out of the living room into the small hall.

Below, in her concrete cell, Libby still huddled, still shaking, eyes fixed on the black plastic that she now knew was her dear friend's body bag.

She'd *suspected* her.

The shame was overwhelming.

Do something, she told herself.

There was nothing she could do. Except sit here and hope to survive. All the while experiencing a kind of hatred she had never known before, had never wanted to know.

She forced herself to track back over Reggie's story. Of Alfred Ashcroft and Frederick Brownlow and their personal sufferings.

Of Reggie's own pain and losses.

But Reggie had done *this* to Marika, had done this to her.

No incapable, still-vulnerable, post-traumatic victim. A highly intelligent, skilled, premeditating, calculating bitch.

Still a victim. Still mad.

Maybe, but Reggie had not needed to do *this*. Not to Marika, a total innocent. To Libby, perhaps; bizarrely, irrationally, insanely, punishing her for being the granddaughter, the heir, she supposed, of Harriet and Jack, who had brought Ashcroft down and contributed to Reggie's family tragedy.

But not to Marika.

Lucas turned over one of the bins, used it as a step-up to help him climb the second tall gate that separated the rubbish area from the presently cluttered back garden. He hauled himself to the top and dropped down on to the other side, landing hard, jarring his knee on the unforgiving wet concrete.

'*Schijt*!' he said – then jumped, startled by a weird sound from above.

It was only plastic sheeting, two floors up on Libby's roof garden, flapping in the strong wind. Painfully, Lucas straightened up, limped over to the glass doors, tried, cupping his hands around his eyes, to see inside, failed, the glass too misted, then stood back, looking up.

'Libby?' he called, and then, after a moment, 'Reggie?'

No one answered. He could hear nothing but the wind in the trees and the flailing heavy plastic.

Now what?

He looked around, saw a pile of broken stone slabs on the grass, picked up a small hunk, felt its weight in his hand. Debated for one more second.

And used it to smash one of the door's glass panes.

If his brand-new sixth sense proved to be crazily out of kilter, if there was no emergency, he could apologize later and pay for the damage.

Upstairs, still helpless, tied up in her bath, Beatrice heard the sound.

Of glass breaking somewhere below.

Hope took flight.

* * *

Lucas found a piece of rag, wrapped it around his hand and wrist, reached through the broken glass to open the door – but the security lock wouldn't let him do that.

So much for his burglary skills.

Though didn't he remember Libby fighting with the kitchen window lock the other week? And he *thought* she'd given up because the key wouldn't fit – and he *thought* she'd left it unlocked.

Beatrice heard more curious sounds from below.

Help coming, perhaps.

Or maybe Reggie Brownlow running amok, breaking up the place.

Hope crash-landed.

Eighty-five-year-old Beatrice Newby, once-upon-a-time survivor of the London Blitz, reasonably courageous victim of the Hampstead Heath dog-attacking brute, remained as still as her infuriatingly ageing and trembling body would allow, hardly daring to breathe, hovering between fragments of optimism and rekindled fear.

Lucas's landing from the window above the kitchen sink was inelegant and painful. He got up quickly, limped around the place, checking every room, still inexplicably jittery – and with no sign of Libby and, more to the point, no sign of even the slightest problem, he was starting to feel seriously ridiculous.

Except, suddenly, he spotted her mobile on its charger on the floor. He picked it up, saw all his missed calls and his last text, put it back.

The alarms already jangling in his mind grew louder.

He went next door to his own flat. Everything was as it had been when he'd left earlier. Everything looked fine.

Everything was *not* fine.

He needed to find Reggie, confess to the smashed glass door, explain his anxieties.

He left his flat, looked at the closed basement door, supposed that Reggie was working down there.

'Reggie?' he called, tentatively.

Receiving no answer, hearing nothing at all, he decided to delay his confession and do a quick check upstairs.

On the first floor, the door to Marika's flat was ajar.

'Reggie?' he called again.

Waited a moment, then went inside.

'Enough,' Libby told herself.

More than enough of cowering in this corner.

She had the knife, after all, and whatever the consequences, the asbestos had already been disturbed, was presumably in her lungs, and *anything* had to be better than just sitting waiting, doing nothing.

Carefully, she moved the stool out of the way, looked at the door.

Scanned it for hinges.

For any possible means of effecting an exit.

FORTY-ONE

No clues in Marika's flat.

Lucas looked across the narrow hallway at Beatrice's closed door.

Something about the lock . . .

It was *clean.* That was it. Almost everything in Calla House not in regular use or covered by polythene or sheeting was presently coated in dust. But there was hardly any on the brass escutcheon covering this lock and, looking more closely, what dust there was had been smeared.

Of course the simplest explanation was that Reggie or Evans or one of the other guys had been in here. Except that, so far as he was aware, the work on this floor was largely finished, only the ground floor left to deal with.

'Hello?' he called. 'Anyone in here?'

For an instant, hearing the voice, Beatrice froze.

Not Reggie. Male.

Could be Evans, or one of the other workmen.

Who might be in cahoots with the madwoman.

Sometimes, though, chances had to be taken.

'Hello!' she called back, her voice muffled by the tape over her mouth.

No one answered.

'*Help*!' She gave it all she had, because she'd be damned if she was going to end her days trussed up like a scraggy old turkey, *and* in her own bath.

One more time, louder still.

'*Help*!'

Lucas heard the cry, odd-sounding, but female and definitely distressed.

Libby?

He tried the door. Locked. He'd never kicked in a door in his life, but he had done *kickboksen* as a student in Amsterdam.

His left knee still hurt and he needed maximum strength to make this work, so he moved sideways, knew he had to attack the weakest part of the door, around the lock, he guessed, near the frame.

'Coming in,' he shouted. 'Stay back from the door.'

He stood on his stronger right leg and kicked out hard with his left foot. Achieved nothing.

More wimp than hero.

He went again, yelling, the way they had in class, and it worked, and one more kick and the door surrendered.

He stood still, panting, both legs shaking, took in the living room.

The plastic covers had been taken off the sofa and dumped on the floor, half covering a handbag and umbrella.

Beatrice's bag, he registered, old-fashioned, its clasp gleaming. *Not Libby.*

In the bath, Beatrice was silent, listening, still afraid.

And then she heard the voice again, closer, clearer.

'Beatrice? It's Lucas.'

Relief flooded through her and she cried out again through the tape, as loudly as she could manage.

'In here!'

Libby couldn't find any blasted hinges. She was sweating, breathless, wondered again, briefly, if sweat and tears might make asbestos more dangerous, decided that right now all she cared about was getting *out.*

She poked the knife's blade into the narrow slit to the right of the door, tried to run it up and down, but there wasn't enough space, and there had to *be* hinges, but she still couldn't find them, and she was trembling again, feeling sick and weak.

She allowed herself a moment's pause.

Then began again.

'My God, Beatrice.' Lucas was appalled.

Her eyes were grateful and imploring.

'It's going to be all right,' he told her, stooped, started to peel the tape away from her mouth, but she gave a small cry. 'Sorry.'

Except her eyes weren't on him now.

Lucas read the shock and fear in them too late, turned, saw Reggie swinging down on him with a claw hammer, and he ducked and twisted, but it caught his left arm and he yelled with pain.

'What the *hell*?'

Reggie swung the hammer again, struck him in the small of his back, and he went down, stunned, blanching with agony.

'Fuck's sake, Lucas, why couldn't you just keep out?'

Reggie tucked the bloody claw hammer back into her belt, bent down and dragged him to his feet, Lucas too weak to fight her off, Beatrice crying outrage from behind the tape, struggling harder than ever.

'Give it up, Beatrice.' Reggie hauled Lucas out through the bathroom door. 'You want Libby so much?' she said to him. 'Come with me.'

Lucas felt as if it was all happening to someone else; he knew that he'd been hurt, that he was bleeding, that this incredibly strong person – this *alien* Reggie Brownlow – was propelling him down the staircase, opening the door to the basement, dragging him down the steps into darkness, and he couldn't seem to summon the strength to even *try* to fight back.

And then halfway down, Reggie stumbled slightly, and that fleeting loss of control was just enough to enable him to pull away from her, but Reggie did not let go and – both of them now totally off-balance – they fell together, the hammer slipping from her belt and bouncing noisily down the rest of the steps ahead of them.

They hit the ground, Lucas's breath knocked clean out of him, the pain shattering, Reggie flat out beside him.

Libby heard it.

Didn't know *what* she'd heard, but she ceased trying to work the knife blade, pulled it carefully, silently, out of the slit beside the frame and put her ear against the door.

Straining to listen, not daring to utter a sound.

Reggie recovered first, hauled Lucas back up on to his feet – ignoring his yelps of pain – and over to the concrete cell, loosening her grip just long enough to get to the keys in her back pocket.

Lucas used the pause, some still clear part of his brain directing him, and he twisted away, brought up an elbow hard, caught Reggie under the chin, and the bunch of keys fell from her grasp.

His eyes adjusting to the dim light filtering down from the hall above, Lucas saw the concrete box, as out of place as a Tardis might have been, took in the lock on its door – and suddenly comprehended its significance.

Reggie reacted, dived for the keys, but Lucas reached them first, kicked out hard at her, connected with her chest, and Reggie sprawled backwards, gasping for air.

There were at least ten keys on the bunch, and Lucas swore under his breath as he struggled, hands shaking, to find the right one, and the first didn't fit, nor the second, and he had no *time* . . .

'*Lieve God,*' he prayed.

The third one slid into the lock.

Lucas turned it.

Libby heard the key turning, saw the door start to open, backed off, the penknife clenched in her right hand ready to thrust. Saw Lucas.

'Don't come in!' she shouted and stumbled out straight into his arms, then pulled away, afraid of contaminating him. 'It's full of asbestos. Reggie's gone mad, she—' She stopped, seeing her captor sprawled on the ground.

'Let's just get you out, call the police.' Lucas dragged her close, looked back, saw that Reggie hadn't moved, looked back at Libby and embraced her hard, and pain from the wounds in his back and arm stabbed at him, but he didn't care, just wanted to hold her.

Libby pulled away again, stared at her palms, saw his blood on them. 'Lucas, you're hurt!'

'I'm OK. We need to get—'

Libby saw the movement first, behind him.

Reggie was up – a second's indecision and then she was at the steps, starting up them, and Libby – without hesitation – went after her.

'Libby, no!' Lucas shouted. 'Wait!'

He tried to move, but his limbs felt leaden.

'Lucas, she's Ashcroft's granddaughter,' Libby called back, not stopping.

'Libby, leave her! Get your phone, call the police.'

'You call them.' Libby was on the top step, framed in light. 'Lucas, she murdered Marika. Her body's in there, in that cell –

Reggie locked me in with Marika's *body*, and I'm not going to let her get away.'

In the hall, Reggie paused again, knew there was no time to unbolt the front door, headed up the staircase instead, and Libby followed, but her leg and the hours of imprisonment and fear and shock were taking their toll, slowing her down, and Reggie was already halfway to the top, and Libby *knew* that she should stop, do as Lucas said, get her phone from the flat, because this woman was deranged and infinitely more powerful than she was, yet right now Libby's rage and grief for Marika were eclipsing all logic, and she was *damned* if she'd stop until—

Top floor.

Her own front door was open.

Libby halted, panting.

Nothing beyond that doorway was remotely identifiable, all familiarity obscured by heavy polythene, like some sinister other-galaxy planet.

A constantly shifting, eerie, *menacing* planet, because the door to the roof garden was open too, the wind blowing through the flat.

Libby stepped inside, walking slowly and unsteadily through what, nearly eighty years ago, during another time of terror, had been Harriet's flat, and what, just a few months ago, had been her own, peaceful living room, but which now felt like some unnerving funfair haunted house because Reggie could be hiding *anywhere* . . .

Lucas had picked up the claw hammer and summoned enough strength to have made it back up to the first floor, back into Beatrice's bathroom, where he gently peeled the tape off her mouth and untied her hands and feet.

'Thank you, Lucas.' Beatrice was tearful, her voice croaky.

He hugged her briefly and then she leaned against him as he helped her out of the bath, gripped her arm, fished for the phone in his pocket and gave it to her. 'Are you OK to dial 999?'

Beatrice managed a stern look.

Lucas nodded. 'Then get yourself out of the house. Can you walk?'

'I'll call, then I'll get out,' she said firmly. 'Is Elizabeth all right? Is that bitch still here?'

'Call the police,' he said.

And was gone.

Libby stood motionless at the open balcony door, feeling rooted to the spot because even her roof garden was unrecognizable with its weird walls billowing noisily in the storm, fat hoses like monster snakes feeding from the house out to the garden's edge.

She knew again that she should stop, that Lucas would have summoned help by now. Except that he'd been bleeding and she didn't know quite how badly, and for all she knew he might have collapsed, might be unconscious, still down in the basement. Just feet away from Marika's bundled body.

If she allowed Reggie to escape, she would never forgive herself.

She thought again of her grandparents and Ashcroft, knew that this was the absolutely right time to channel Harriet.

She edged forward through the doorway on to the first paving stone, and the wind whipped hard at her hair.

Reggie stepped out right in front of her.

Unmasked, features sharp and hard, eyes remorseless.

No words now, just a tall, athletic murderer, facing down her prey.

Logic returned, fear annihilating Libby's courage and she turned to run, but the unsheathed blade of the Stanley knife in Reggie's right hand found her throat and the killer's strong left arm dragged her close again.

'Should have stayed put, Libby.' Reggie pulled her further out into the garden. 'Nice and snug in your box.'

'It's finished, Reggie.' Libby's voice was choked with terror. 'Lucas has called the police.'

Reggie gripped Libby more tightly, moved the blade away from her throat to slice at the plastic wall to their right, and Libby used the instant to struggle, but the blade was swiftly back on her neck, below her right ear.

'Carotid or jugular,' Reggie said. 'I'm never sure exactly where.' She dug the blade in a fraction and Libby gasped. 'I might have settled for jail, you know . . .'

She withdrew the knife again, took another, deeper slash at the plastic, and this time she broke through to the outside world, and the wind lashed even more furiously at the sheeting and at the two women.

'If only you'd stayed put, suffered in there just a little longer.'

She stepped sideways, expanded the slit vertically, yanking Libby downwards as she sliced, creating an opening, and then she began to drag her through the space towards the outer stone wall.

'What are you *doing*?' Libby cried out.

'But your very own hero had to come, didn't he?' Reggie said. 'Just like your Grandpa Jack.'

'That's right, he did.' Lucas's voice came from behind them. 'So time to let her go, Reggie.'

The killer turned, still holding Libby tight against her.

Lucas stood in the doorway, blood-soaked and weakened, terror for Libby keeping him on his feet, the claw hammer clenched in his right hand.

'I rest my case,' Reggie said. 'Good old Jack and Harriet all over again.'

Lucas took two steps out on to the roof garden. 'Police are on their way, Reggie. No point making this worse than it already is.'

'Won't be worse for me.' Reggie dragged Libby right through the opening in the plastic and made straight for a pile of timber over by the outer wall, kept the blade at her prisoner's neck and put one foot up on the top plank.

'No, Reggie, *please*,' Libby protested.

'For God's sake, Reggie.' Lucas stopped moving, too terrified now for Libby to risk getting any closer. 'Let her *go*.'

A huge gust blew a heavy section of severed, loosened sheeting into Libby's face, striking her hard, shoving her sideways and right out of Reggie's grip.

'Libby, come to me!' Lucas yelled.

He launched himself forward, but Reggie caught Libby again by her right arm, twisted her around and back to the outer wall, got one foot back up on the pile of planks, then the other. The gale shrieked, sending weighty plastic swinging back again with even greater force. Reggie saw it coming this time, moved to evade it but lost her footing on the top plank. She let go of Libby, dropped the Stanley knife, caught at the sheeting to save herself, realized too late that it was ripping away from the rest of the wall . . .

She began to fall, still clutching the plastic . . .

'Reggie!' Instinctively Libby reached out to save her.

'No!' Lucas dropped the hammer, grabbed Libby, hauled her back, away from the edge, held her tight.

She let him hold her. Closed her eyes, hearing sirens from arriving patrol cars and ambulances.

The killer went on falling, the storm still lashing at the thick polythene, slowing her descent, the plastic twisting itself more and more tightly around and around her body, wrapping her face, sealing her nose and mouth, half suffocating her even before she hit the ground.

And died.

Regina Brownlow.

Wrapped in her own, self-made shroud.

FORTY-TWO

A few weeks after her funeral in Hungary, a service of thanks-giving for the life of Marika Szalet was held at the small but lovely Unitarian chapel in Rosslyn Hill.

A beautiful, sad service, followed by a bittersweet homecoming.

It was late November and gloomy, but Calla House looked normal. All signs of Regina Brownlow's handiwork gone.

All traces of asbestos gone too. It had been of no major signifi-cance in any case, they had since been informed. As Reggie had told Libby during that long afternoon of horrifying revelation, what there had been could have been left in place, presenting no risk. Had Libby called in another firm and had Reggie not gone to such painstaking lengths to gain certification for Brownlow & Daughter, Calla House would have been left intact, Marika would still be alive, and Reggie would presumably have acted professionally, admitted her error and waited, perhaps, for some other future opportunity to wreak her vengeance.

Libby took that news very badly, felt that it rendered her guilty for all that had happened, blamed her poor judgement skills and a naiveté that had placed them all in such danger.

That had resulted in her dear friend's murder.

'But she trusted Reggie too, at the outset,' Beatrice had reminded Libby. 'As did I. I admired the woman.'

'And Marika would be the first to tell you not to blame yourself,' Lucas had added.

They had concluded that Marika had probably gone down to the basement at some point to deal with the cause of those bothersome night-time sounds, had seen instead – perhaps tried to investigate – the soundproofed concrete box and had found herself at the hands of a ruthless killer. Who must have forced Marika to write that letter to Libby before she died; who probably even drove to Gatwick to post it for the sake of authenticity.

Yet part of the craziness of the tragedy, it seemed, was that Reggie might not actually have intended to kill anyone, might have wanted no more than to punish Libby with her elaborate, obsessively planned hoax, a monstrous trick – punctuated by other, smaller mind games – to cause maximum long-term psychological suffering.

The pulmonologist to whom Libby had been referred had said, following a number of medical tests, that even if she had inhaled some asbestos fibres in Reggie's custom-built cell, it was unlikely to create a long-term health problem.

'Unlikely,' Libby had repeated.

'Hopefully,' the consultant had said. 'No guarantees, of course.'

Libby had wavered, for a while, about keeping Calla House, but Lucas and Beatrice – and Sylvie, too, over from Hong Kong directly after the traumas – had all persuaded her that abandoning the house would be a kind of posthumous victory for Reggie and even Ashcroft.

'Not the daughter I know,' Sylvie had said, 'to give in to terrorists.'

'God, Mum, she was just so messed up,' Libby had said.

'But not by you,' Sylvie had said. 'Nor by Harriet or Jack.'

With Sylvie already back in Hong Kong, they were finally coming home. Beatrice and Nelson – the dog having been found late on that terrible day, drugged and shut into Reggie's van – were taking over the garden flat. And Lucas, fully recovered from his injuries and ready to go back to work, was moving in with Libby on the top floor. Three flats, therefore, needing new tenants; good, practical work for Libby to focus on.

Easier said than done, after all that had happened.

She took a slow walk around the house one afternoon, on her own, moving from flat to flat, from floor to floor, memories of terror stabbing at her almost everywhere, even on the staircase. Libby needed Calla House to feel like *hers* again: a safe place rather than a house of horrors, needed, she supposed, to confront the flashbacks.

She stood in the garden flat for a while, looked at the room in which Marika had stayed, knew now that Reggie must have planted the family photo there in order to provoke suspicions in Libby. She hovered in the doorway of the shower room, where she guessed – though she could never really *know* – that Reggie had probably tripped the light fuse and maybe messed with the door so that Libby would be trapped in the dark – Mal Evans's rescue entirely innocent, as it turned out.

She moved on into the garden, November-bare but still lovely, emptied of builders' debris. She looked at the bench, as sure now as she could be that it had been Regina Brownlow who had moved her crutches as she dozed that afternoon; she spent time staring at her laptop, wondering if Reggie had actually been snooping on her researches into the Ashcroft family – *her* family – and Libby had all but accused Lucas of that, hadn't she? – and deepest shame overcame her when she thought of that . . .

She stood in the hall looking at the closed basement door for the longest time, but that challenge, at least for now, seemed beyond her courage.

The 'Private War' paintings had all been put back in place upstairs, including the one that Reggie had installed in the cell. The normality of their return was of some comfort to Libby at times of need, when Lucas's arms around her did not seem quite enough, or when she heard the old house making odd sounds at night.

It was Lucas who convinced her at last to go down to the basement with him so that she could lay her ghosts. To see for herself that the concrete and steel box was gone, that all was clean and freshly painted, a solid handrail on the repaired steps, lighting rewired.

One thing still to be dealt with.

The wheelchair, returned by the police and in demand, grotesquely, by collectors of crime memorabilia, was to be taken to a scrap metal yard, and crushed before their eyes.

'What will happen to it now?' Libby asked after it was done, and was told that it would be melted down for recycling.

Gone for good.

Yet still, now and then, it returned to her in vivid dreams. In one recurring nightmare she was tied to it again in pitch-darkness, unable to move. In another, she was walking along Belsize Avenue in the wartime blackout when she heard a hideous creaking and looked back – and it was there, moving by itself, a haunted wheelchair speeding towards her, and Libby would wake beside Lucas, terrified, heart pounding, and for the next few nights she would feel almost too afraid to go to sleep.

'Maybe you could do what Harriet did,' Lucas suggested. 'Paint it.'

'I draw cartoons,' Libby said.

'Then draw it.' Lucas kissed her shoulder. 'A very dark cartoon, perhaps.'

'I suppose it might be cathartic,' Libby said.

'Worth a try,' Lucas said.

She began next day.